T0157752

Devil's
VERSE

Devil's
Verse

Joseph Nicholas

iUniverse, Inc.
New York   Bloomington

Devil's Verse
Natasha Azshatan Unlocks Ancient Mysteries, Reveals Secrets,
And Wrestles With Demons As She Fights To Stay Alive

Copyright © 2008, 2009 Joseph Nicholas

All rights reserved. No part of this book may be used or reproduced by
any means, graphic, electronic, or mechanical, including photocopying,
recording, taping or by any information storage retrieval system
without the written permission of the publisher except in the case
of brief quotations embodied in critical articles and reviews.

This is a work of fiction. All of the characters, names, incidents,
organizations, and dialogue in this novel are either the products
of the author's imagination or are used fictitiously.

iUniverse books may be ordered through booksellers or by contacting:

iUniverse
1663 Liberty Drive
Bloomington, IN 47403
www.iuniverse.com
1-800-Authors (1-800-288-4677)

Because of the dynamic nature of the Internet, any Web addresses or links
contained in this book may have changed since publication and may no longer be
valid. The views expressed in this work are solely those of the author and do not
necessarily reflect the views of the publisher, and the publisher hereby disclaims
any responsibility for them.

ISBN: 978-1-4401-4953-5 (sc)
ISBN: 978-1-4401-4952-8 (dj)
ISBN: 978-1-4401-4951-1 (ebk)

Printed in the United States of America

iUniverse rev. date: 06/26/2009

For my wife and daughter

Acknowledgments

My wife is my inspiration. She is a brilliant, active, and loving person. She gives me unconditional love and the courage to believe that I can achieve great things—even the accomplishment of goals that others might believe to be improbable. She is the most wonderful wife and mother.

Dad taught me the true meaning of a hero. There were many times in my life that I witnessed him give generously of himself in order to help a person in need. He is a good father who taught us kids to work hard and care about other people. He always reaches out to us with an encouraging and guiding hand.

Similarly, my brother has shown me a quiet and humble heroism. When my mother came down with cancer, he quit his lucrative career and moved across the country to take up the mission of caring for our mother during her final two years.

My mother was such a wonderful person. She was also a source of unconditional love and encouragement. She loved life and everyone in it. She also taught me about matters of faith and soul. She was so brave. Cancer took her life, but it could not take her spirit; she stays with us, in our memories and in our broken hearts.

My daughter is my greatest inspiration. When I see her smile, I want nothing more than to be the best daddy in the whole world and to care and provide for her. Her little hugs heal me from all troubles and her little kisses make my heart larger. In her, I see the greatest promise—the hope of our future.

Prologue

In February 1798, the new Republic of France waged war against the Vatican. Giovanni Angelo Braschi had reigned twenty-three years as Pope Pius VI. At the age of eighty, he was neither frail nor sickly. To all who knew him, he did in fact seem younger and stronger than a man of so many years.

Braschi held his spyglass with a steady hand and watched from his window as the French general, Louis Alexander Berthier, and his army marched through Saint Peter's Square.

"We prevailed our lawsuit for peace and yet they halteth not," Braschi remarked.

"Yes, Your Holiness," the Cardinal Secretary of State answered.

Braschi continued to observe, seemingly detached, as the invading army entered the Vatican and arrested his cardinals. He paced over to the corner of the room near the fireplace where a birdcage stood as home to his pet doves. He reached into the cage and carefully pulled out two of the peaceful creatures. He gently held them in his cupped hands as he walked back to the window and released them.

Braschi closed the window and deliberated as he watched the birds fly out of sight. He heard the footsteps of the approaching General Berthier and his soldiers. The doors of the Pope's apartment burst open and Berthier and his officers entered.

The General was an imposing presence—a tall man with thick brown hair and a serious gaze—his voice, stern.

"*Monsieur* Pope, *la* lettre *de* Napoleon."

He handed Braschi the envelope. Braschi put on his spectacles, broke the seal, and looked down. Napoleon's communiqué: two sentences, a direct quote from the prophetic scripture of Revelation.

> He who leads into captivity, shall go into captivity;
> He who kills with the sword, must be killed with the sword.

Braschi looked up at Berthier with surprise and a mixture of anger and betrayal. His prominent forehead wrinkled, his dark eyes burning, "What is this?"

"*Messieurs* Giovanni Angelo Braschi," Berthier declared. "By the order of Bonaparte, thou art henceforth a prisoner of war of the Republic of France."

The iron chains clinked as Braschi's hands were bound.

"Ye needeth not do this. I canst be an ally."

Braschi feared his fate as he saw the soldiers plunder his apartment and loot his personal belongings with complete disregard.

General Berthier pulled a soldier's New Testament from his vest pocket and began to read aloud from Revelation as Braschi was dragged out against his will.

> I will show unto thee the judgment of the great whore with whom the kings of the earth have committed fornication, and the inhabitants of the earth have been made drunk with the wine of her fornication.

Braschi fell to his knees and bent forward, suctioning his palms to the smooth marble floors to prevent his capture. Imprisonment was the most terrifying fate he could imagine. He tested the strength of his chains and tried to break them as if he thought it were even possible, his face red with effort.

The French soldiers laughed at him. "He is soiling himself," one of them mocked.

Berthier continued his sermonizing to the dethroned pope as if he were reading him Miranda Rights written by the hand of God.

> And the woman which thou sawest is that great city, which reigneth over the kings of the earth.

Braschi was pulled to his feet. A soldier by his side locked an iron collar around his neck. "Thou shalt not escape," he snarled and heaved on the chain.

Braschi shouted out as he was forced to suffer these indignities. "Thinkest thou, that while we sued for peace that we wouldst not also take precautions?"

Berthier ignored Braschi and continued to read aloud.

> How much she hath glorified herself, and lived deliciously, so much torment and sorrow give her: for she saith in her heart, I sit a queen, and am no widow, and shall see no sorrow.

The guard in front heaved on Braschi's chains as if he was pulling on an unwilling mule. The soldiers laughed and mocked Braschi. They cheered as he was ejected from his palace and pushed into his horse-drawn cage.

Braschi turned and gazed upon his conquered city. Snow fell and smoke poured out of the Vatican windows as he and his Cardinals were carried away in the middle of the night. Braschi watched the fires burn and chanted the mystical words writ by a phantom hand in the presence of King Nebuchadnezzar. The very words of which, half a millennium before Christ, foretold the fall of the kingdom of Babylon.

Mene, mene tekel upharsun.

Mene: Your kingdom has been assessed.

Tekel: It has been weighed in the balance and found wanting.

Upharsun: Your kingdom is to be divided. And given to your enemies.

Giovanni Angelo Braschi, who had reigned longer than any other Pope in historical times, died in prison eighteen months later. His funeral was postponed for three years because his corpse had vanished.

"Dr. Azshatan," the counsel for the defense addressed her. Natasha raised her eyebrows and leaned forward, willing to answer whatever question Sidney Delaware desired to ask. He was a tall, skinny man who liked to stroke his smoothly shaven chin as he paced in front of the jurors. Mr. Delaware had a long face and a mouth and teeth that were too wide for his narrow head. "Please explain to the court the term 'paleography.'"

Natasha looked at the grotesquely deformed man who sat in the defendant's chair. She was certain that he was the killer of the young woman Katrina Dunlap. She knew that her testimony would be a key element for the prosecutor to secure a conviction.

"Paleography is the study, analysis, interpretation, and authentication of ancient handwriting. Specifically Greek and Latin," she answered.

Natasha turned her attention back to the jury and briefly wondered if she appeared to be what they expected in a paleographer. She was an attractive woman with mid-length golden hair, and intelligent brown eyes. Wearing an ivory suit, she thought she looked enough like a stereotypical linguistics academic. "Smart Babe," her girlfriend Lucy had teased. Natasha found herself wishing that she had her pair of reading glasses to flip open and push up the bridge of her nose—in order to look more like doctor and less like a babe.

Delaware continued, "And isn't it true, Dr. Azshatan, that your seemingly impressive academic credentials from Georgetown and Oxford are actually in the specialization of paleography?"

"It's true that my doctorate is in paleography. However, paleography is a sub-specialization of graphology in general," she explained. "I am an expert in the analysis of handwriting."

"You are an author, aren't you? Your most recent book is a bestseller, isn't it?"

"Objection. Relevance!" the prosecutor protested.

"Your honor I will show relevance," Delaware answered.

"I'll allow it for now," the judge ruled.

"Dr. Azshatan," Delaware continued. "Isn't it true that this latest book is about insights that you arrive at by means of not only your study of ancient writings, but also by means of your self-proclaimed psychic abilities?"

Natasha didn't know how to answer. Mr. Delaware had grossly mischaracterized her book.

"That's not exactly how I would put it," Natasha answered. "It's about using one's intuition and life experience to discern personal meaning from ancient writings."

"Yes. But isn't it true that you consider yourself to be psychic?" Delaware probed.

"I'm not a fortune teller, but I feel I have a heightened intuition and sensitivity to the spiritual."

"Heightened sensitivity to the spirit realm," Delaware repeated. "So do you feel that you are communicated to by spirits?"

"Objection. Relevance!"

The prosecutor stood up.

"I'm allowing it."

The judge looked over to Natasha to answer. Natasha bent back to the microphone.

"Yes. Whether we realize it or not, we are all communicated to by spirits."

"And what about the spirit of the deceased in our case? Do you believe she assisted you in *discerning*—as you put it—the truth?"

"I strictly analyzed the handwriting, Mr. Delaware," she answered.

"But why? If my client were guilty, wouldn't the victim be screaming at you of his guilt? Did you perceive any communication from the victim as to my client's guilt?"

Natasha looked at the defendant, Gilbert Carver. He avoided her glance and lowered his bald, misshapen head.

"No. The communication I received as to Mr. Carver's guilt came from Mr. Carver, in my opinion. I concluded that the handwriting was his," Natasha answered.

"So what are you, Dr.Azshatan, a handwriting expert or a psychic investigator?" Mr. Delaware vigorously shook his head with a look of condemning disapproval. "No further questions, Your Honor," he hollered to the courtroom on his way back to sit next to Gilbert Carver.

~

William Jaimeson awoke from another one of his bad dreams. His eyes had changed from their brilliant cobalt blue to a bright red in his dream. Red from the rage he had felt. He believed in dreams. After all, they had taken him this far, hadn't they? But the bad dreams were more frequent these days. *Probably stress. It's been pretty busy lately.* William caught his mind drifting. *I must get back to sleep and undo this dream. I must make it better.*

You always make it better. A voice inside him said. *That's why you're the most popular governor in Washington State history. That's why you're the next president of the United States.*

It was his mother's voice. She was gone now, but she never stopped encouraging her boy Will.

He filled a quarter of a bar glass with water and added vodka. *That's right, baby. You can have a nightcap. Forget that bad dream. Instead, dream about your beautiful wife or your good old Mommy.* He finished his drink and went back to his dream, trying to undo it and make it all better.

Nevertheless, he didn't make it better. In the dream, he watched a hijacked airplane. He could see the terrorist pulling plastic explosive material out of specially machined American quarters. The quarters were hollow. Each one held just a few grams of explosive.

That's how they'll sneak it on the plane. It'll look like a handful of pocket change.

The terrorist went to the lavatory, extracted the explosive putty from the coins, and assembled the bomb. When he came out, he was joined by four others.

"I am Ahmed Ahmad," the terrorist announced as he began his takeover of the plane. He spoke with a cultured British accent. "Today, Allah will drink the blood of the Great Dragon. Allah has given us a great honor to be his cupbearer. At the end of this day, we will fly this plane into the United Nations Building—but that doesn't mean you have to perish. If you cooperate with us, you may live.

Under each of your seats is a parachute. Give us the plane freely and we will fly to a low altitude and you may skydive to safety. If you do not give up the plane, it will be exploded—and we will all die together."

He held the bomb up for everyone to see. It was a walnut-sized ball of gray putty with wires sticking out of it. In his other hand, the terrorist held a modified RC car remote. He stuck the plastic explosive to the window.

"Give us the plane and skydive to safety or you will die a horrible death. Your bodies will be burned alive—or perhaps your flesh will be sucked through small holes in the plane. Think about your families. Think about the ones you love."

"Don't do it!" a beautiful woman screamed from the rear of the plane. She had wavy light hair and intelligent brown eyes. "You're all going to die anyway. The chutes won't open. He's going to turn you all into falling little bombs. He will use your bodies flying through the sky and splatting all over the city to magnify the horror! Don't you understand?" she shouted. "You're part of the horror! You are the bombs! Your deaths are part of the diabolical scheme of horror!"

The passengers decided to save themselves.

"You have chosen wisely!" Ahmad shouted. The plane flew low and Ahmad opened the emergency exit door. He shouted, "Hurry! Save yourselves. Tell the world our cause is just."

The passengers lined up and one by one jumped out of the plane. Will saw the horrified expression on their faces as they pulled their parachute ripcords, only to realize that they didn't function. He heard them scream as they plummeted to their deaths.

The 321 passengers sprayed across the skies of the city like the falling tail of a comet. Will could hear their screams. He saw them landing on cars and on buildings. He saw them landing on unsuspecting pedestrians. He saw their eyeballs shoot out of their sockets. He saw their spines eject through the tops of their heads like skewers through pieces of marinated pork.

Will screamed, "Ahhhh! You monstrous psychopaths!"

He saw the general assembly of the United Nations. With no warning, the plane burst through the walls with an explosion. The General Assembly was vaporized.

Will screamed, "Ahhhhh! Those poor people."

He shed tears into his pillow and swore vengeance. Rage burned under his eyelids.

The next morning, Will began to think of a way to finally end his terrible dreams.

~

Natasha couldn't help replaying her testimony. She despised the memory, but she was a slave to it. It kept replaying in her mind just as this dream that had awakened her once again in the middle of the night. She looked up at the ceiling and renewed her vow that she would never again offer handwriting testimony in a court of law. Her disastrous testimony led to the eventual acquittal of the notorious killer Gilbert Carver. He was out there somewhere, hunting for his next victim.

Natasha made a decision to change her thoughts and to think about something positive. She looked over to Tom. He lay sleeping peacefully on his back, his straight nose and bearded chin pointed to the ceiling. The silhouette of his face seemed to her like a moonlit range of mountains. His full head of dark brown hair tempted her caress. She imagined he was dreaming about the new life they were about to start in the Pacific Northwest. After twenty long years as a diplomat in the Foreign Service, Tom was ready to retire at the young age of forty-two.

Natasha arose quietly and walked to the master bath. She filled a glass with cold tap water and drank it. She quietly made her way back to bed and snuggled beneath the covers. *Soon we'll start our new life,* she thought, just before sleep overtook her. *Soon we'll journey to that enchanted island.*

~

It was raining hard the day that Tom and Natasha first saw Jerrell's Cove and Harstine Island. Natasha reclined in the passenger seat, napping while Tom drove.

She was fatigued from the travel; first from Maryland to Seattle. After Seattle, a one-hour ferry ride to Bremerton.

From Bremerton, Harstine Island was just thirty minutes drive south. They were on their way to meet with Vernon Cook and to inspect their dream home for the first time.

As they crossed the bridge to the island, Natasha breathed deeply and dreamed of the days ahead. Vernon's description echoed in her mind with the rich, toned voice of a man whose success was dependent upon building relationships with people over the telephone.

"Jerrell's Cove is a gated community. It has all the amenities of a resort. Most of the homes have stunning views of the water and the surrounding mountains. And to top it all off, it's got its own private marina with assigned moorage for each property."

Tom spoke up. "After we settle in, I'll find us a boat and we'll sail to endless destinations."

He watched the road. Silent but for the hum of the engine and the squeegee of the wiper blades back and forth along the windshield, Natasha imagined all the places to sail.

Seemingly out of nowhere, Tom continued again out loud, "We could sail to Seattle, Bainbridge Island, or the San Juans. Port Angeles and Hoodsport are gateways into the Olympic Mountains. We could moor at their marinas and go on backpack adventures."

Natasha smiled, thinking of Tom out on the hunt for his boat. He would find it in the classifieds, on a bulletin board, or parked near a busy intersection with a big for sale sign on it.

"You'll find it honey," she told him. She smiled big, stretched, and let out a howling yawn.

"No one can bargain like you."

"Yeah, all those years in foreign marketplaces have honed my negotiating skills pretty good, haven't they?"

"Oh, yeah. I'm sure you'll find us the perfect boat."

With the success of Natasha's writing career and Tom's own success as a career diplomat, they had plenty of money to buy a new boat, but that wasn't Tom's style. He preferred the buying of a thing—such as a boat from an individual—rather than a corporation or a professional salesperson. Perhaps it was the personal negotiations and the opportunity to test his skills at reading body language. Perhaps it was the opportunity to make a new acquaintance or a new friend. Possibly it was the fulfilling sense of coming to the rescue of a person who needed to sell in order to raise cash for some reason or other.

Vernon was waiting for them from inside his dark green Jeep Cherokee, at the Jerrell's Cove entrance gate. The gate seemed out of place in its setting—a black iron monstrosity connected to black iron fencing that extended out in both directions until it was engulfed into the forest of cedars, Douglas firs, and tall sword ferns. An intercom and keypad device stood about four feet high, like a fast food drive-through menu. Natasha looked up and noticed video cameras mounted high above the gateway.

After they entered, they followed Vernon's Jeep along a narrow winding road. Natasha gazed out the windows to see what wildlife might be out there.

"Now I know what Vernon meant when he said, 'enchanted forest feel,'" she said.

Jerrell's Cove was abundant with deer and friendly families of raccoons. Majestic old-growth cedars lined the edge of the roadway. It was as if the road was made to meander around and through the trees.

Narrow asphalt bike and walking trails crisscrossed through the entire forested community. As they drove, they noticed trailhead entrance signs every so often.

They turned right and passed the clubhouse on the left.

"That must be where they have the swimming pool," Natasha pointed out.

A few moments later, they passed a little village church on the right. As they parked in front of the home, Natasha and Tom smiled at each other.

The house was fantastic. It was Pacific Northwest lodge style with exposed timber, a river-rock fireplace, and awe-inspiring views from enormous cedar-framed windows. It felt warm and down to earth. The pleasant scent of consumed cedar lightly affected the atmosphere.

"Vernon, it's even better than we imagined."

Tom and Natasha looked out the large bay windows at the view, turned to each other, and embraced.

The seminar in Olympia, Washington, was her last for the year. It was a small venue, but it was located only thirty minutes drive from their new home.

Natasha was a stunning presenter. Speaking in public did not come easy for her, but careful practice for her presentations helped immensely.

At larger venues, the seminar was almost always a double feature. The distinguished psychic medium, Grant Nuby, would give the introduction for Natasha. When Natasha ended her presentation, there would be a short intermission and she would give the introduction for Grant.

By 5:00, most of the audience had arrived and been seated. Inspirational, up-tempo music softly flooded the room and cued the audience that the show was about to begin.

Tonight, Tom Azshatan filled in for Grant. Although Tom was a moderately handsome man with dark hair and eyes, and a medium build, his most notable characteristic was his wide, genuine smile. It beamed out of his full-faced beard as sunshine through clouds. He walked energetically up the side stairs to center stage and grinned widely to the audience.

"Welcome, ladies and gentlemen!" he called out.

The music intensified.

"She has traveled the world as a United States diplomat and has delighted audiences all around the world with her positive and hopeful messages. She is both an old-time scholar and a spiritual visionary."

Natasha felt a wave of anxiety and adrenalin wash over. She loved the sensation, but it also made her want to run away. Her heart was pounding. She breathed in deep and remembered to smile.

The music was rising to its climax as Tom continued, "Ladies and gentlemen, you are about to experience a life-changing event. It will answer some of the greatest questions of our time. It will take you on a journey of mind and spirit and unlock for you the mysteries of inspiration! Welcome to the dynamic presentation, 'Inspired Revelations.' Please put your hands together to welcome the one and only Natasha Azshatan!"

A healthy cheer of applause thundered as Natasha jaunted to the front of the stage.

"Thank you. Wow. Thank you very much," Natasha responded to the applause.

Behind Natasha, the giant screen glowed and the title "Inspired Revelations" faded onto screen. It appeared as if it were written in calligraphy on ancient paper.

She began solemnly, "The actual title for what we know as the Book of Revelation is the Greek word Αποκαλυψισ. The Apocalypse. The Revealing. And within its pages is a passage that is actually quite revealing in regards to the process of inspiration."

In the back of the room, a tardy audience member entered quietly. She was an upper middle-aged woman with long, dark, but graying hair, pulled up into a tight bun at the back of her head. Natasha made brief eye contact with her, noting that her eyes were a cloudy hazel. The woman made her way to a rear corner seat and dropped her backpack on the floor next to her feet.

Natasha clicked the control in her fist, and transitioned the slide to Revelation 20:10, and continued her presentation.

"Revelation chapter twenty, verse ten. In the New King James version of the Bible, it reads:

> Blessed are those who keep the commandments, for they shall have right to the tree of life.

However, in the New International Version of the Bible it reads this way:

Blessed are those whose robes are washed, for they shall have right to the tree of life.

How can the same verse be translated so differently in two different, yet widely accepted, versions of the Bible?

Natasha looked around at the faces in the audiences and searched their expressions as they pondered her question. She noticed the woman in the back wasn't paying any attention; instead, she was fumbling around with both her hands in her backpack. It looked almost like the woman had a pickle jar she was trying to open.

Natasha continued, "The answer is simply that scholars cannot agree on which version is correct. The controversy goes back to the ancient Greek manuscripts themselves. The King James version and the New International version have each made the decision to rely on different texts."

Natasha noticed a man who sat a few empty chairs down from the cloudy eyed woman; he looked distracted by her fumbling about in the backpack. He was watching her with a look of concern and annoyance. She clicked the next slide.

"Let me show you the corresponding versions of the subject sentence side by side as they appear in the Greek."

Plunantes	stas	tolas	auton
πλυναντεσ	στασ	τολασ	αυτον
Poinantes	tas	entolas	autu
πο ιναντεσ	τασ	εντολασ	αυτ υ

"As you can see, the two versions optically appear very similar when compared. The variance between the two versions is the result of an extraordinary and yet understandable scribal error. This one, of course, magnified by its profound effect on the meaning of the text."

The woman in the back stood up and put her backpack on.

"Bravo!" she shouted sarcastically. "You think you're so smart! Don't you?"

Natasha stopped. She clenched her teeth tightly while trying to maintain calm and searched for security. Tom stood up. He was in back, but on the opposite side of the room as this woman had been.

Natasha tried to ignore the woman and hoped someone, either Tom or security, would escort her away. Natasha continued, "So how can one discern personal meaning from inspired sources if one is not certain of its accuracy?" Light instrumental music faded in. It sounded like puzzle-solving music. "The answer? Test all things."

The woman began approaching up the center aisle.

Natasha continued, "It's all right for a product of inspiration—such as scripture—to be sprinkled with mistakes here and there.

The woman interrupted suddenly, "Did you read the part in Revelations where it says the smoke of their torment will ascend forever and ever?" As her face turned red, she continued her approach. "Who do you think it's talking about, Mrs. Smarty Pants?"

Natasha put her hand out, motioned to the woman to sit back down, and attempted to continued with her presentation, "It's our job to discern."

Natasha looked back at Tom.

"Simply test it against these three criteria. Does it harmonize with science? Does it harmonize with personal experience? Does it harmonize with other known truths?

The woman walked closer, brandishing a spraying wand—the kind used by gardeners to apply pesticides and fertilizers. "It's talking about people like you!" she pronounced in a strained holler and smacked her lips again, chewing her gum. "You're gonna burn!" The woman pointed the wand at Natasha.

Suddenly, Natasha was petrified in terror at the realization that she was being doused with gasoline. Tom ran up the center aisle, but it was too late. Almost in slow motion, Natasha watched the woman pull out a giant lighter with her left hand and click the trigger as its tip entered the stream of gas. A spray of flames shot up toward Natasha and engulfed the podium in a fiery blaze. Natasha screamed and dived off of the stage to her right, narrowly avoiding being ignited.

A young, bearded orthodox priest sitting in the second row reacted swiftly. He saw the hose that led from the wand to the gas tank in her backpack. He jumped out of his chair, grasped the tubing, and yanked it down with as much force and velocity as he could, knowing that if he failed to disconnect the hose, the crazy lady could turn her flame shooter on him next.

He ripped the tubing right out of the backpack and, an instant later, Tom rushed up from behind and wrestled the crazy woman to the ground. The building's sprinkler system reacted and began showering down on the audience. Other audience members pulled fire extinguishers off of the walls, and covered the stage in white foam putting out the flames.

The orthodox priest, Father Elijah, looked over at Natasha to make sure she was okay and turned around to where Tom was wrestling with the woman on the floor. Elijah, with the rubber tubing still in his hands, pulled a slipknot, and bound the woman's arms behind her back with great effort. The woman, with incredible strength for her size and weight, fought wildly.

Most of the audience was about to—or already had—abandoned their seats to head for the exits. Natasha returned to the stage and addressed the audience, "Stay calm, everyone. It's all over. I'm very sorry for the inconvenience, but obviously we won't be able to continue."

Security guards ran in and pulled the woman to her feet.

Natasha continued, "If anyone is interested, I'll be available for book signing and discussions at the hotel fireside lounge in one hour."

Natasha joined Tom and Father Elijah; they had just finished shaking hands and introducing themselves to each other. The fire alarm and sprinklers had turned off. Tom and Natasha embraced. "Are you okay?" he asked.

"Other than the fact that I'm wet all over and smell like gasoline and a little shook up, I'm just fine. Thanks to you two, I'm fine," she added before turning to Father Elijah with a smile. "Father. How can I ever thank you?"

Father Elijah blushed slightly. He was a mildly chubby man in his mid-thirties. His wavy brown hair was pulled into a ponytail and his beard was wild and untidy. His skin was smooth and pale—except for his pink cheeks—and he wore golden, small-framed, round glasses.

On his chair, he had left his hardback edition of *Inspired Revelations*. He plucked the book up, extended it to her, and smiled back.

"Dr. Azshatan, it's a pleasure to meet you. I'm Father Elijah from Jerrell's Cove. It hardly seems appropriate, but…"

"Oh, no. The pleasure is all mine," Natasha assured him. She pulled out her pen and scribbled an autograph. Natasha recognized him as the priest of the small church near her home. "It's not often that a member of the clergy attends one of my seminars."

She handed him the book and they began walking out of the conference room with Tom.

"I have to say it's very interesting and thought-provoking," Father Elijah said. "Of course I don't agree with everything, but you might be surprised by how much I actually agree with you."

As they passed through the exit and turned toward the lobby, Natasha smiled at him. "Thank you, Father Elijah. What especially did you like?"

"Well, you probably already know that the Orthodox Church also holds a historical, metaphorical interpretation of the scriptures."

Natasha nodded. She did of course know that. The majority of Christendom, in fact held the historical, metaphorical interpretation of scripture.

Elijah continued as they walked, "But what I really like is the idea that you bring up about appreciating the scriptures for what they are. The fact that they are imperfect may be by God's design. The imperfection drives us to seek wisdom and understanding through prayer."

Natasha nodded and smiled widely now. *He wasn't just being agreeable—he really does appreciate my ideas.*

"Yes, exactly. Thank you, Father. You know that wasn't what I expected you to say."

They all stopped just a few feet in front of the reception desk. "What did you expect?" Father Elijah asked.

"Well, I thought you were going to ask me to stay away from your flock."

He shook his head and smiled.

"No *flocking* way," he joked.

The joke hit their funny bones just right after such a stressful event and a serious conversation, causing them all to break into short, but vigorous, laughter.

When it subsided, Elijah continued, "No, no. On the contrary, I would be honored if you and Tom would join us this Sunday for Divine Liturgy."

"Well, thank you. Since we have so much in common, we might just take you up on that offer. I'll discuss it with Tom and—who knows—you might just see us there."

Tom was standing at Natasha's side and gave her a squeeze.

"There's one other thing," the priest said. He curled his newly autographed book up into his arm like a football.

"What's that?" Natasha asked.

"I have come across some material that I think may astonish you."

Natasha raised her eyebrows.

"What kind of *material?*" Natasha teased.

"Come to church and I'll show you," Elijah answered.

"Well, you've definitely got my attention."

"Good. Divine Liturgy begins at ten."

Elijah shook hands with them, turned to go, and waved, before walking out. Natasha and Tom walked up to the reception desk. They had less than an hour for Natasha to buy a change of clothes, shower, change, and be back at the hotel's fireside lounge.

∼

Natasha and Tom awoke to a clear, sunny winter's day. The sky was blue and the mountains seemed even closer than usual. The air smelled fresh and little like snow.

They awoke earlier than they normally would on a Sunday because they intended to go to church—despite the fact that Natasha and Tom weren't exactly churchgoers. However, Father Elijah's friendliness had managed to make them feel comfortable and also they enjoyed the traditions of Christmastime—especially singing Christmas hymns.

Natasha supposed that perhaps it brought back to her the magical memories of her childhood before her father had passed away. He had loved Christmas.

It was the people at her childhood church who had been the only ones who had helped her and her mother during the nightmare of her father's death. It was probably the childhood loss of her father that had something to do with the ease at which she made friends with Father Elijah, and before him, Father Francis Charles.

After several changes of mind, Natasha decided on her red outfit. "Tis the season to wear red, fa-la-la-la-la-la," she hummed. A short walk later, they arrived at the small church to the sound of the choir singing hymns.

The atmosphere was special and reverent. Under dimmed lights, people quietly lit candles, placed them in sand, and silently prayed. At the front of the church, a gold-painted dividing wall with an arched doorway stood between them and the altar.

A large icon of Jesus Christ was painted in distinct Eastern Orthodox style to the right side of the doorway. He had caramel skin, a ski-sloped nose, and a narrow, gaunt face with long narrow eyes and small lips. His right index and middle fingers pointed upward as if he was saying the Boy Scout oath.

The spicy, clean scent of sandalwood incense and the soft chimes calmed her.

Natasha noticed a box of candles with a handwritten placement card in the lobby. "Let's burn some candles," she whispered.

Tom shrugged his shoulders in agreement.

He stuck a five-dollar bill in the collection box and Natasha grabbed two candles, handing one to Tom.

"Do I get to make a wish?" he whispered jokingly.

Natasha jabbed him with her elbow. They entered the sanctuary and sat in the last pew in the right corner.

Father Deacon Jim Worley entered and walked down the aisle to the podium. He was a tall, round man with thick glasses and a comb-over hairdo. Despite his somewhat unkempt appearance, Natasha sensed the church members respected him.

"Everybody, may I have your attention?" Jim paused and looked about the congregation. "Father Elijah has not arrived yet. I just got back from his home and he's not there either, but his car is. I'm afraid that something's wrong. Father Elijah has gone missing. I just called the sheriff; he and his deputy are headed over right now."

A woman sitting in front of Natasha buried her head and began to sob. Natasha felt a lump in her own throat.

I'm sure he's okay. Natasha tried to reassure herself, but her instincts told her different. *Nobody knows why he would have no-showed church this morning, but a lot of things could have happened.*

Tom squeezed her hand. "Are you okay?" he asked.

"No, I've got a bad feeling about this," she whispered.

Sheriff Darwood arrived with his deputy, Ben Green. The sheriff's silver hair and healthy skin complexion made him appear to be fiftyish to Natasha. She had a feeling he might be a retired Marine officer. He appeared confident, strong, and in good physical condition for his age. Deputy Green appeared slender and he nervously twisted the ends of his brown mustache as he surveyed the room.

At the front of the church, Jim yielded the podium to the sheriff.

"Listen up, everyone," Darwood announced. "Jim Worley has filled me on the details. Based on my experience, I believe we need to begin a search for Father Elijah in the woods immediately. I have a hunch he may have either gotten lost off a trail or possibly caught in an animal trap.

"All of his belongings are still at his residence and his car is still there. We've called all the taxi services in the area; no one took a taxi out of here last night. Does anyone have any idea what might have happened?"

Again silence.

"All right, then. He may very well be freezing out in the woods."

Sheriff Darwood led the congregation back to the community center where the priest had last been seen.

"Everyone, stay far behind us and let the dog do its work."

He took a piece of clothing, bunched it up, and put it to the dog's nose. Bear was a fluffy, bulky mixture of Black Lab and perhaps a little Husky.

" Okay, Bear. We're counting on you. Let's go find our man. Let's go!"

Bear immediately took off down the street past the church and down toward the Azshatans' place. They passed the home and continued around the circle before stopping at the marina trailhead. He sniffed around momentarily and ran toward the marina.

The canine barked confidently as he charged down the snow-packed trail, finally stopping near the spot where, two weeks earlier, Tom and Natasha had photographed a deer. Later, they had discovered the small outbuilding hidden in the trees and bushes—just barely out of view from the main trail.

"Father Elijah, are you here? Father Elijah, can you hear us?" Darwood shouted.

Bear ran up to the outbuilding and jumped up on his hind legs. He scratched at the door and barked, trying to push the door open.

"Everybody stand back. Father Elijah, are you in there?" Darwood shouted.

Silence was the only answer.

"You all get back home right now!" he ordered. "What's behind this door is police business."

Nobody moved. Nobody was about to go home. The sheriff shook his head at the crowd for defying his order and turned back to the door. The young deputy drew his pistol, taking position behind and off to the side, ready to cover as Darwood opened the door.

~

Father Elijah's frozen body slumped in the far corner of the pump house. His neck was cinched in a belt, which attached on the other end to a water pipe a few feet above his head. A clear plastic bag, the sort one might find in the produce section of any grocery, snugly covered his face. Frozen blood covered his hands. Above his head, a bloody finger-painted message screamed out from the wooden planks:

IN GIRUM IMUS NOCTE ET CONSUMIMUR IGNI

"Dear God in heaven!" Sheriff Darwood exhaled and whipped around. "I want everybody out of here right now. Go back to the community center. He's dead. I'm going to have to secure the site and then I'll have questions for you all. Deputy Green, tape off this area. Does anybody here know Latin?"

Natasha reluctantly stepped forward.

"I can help."

Testifying in the Gilbert Carver trial had set a killer free. Now, she felt the possibility of redemption. She could never allow herself to testify, but that didn't mean she couldn't try to be helpful.

"Okay then, you two stay here!" Sheriff Darwood commanded. "Everybody else, go back to the community center if you think you might have any valuable information. Otherwise go home."

Once everyone else was gone, Sheriff Darwood turned to Tom and Natasha.

"The details of Father Elijah's death are a matter of police business. What are your names?"

"I'm Natasha Azshatan," Natasha said as she offered her hand.

The Sheriff's eyes sparked in recognition when Natasha introduced herself. He shook her hand and turned to Tom.

"I'm Tom."

Darwood said solemnly, "It looks as if he hung himself. He wrote a note in his own blood. I need to know what it means."

Natasha wanted to explode in tears, but she fought it. *You must be strong. If you show any weakness now, the men will just tell you to go back with the others.*

Darwood opened the door. Natasha gasped. "Oh no, oh no, oh no. This can't be. This can't be. Last night at the Christmas party… he seemed fine."

Tom held her as she sobbed into his shoulder for a moment before composing herself.

"Are you gonna be okay, honey?" Tom asked.

"Yes. I just can't believe it," Natasha answered and wiped her eyes with her sleeve.

"See his writing just above his head?" Darwood asked.

Natasha nodded.

"I can translate what he wrote, but it doesn't make much sense. He wrote, 'We wander in the night and are consumed in the fire.'"

Darwood repeated the sentence and momentarily broke eye contact. When he looked back, his eyes had a different—less friendly—look.

"Thank you for the information," he said. "Don't worry. We'll do a thorough investigation, but I think what we have here is a pretty clear case of suicide. The writing's on the wall. Believe it or not, a lot of people die like this."

"Why would he want to be found like this?" Natasha asked.

"Who knows? He might have been *really* sick," Darwood answered.

"Sheriff, I'm a paleographer. I'm an expert at authenticating, and analyzing handwriting—in particular, handwriting in ancient Greek and Latin. If you provide me handwriting samples, I will be able to tell you with certainty whether or not Father Elijah wrote that note."

"No offense, Mrs. Azshatan. I appreciate your offer, but your reputation precedes you. Just leave the police business to me. You two go back home now. As far as handwriting analysis goes, the Washington State Patrol has a lab for that if we need it."

~

When they arrived home, Natasha drew a steamy hot bath while Tom kindled a fire and made a fresh pot of coffee. She leaned her head back and sunk deep into the suds so that only her face and breasts were not submerged. Massaging her scalp, she exhaled slowly, opened her eyes, stared at the ceiling, and tried to relax.

Natasha could hear the Elvis Christmas music playing from the living room; "singing choirs of angels sang with exaltations" as Tom watched the Seahawks score a touchdown. The game-play hollering mixed with the music and channeled to her ears through the bathwater made for a unique audio experience. Natasha could tell he had already turned his mind free of today's horror. She wished she could do the same, but she couldn't.

Natasha sat back upright, wrung out a washcloth, and wiped her face repeatedly.

It just didn't add up. There's no way he committed suicide. Last night at the party, he seemed perfectly happy. I'll bet Father Francis Charles could shed some light.

Natasha had mixed feelings about contacting Francis Charles. Part of her still loved him and missed him, but on another level, there was hurt and heartache. There was also a destructive secret that they both shared and tried to forget.

Natasha's mind drifted. She felt a little excitement remembering those times. She was barely out of university and the job at the embassy in Italy was a dream come true. During the day, she was a government paper pusher, but after work she enjoyed all that Rome's nightlife had to offer. Father Francis Charles was the embassy chaplain and, through the ordinance of confession, he had special privy to her personal affairs.

Father Francis was the most eminent scholar Natasha had ever known. She had met many intelligent and gifted people both in university and during her tenure in the Foreign Service, but none like Father Francis Charles. He was fluent in ten languages and was a walking, talking encyclopedia. They could talk for hours.

Natasha believed he started to fall in love with her the night he encouraged her to discuss her romantic life during confession. She thought back to that night and remembered.

Francis showed up at her apartment late that night, claiming that he felt alone and needed a friend. They talked until late. When she offered him the couch, he counter-offered that they could share the bed as platonic friends. He told her that, as a priest, he felt so lonely and starved for human contact; just for once, he would love to fall asleep within the comfort of an affectionate snuggle.

Natasha empathized with Francis and didn't have any objection to snuggling with the handsome young priest in her bed.

Later that night when she felt his arousal, she decided that she felt the same way. She turned to him and they kissed. Then, they made love—and it was *good* love. Love that was like water in the desert. Love that only people who had ever been so lost and lonely could also understand.

When he came back over the next night, she ended it with him. Despite his smile, Natasha could tell he was disappointed.

When she found out she was pregnant, she didn't know what to do. After all these years, she had still never told Francis that she had conceived and bore him a son. In her seventh month of pregnancy, she took a furlough to the coastal town of Rimini. Six weeks later, she gave birth to her only son. She had checked into the hospital using an alias and had given her baby boy over to the sisters.

Natasha's heart ached from this memory. She felt a dull, weighted pressure on her chest and she knew what was meant by a broken heart. There was the heartache of losing her son—and there was another pain too. Giving birth at a quaint coastal medical center had a high price. The substandard medical care had caused her to be barren. The boy she gave away was the only child she was to ever have.

When she returned to Rome, she avoided Francis Charles and found comfort in the arms of Thomas Azshatan. Tom and Natasha fell in love while Francis Charles watched from the sidelines. He watched her fall in love with another man. When Tom and Natasha decided to get married at the Embassy chapel, Francis performed the ceremony. He smiled all the way through. He also *envied* Tom Azshatan all the way through. He had pronounced them man and wife—and watched them kiss after telling Thomas that he may now kiss the bride.

Natasha had always felt a strange mixture of thankfulness, pity, admiration, and guilt when it came to Francis Charles—but she had especially felt guilt. She knew deep inside that she had robbed him of his only son. She had robbed them both.

Natasha again thought back to what he had told her in the confessional booth the night before they had first made love. "You must control your mind—it's the key to controlling your life. Is there anything else?"

"No, Father. Other than that, I've been a good girl."

"Then your confession is penance enough. You are forgiven. Go in peace, child."

His words still echoed in her mind all these years later—and they seemed to offer her the forgiveness she longed for, but could never have asked for.

She wiped her face with the washcloth again. She felt peaceful already. She got out of the tub, pulled on her robe, wrapped a towel around her head, and fell back onto her bed to air dry.

"Go in peace, child."

His words echoed as she fell asleep.

~

Darwood stood in front of the outbuilding, facing the trailhead. His eyes followed a squirrel running up a tree trunk. When his gaze wandered higher, he noticed a winter hawk circling in sky far above.

He grasped his radio from its holster and held it to his lips. "Deputy Green, this is Darwood, come in. Over."

K-s-hhh , K s-s-s-sh-sh-sh crrhrhk.

"Green here. Over," the deputy responded.

"Deputy Green, before you start asking questions, I need you to bring the crime kit down here pronto. Over."

"Affirmative. Be right down. Over."

"Roger. Over and out." Darwood spun the radio in his hand and landed it in its belt clip like an Old West gunslinger.

A few minutes later, Deputy Green showed up with the crime

kit. He walked up to where the sheriff waited for him just outside the outbuilding.

"You want me to stick around with you here and interview the folks later?" Green asked.

"Negative. I've got this covered. Go back and interview them. See if anyone has anything to share that's of value. I'm worried about what Father Elijah did that was so bad that he couldn't live with himself."

"One other thing. Get on the horn with Red at the mortuary. We'll be running out of daylight soon and the body needs to be secured."

"Understood."

"Call me if you need me!" the deputy shouted as he left.

Darwood reached into the crime kit duffle bag, pulled out latex gloves, and snapped them on. He cracked his knuckles, pulled out the Polaroid, and began taking photos of the snowpack around the shack.

Doggone it! Too many footprints in the snow now. Shouldn't have let anybody approach the shack at all. There were at least four sets of footprints leading up to and around the shack. If the priest's tracks were present, or if the tracks of a mysterious stranger were there, it was impossible to prove.

His photos of the snow would be useless. He thought back to when he approached the shack with the dog.

Had any footprints been observed? No. I don't think so, but I can't remember for certain. It was snowing last night. Most likely any footprints were covered by the fresh snow.

He opened the shack, turned on the light, and began shooting photos. He took close-up shots of the significant parts of the scene. The priest's head wrapped in plastic. The Polaroid made its familiar sounds. The father's neck. His left hand. His right hand. *Hmm. He left his multi-tool knife on the workbench.*

Darwood stepped backward to get a wide shot. A creepy feeling came over and he froze. He sensed someone lurked in the corner behind him, hiding behind the door.

His chest felt heavy, his stomach dropped, and he couldn't breathe.

Damn! The murderer was behind him. He reached for his gun, but it was too late.

Before the sheriff could react, the evil in the shadows whipped a plastic bag over his head and pulled him backward. The killer flung the sheriff sideways over his own hip and facedown into snow outside. He jumped on top of the sheriff's back and pinned Darwood's arms down under his knees, pulling the plastic snug.

Darwood struggled, but it was useless. He tried to buck the killer off, but he couldn't. The sheriff's lungs burned. His chest felt as if it were exploding. "C h h h h c h k k k h, ckkhckkk, k hhhhhh"

He tried to roll sideways.

"Chkuhhh svvffkhh, kkkuh."

He snapped his legs up in hopes of being able to kick the killer off or pull him off with his feet.

"Khuu, khuuu svchuih, ahh, ahh."

Darwood's legs dropped.

The killer sat on his back and arms a few more moments to make sure the sheriff was dead. *Perfect kill. They'll assume he just had a heart attack and collapsed in the snow.*

The killer thought of an idea. He had heard just enough of the sheriff's radio call to Green to know how they spoke on the radio.

He practiced the sheriff's voice.

"Green this is Darwood. Having ... hear-r-rt att-t-ta-a-a-ck. Get an ambulance. Over."

Sounds good. He pulled the radio off the sheriff's belt, held it to his lips, and did his best to imitate what the sheriff would sound like if he were having a massive heart attack.

A voice much like the sheriff's came out of his mouth.

"Green, this is Darwood. Over."

"Green. Go ahead," the deputy answered.

The killer smiled.

"Green, this is Darwood. Having-g-g. Hear-r-r-t-t-t atta-a-a-ack. Ahhh. Ahh. Send an ambulance uhhh uhhh uhhhhhhh."

The killer put the radio back in the sheriff's hands and pulled the plastic bag off his head. He then backtracked hastily through the other footprints. Once on the trail, he made his way to the marina. It was mainly deserted this time of year. He would wait until dark and then escape by boat.

~

Deputy Green and Jim Worley jumped in the sheriff's car and sped toward the trailhead. Green snatched up the dashboard-mounted radio handset and called out.

"Dispatch, this is Green. Over. Get an ambulance over to the marina trailhead at Jerrell's Cove right now. Sheriff Darwood has had a heart attack. I'm on my way right now."

"Darwood, are you there. Darwood are you there?"

No answer.

"Damn!"

He slammed the radio and looked at Jim. Jim just shook his head. The sheriff's car sped past Natasha's home with its sirens screaming and its lights flashing.

The commotion woke Natasha from her nap and startled Tom from his game. They looked out their window to see as the sheriff's car flew past.

"I wonder what that's all about," Tom said. "Why the rush?"

"Let's go see," Natasha suggested.

They were lacing up their boots when the ambulance sped by ten minutes later.

"Something's going on," Natasha exclaimed.

They ran down the street to the trailhead. The paramedics were already on their way up to the shack. Natasha ran ahead of Tom. She was six years younger and a *lot* more athletic.

Natasha arrived to see the paramedics rolling the sheriff onto a transport board. They strapped him in.

"One, two, three."

They hoisted him into the ambulance gurney.

"Out of the way. Out of the way!"

They ran Darwood down the trail and back to the ambulance.

"Oh my goodness. What happened, Deputy?" Natasha asked.

"Darwood had a heart attack and collapsed. He wasn't breathing when Jim and I arrived. I performed CPR on him until the medics came," Deputy Green choked up. "He was like a father to me."

Jim Worley put his hand on the deputy's shoulder. He didn't say anything. Just gave the deputy a pat on the shoulder.

"They shot him with adrenaline and they'll continue to try to resuscitate him on the way to Mason County. Since the snow kept him cold, he may not even have brain damage if they manage to bring him back."

Tom arrived in time to hear this last bit. The ambulance's sirens sang out as it sped off.

"Is there anything we can do to help?" Tom asked.

"Well, Red from the mortuary is on his way to claim the priest's body. I need to stay here and wrap up the scene here for the file."

"Jim," The deputy turned to him. "It appears the man committed suicide."

Jim clamped his teeth down, looked at the earth, and shook his head.

"I'm sure that when I look inside, I'll see the same things that make you think that. But it's pretty hard for me to believe that."

"I think so too," Natasha affirmed.

"I'm gonna finish taking pictures of the scene, then I'd like you to take a look and tell me if anything pertinent comes to mind. As far as suicides go, it's a strange one."

When Jim saw the condition of the priest, tears burst from his eyes. He silently shook his head and dropped to his knees next to the body.

He clenched his teeth, and shook his head.

"Can I?"

Jim gestured to Deputy Green that he wanted to untie the man's neck and take off the plastic. Green nodded.

Jim loosened the priest's neck from the belt and held the man's head to his chest, weeping deeply. He clenched his teeth and shook his head. His throat locked with pain. His eyes squinted—facial muscles quivering—as he hugged the man's head and wept.

The sight was overwhelming and, at that, Natasha cried too. Tom and Deputy Green tried hold in their emotion, but they also could not hold back their tears.

Nobody spoke for a few minutes. Tom held Natasha and the deputy patted Jim's shoulder.

"How about if I give you a hand up, Deacon?"

Jim gently lay the priest's head back against the corner of the wall.

Deputy Green extended his hand and helped Jim pull himself up from the floor. Jim wiped his eyes with his shirtsleeves and gave the Deputy a hug.

"You two go on home now. Jim, if you'll stay with me, I'll just gather what I need and we'll head over to the Father's parsonage."

"Um hum," Jim agreed.

The phone rang at Tom and Natasha's house on Monday afternoon.

"Hi, Natasha, it's Jim Worley. How are you and Tom doing?"

"I didn't sleep too much last night. Tom was up, too."

"Me, too, I guess," Jim continued. "One thing I'm certain of. The man was murdered."

Tom was in the garage situating his tool area. He hammered a nail as if to punctuate Jim Worley's statement and a chill ran down Natasha's spine.

"Who do you think might have done it? And why?"

Jim took a deep breath and sighed.

"Wish I knew. All I do know is that Father Elijah didn't commit suicide—and that leaves only one other possibility."

"Did you tell Deputy Green?"

"Well, the deputy's pretty headstrong. He thinks it's a suicide. Of course, there's no evidence to the contrary. Ruling the death as a suicide is a lot less work than a murder investigation. When he talks about looking for clues, he's really just looking for clues as to why he might have taken his own life."

"How do you know?" Natasha asked.

"I was with him at the scene and also at Father Elijah's home."

"I, on the other hand, was looking for clues as to who would have wanted him dead. Two very different mindsets. I observed his home and personal belongings carefully. Now I'm just trying to put the pieces together. I did see some things that created some ideas for me."

"Did you retrieve any handwriting samples?" Natasha asked.

"Not a single scrap. He was all digital."

"What was it that you found?"

"I'd rather not say for now. If that's okay."

Natasha invited him to dinner and Jim agreed.

～

"I was thinking last night that maybe you could shed some light on the note that Father Elijah left behind," said Natasha as they sat down to a roast beef dinner.

"Have you considered the possibility that it wasn't Father Elijah who left the note?"

Tom and Natasha looked at each other and their eyebrows raised.

The thought did cross our minds," Tom answered. "But it looked like he wrote it."

Jim continued, "Well, it looked like he wrote it because at first we assumed he was the only one present at the time of his death, since the sheriff hastily ruled it a suicide. But if you open the possibility that he was murdered, then that means there was someone else was there with him."

"And that person may have been the one who left the note," Natasha agreed.

"But it was written in the Father's blood—with his own fingertip," Tom raised some doubt as he poured another glass of red wine.

"We assumed that too," Natasha took over to Jim. "Just because his hand has blood on it doesn't necessarily mean he was the one who wrote the note."

They all thought for a moment.

"Jim, when we spoke earlier, you mentioned that you might have seen something at the Father's home that gave you some ideas."

"Truth be told, it's partly what I didn't see that gives me some ideas," Jim answered. "As I mentioned earlier, his home was completely devoid of any scrap of handwriting. We turned on his computer and discovered that all of his documents had been erased from his hard drive. And the Internet browsing history had been erased, too. There was no trace of his pet project either."

"What project was that?"

"The father was writing a series of sermons. He was going to call the series, Countdown to the End Times. Or Count Down to the Apocalypse. Or something like that. It had to do with the interpretation of the prophecies of Revelation. Specifically the seven seals."

"Are you saying you think he might have been killed over that manuscript?" Natasha asked.

"The question is *why* was his computer erased? Where was all his research? Where was his sermonic calendar? Where were his manuscripts?"

"But why would someone want to kill him over a book about the end times? There are hundreds of such books already," Tom said.

The idea that Jim put forward was interesting, but Natasha began to wonder if maybe Jim was letting his imagination go a little too far.

"Do you have any idea what the message is all about?" Tom asked. "Why would the killer have written that?"

"That's a good question," Jim responded, wagging his empty fork at Tom as an extension of his pointer finger.

Natasha answered, "The Zodiac Killer used to leave puzzling messages for the police to figure out. Maybe this phrase is a clue to the killer's identity."

They all thought silently for a moment. Jim looked as though he had thought of something, but then he stopped.

"What?" Natasha asked.

"Well, I thought of something else that could be relevant. I guess I better tell you now, rather than have you find out later."

"What?" Natasha pushed.

"Oh. About twenty years ago, there were a lot of mysterious cattle mutilations—and a lot of talk about devil worshippers in the woods of Mason County."

"Devil worshippers. Hmm. The wandering in the night and the fires seem like it could be cult or demonic related. It's something worth checking out."

"Yes—and it might explain motive as well," Jim agreed.

"Maybe I'll pay a visit to the *Mason Journal* tomorrow," Natasha suggested.

She cleared the plates, turned on the teapot, and sat back down.

"So, Jim. Tell us about your boat," said Tom.

"Oh. She's nothing fancy. But she's comfortable. Named her Foresta because when you sail around here, it's so peaceful to look at the edges of the forest as it meanders along the pristine beaches."

"Sounds nice," Tom said.

"Any time you want, we can take her out."

The teapot began to whistle and Natasha got up.

"I think you'll like this tea, Jim. It's called holiday spice."

"Sounds good. Thank you, Natasha."

Natasha smiled. She loved introducing people to her favorite unique teas.

Tom got up, pulled the cookie jar off the counter, and put it out on the table. It was filled with Natasha's homemade chocolate chip and walnut cookies.

Natasha walked carefully back with the three hot mugs and sat back down.

"I think we need to have a talk with Deputy Green."

"Won't work," Jim countered. "I know the man. He lives in a world of black and white. And all we have is unproven conspiracy theories."

"If all we have is conspiracies, then we better find something pretty fast. Because we only have two days before the funeral. And I think he deserves better than for the whole town to think he committed suicide."

"And we deserve better than to have to live in fear of an unrestrained murderer in our midst," Tom added.

"Um humph," Jim agreed. "We'll need to gather the facts and present the case to Green no later than Wednesday night. So we need a plan."

They all thought for a moment until Natasha broke the silence.

"Tom, I know you didn't want to split up, but you know I can very well defend myself. And as I see it, we have three separate places to cover. The newspaper, the library, and Jerrell's cove. How about if you take the newspaper; I'll take the library; and Jim can cover the church and the crime scene? Jim, how about if you call Deputy Green tonight and see if there have been any new developments? And one way or the other, get him to open the crime scene up to you as early possible tomorrow."

"Sounds like a good plan," Jim said.

"Who said I was worried about you?" Tom joked. "You're the one who studied karate not me."

"That's right. So you better watch out, old man," Natasha teased. She made a karate chop gesture.

"I best be going then," Jim said as he sat up. "Tomorrow morning comes awfully early for me."

He made his way to the door and put on his jacket.

"Thanks for that delicious dinner. And it was a real pleasure getting to know you better."

"Thank you for being our guest."

Natasha reached into a side drawer, grabbed one of her business cards, and gave it to Jim. It was a plain white card with her name and number.

"This is my toll-free business line and it forwards to my cell phone. Call me as soon as you can tomorrow with any updates. And I'll get Tom on the line for a three-way call."

"What kind of business?"

"Inspirational, motivational, you might say."

"It was nice to get to know you better, too. And I'll definitely take you up on that offer for a day on your boat."

"Any time you wanna take her out, just give me a holler. I leave the keys under the captain's chair."

"Good night," Natasha said as she gave him a hug.

He and Tom shook hands.

"Good night. See you tomorrow."

Jim turned around to go and Tom closed the door behind him.

The next morning, Tom made cappuccinos. They sipped them on the back deck while they enjoyed the mountain and water views.

"So," Tom said. "You really want to get mixed up into this?"

"We already are. Besides. Whether I like to admit it, or not, Sidney Delaware was right. I am kind of a psychic investigator."

"This is serious."

"I *am* serious. I may not be psychic like Grant Nuby, but you know I have a gift. Even if it's just a glorified woman's intuition."

"What's your intuition tell you now?"

Suddenly, an ugly, dreadful feeling manifested in her core. It was heavy and oppressive. She recognized what it meant—she knew that someone had died or was in danger of dying. Perhaps someone she loved.

Natasha bent over in response to the feeling.

"Honey, are you okay?"

Tom put his hand on her back. Natasha didn't answer right away, but after a few moments, she straightened up.

"Something bad has happened or is going to happen. I can feel it."

"What do you think it might be?"

"I don't know."

Tom kissed her on the lips and on her forehead.

"Thanks, babe."

"Of course. Don't forget to eat the breakfast I cooked you."

Tom went back to the living room and turned on the news channel. Natasha walked back to the bedroom and slipped into her favorite blue jeans with the red sparkle beads on the right thigh. She looked in the mirror and smiled to herself. She didn't feel like smiling, but she hoped it would help her feel better. She pulled her hair back into a ponytail and pulled on a tight-fitting, white turtleneck sweater.

"Hey, honey?" Tom shouted from the living room. "You better come in here. I think I know what's made you upset."

"What?" Natasha demanded as she entered.

She looked at the TV and she understood why she felt sick. The feeling intensified and felt heavy on her heart. She sat down on the living room couch, and watched in horror as the news helicopter showed footage of the ferry victims floundering about in the water.

"A Seattle ferry just capsized," Tom said. "As many as 1,100 people may have been aboard."

"What caused it to capsize?"

"I don't know yet—I just started watching."

The news anchor appeared behind his desk. Behind him was a window that showed a view of Seattle with a backdrop of the Olympic Mountains.

"KOJO's reporter, Mitchell Johansson, is at the ferry terminal. Let's go to him right now."

"Thanks, Dan. Yes, as you can see, behind me is where the ferry went down. The helicopters are pulling out as many survivors as possible. Here's what we know so far. At 7:15 this morning, an explosion occurred somewhere in the center of the Bainbridge to Seattle Ferry. As many as 1,100 people may be aboard. So far, less than one hundred are known to have survived.

"The Department of Transportation has suspended all ferry routes, effectively isolating some hundred thousand who live on the islands and depend on ferry transportation.

"We are told that A.I.M., the American Islamic Militia, has taken credit for the attack and has warned that there will be more attacks to follow. We have to take a break. When we come back, an interview with Washington's director of Homeland Security, Darrel Burns."

Natasha cried and Tom held her. She was strong, but extremely sensitive.

"All we can do is be thankful that it didn't happen the last time we took the ferry. Let's stay home today. I'm sure we can do our research from the Internet and, if we need to, we can drive to Shelton together."

Natasha nodded and wiped her eyes with her sleeves. She went to the kitchen and popped an English muffin into the toaster.

"Water's still probably hot enough for your tea," Tom yelled helpfully.

Natasha had at least twenty different types of teas. She pulled out a calming tea and poured the hot water and tea into her favorite white mug. The mug was wide and shallow, almost like half bowl and half mug. It was great for slurping soup out of, too.

The English muffin popped up. She put them on her plate and scooped onto them the cheesy scrambled eggs that Tom had made.

"Tom?" she said loudly. "Can you turn the TV down? The news is too upsetting."

"Okay," he hollered back. "I'll let you know if they say anything that's really important."

Clear your mind. Focus on your goals. She closed her eyes, breathed deeply, and exhaled slowly.

She opened her eyes, and looked down at the teacup. A little hill of pulverized tealeaves was surrounded by a moat of the remaining few tablespoons of tea. She moved the cup in a circular motion and swirled around the liquid. As the tea swirled, she tipped the cup back and drank what remained. The particles were left clinging to the surface of the mug. She looked down at them and gazed. She tried to clear her mind and discern any shapes or symbols in the remains.

At first, she didn't see anything, but after a moment, she saw what looked a little like the face of cartoon cat. Natasha smiled a warm, genuine smile.

Natasha stood up, stretched, and looked out the window again at the view. The fog had burned off again or moved away. She put the cup and plate inside the dishwasher and went into her office.

~

Natasha sat down at her desk, pulled out a yellow tablet and a felt-tipped pen. *What's the plan for the day?* She remembered that she wanted to call Cardinal Charles in Vatican City. If anyone can help me with the "wander in the night, consumed by fire" note, it would be him. She wrote on the pad. #1. Call Cardinal Charles. #2. Research connections concerning anything to do with the occult and Mason County—starting with cow mutilations. # 3. Call Jim and see how things are on his end. #4. See where we are at that point.

Natasha dialed Cardinal Charles. As the phone rang, she heard the telephone line's clicks and crackles before the line disconnected. "Ur!" She dialed again. This time it went through.

"Hello, this is Cardinal Charles."

"Hello there, Cardinal. Do you know who this is?"

There was a short silence. The line crackled and clicked.

Francis smiled. "I'd know that voice anytime, anywhere. Natasha! So nice to hear from you! Congratulations on your writing success. I always believed you'd be a great leader."

"Thank you—and congratulations on your promotion, too. You're really famous now."

"I'm honored to serve Christ in this position. It's the most challenging and interesting work that I do now. It's really just incredible. I heard about the A.I.M. attack on that ferry. Horrible. You just never know where they'll strike next."

"Actually, Tom and I moved to the Pacific Northwest earlier this month. We just got here—and *this* happens. It's ironic because one of the reasons we wanted to leave DC was because we were sure it was the number one target."

"Yes. These extremist Islamic radicals will take advantage of any target of opportunity. Thank God you weren't aboard that ferry. Do you live close to Seattle?"

"We live on a small island community southwest of Seattle. It takes us about 1.5 hours to drive there, and about forty minutes by boat."

"Really? You know I'm very good friends with someone else who has a house in that area. What Island?"

"Harstine Island."

"What an amazing coincidence. He and his wife own a home in Jerrell's Cove."

"Wow!" Natasha slapped the desk with the palm of her hand. "That is a coincidence. That's where we live, too!" Natasha smiled in disbelief. "Who are they?"

"Well, I hate to namedrop, but you probably know of them. President-elect Jaimeson owns a summer home there. Every time I talk to him, he's telling me how I have to come out and visit. I nearly took him up on the offer last summer."

"Wow. I haven't met him yet. But I heard he had a place in Jerrell's Cove."

"He's retired foreign service too. That's how I know him so well. I met him way back shortly after I married you and Tom. We served in Istanbul together."

"Small world, huh?"

"Yes. It certainly is. If America had more consular officers like Will, the membership numbers of the A.I.M. would be much lower. He was tough, but always fair. Who knows? Maybe he saved some lives. Radical Islam is the most imminent threat to our civilization. I'm using my influence at the Vatican to toughen our policies and to help the western governments to defend against this threat."

Natasha sensed that the cardinal was barely restraining himself from digressing into a raging rant. He cut off his last sentence and inhaled deeply in effort to calm himself.

He changed his tone and continued, "And it's funny you should call, because you've been in my mind and prayers lately. Are you okay?"

"It's funny how that works, isn't it. I've been thinking of you too. And I do need your help on something."

"I'm at your service."

"Thanks, Francis. Since moving here, I made a good acquaintance with our village orthodox priest, Father Elijah."

Natasha's voice choked up.

She took a breath and continued, "Well, he was discovered dead on Sunday."

"Oh. I'm so sorry."

"Me too. The sheriff ruled his death a suicide, but then died from a heart attack the same afternoon while taking the crime scene photos. It's a very strange situation."

"Yes. Go on."

"There was a note written on the wall in his blood. *In girum imus nocte et consumimur igni.* I translated the Latin—*We wander in the night and are consumed by fire.*"

Natasha waited for his response.

"It can also be translated 'at night we move in circles, and are consumed in flames.' Hmmm, very interesting."

"The thing is," Natasha continued. "I don't think this is a suicide. I'm wondering if he was murdered. And if it was the murderer—who left this note?"

"Handwriting is of course your expertise. Have you told any of the local authorities?"

"Just the sheriff, hours before he died."

"Anybody else?"

"The head deacon Jim Worley. I'd say we both agree. He tried to convince Deputy Green, but the deputy is young and headstrong, and is sticking by the sheriff's hastily declared suicide. There's another problem. The father didn't leave behind any of his own handwriting samples. At least none readily available."

"He must have left evidence of his signature somewhere. On a car loan or a credit card slip."

"I'm sure in time something could be found, but only if the deputy sees fit to pursue the issue. In any case, a signature would not be enough. A credible analysis would require a large sample of writing."

"But still. His signature may reveal either similarities, or dissimilarities."

Natasha wished she could figure out where she could find a sample of Father Elijah's printing.

"That's true—but there are some things that don't add up. And I really have a hard time believing it was suicide. I was at a Christmas party with him the night before. He seemed fine—he seemed joyful. He was still inviting people to his church. When the deputy and deacon went to his home, the deacon noticed that all of his documents and his browsing history had been erased."

"This is very mysterious. You think he might have been murdered—and the message is actually from the murderer?"

"Yes. And the funeral is the day after tomorrow. I really want to clear his name of suicide, in time to set the record straight for his burial. And also to bring the murderer to justice before the evidence trail grows cold."

"Didn't the deputy think it was suspicious that the documents were erased along with his Internet history?"

"The deacon said the deputy just explained it away."

Francis digested the information for a moment and then answered.

"Yes. The deputy might be right. A lot of what you have told me can be accounted for and still be consistent with suicide."

"How old was he?"

"Mid-thirties I'd say."

"And unmarried?"

"Yes. How did you know?"

"You're not the only one with good intuition. The Orthodox Church allows its priests to marry, but he was still single in his mid-thirties. Did he have a strange personality? Was he shy?"

"No. I'd say he was outgoing and had a very well rounded personality. He liked my books."

"Hmm."

"What are you thinking?"

"Just a scenario that might fit the facts is all, but I don't know if you really want to hear it."

"No. Go ahead."

"Suicides often act joyous and outgoing before they kill themselves. It's because they've considered suicide for a long time, but they finally make their peace with death. Once they make their decision, it's as if a weight has been lifted off their shoulders. They will often call old friends and loved ones and have great conversations. They will give precious items away. In the midst of those last interactions, they will hide their suicidal intentions because they don't want to be stopped.

"As far has his computer and writings are concerned, it's probably just a matter of time before they turn up. I'll think about this mysterious note. One way or another, we should find out what it means. I'll call you as soon as I can come up with anything. I think you have to work on getting a writing sample."

"Thank you, Francis. Is it okay to call you Francis? I don't know what to call you anymore," Natasha laughed.

"No problem. I know you're not exactly Roman Catholic anymore, so Francis is fine. Besides, I wish everyone would call me by my first name. I'm so glad you called. Please call me anytime. And actually, definitely call me if you have any updates."

"Thank you, Francis."

"You're welcome. Peace be with you, Natasha."

""Mm, bye-bye."

Maybe father Elijah really did commit suicide. Maybe I'm looking too much for hidden meanings.

She suddenly grabbed the Polaroid and ran to the kitchen. Tom was putting the cups and plates in the dishwasher.

"Wait!" Natasha yelled at him.

Tom looked at her as if she was crazy.

"There was a kitty cat face shape in my tea leafs and I meant to take a picture of it."

Tom raised his eyebrows and shook his head amused. He backed away with his hands in the air like a burglar caught by the police.

Natasha shoved at his chest.

"Don't you make fun of me!"

She understood how ridiculous she must seem at times. She opened the dishwasher, pulled out the teacup, and looked inside. Kitty cat face was still intact. She turned on the overhead light, aimed, and pushed the button. The Polaroid went flash, snap, whine. Now her kitty cat face was preserved for all time.

~

Natasha sat in her study and looked out the window. An evergreen tree near had a healthy layer of snow. The snow rounded the edges and had the effect of making the tree chubby.

She thought about Father Elijah. She could hardly believe he was really dead. Whereas before she felt certain that he hadn't taken his own life, after speaking with Cardinal Charles, it seemed like a real possibility.

She tried to remember anything he said that would help her make up her mind.

She remembered the day he first met her at her book signing. He was so charismatic. He was so excited to show her his "astounding" material.

As farfetched as Jim's connections had been, they seemed to draw her attention. They seemed to urge her to look deeper. She sensed truth in the idea that he was murdered—as horrible as that seemed—in all of its possible ways.

All right. Last night we made a plan. There is no reason to not dig into the research that I committed to.

She launched Internet Explorer and searched for results on cattle mutilations, satanic activities, and mysterious deaths in Mason County, Washington. Of course, fourteen million results showed up. She sifted through all of the garbage. She really hated the sites that pretended to be what she was interested in, only to click on it, and discover they're selling something.

Finally she hit pay dirt. It was an article from the November 30, 1986 issue of *The West Sounders Journal*—"Lucas Phillip Renard arrested for the ritualistic killing of Belfair teen Jeanette Downy."

A mental image flashed in Natasha's mind. She saw a thin, rugged man in his late-twenties wearing faded blue jeans and a flannel shirt. He had long, greasy blond hair. He was hiding in the woods. Waiting. He was crouched behind a huckleberry bush and his lips curled into an evil smile.

Natasha felt like she was inside Jeanette's mind—experiencing what she experienced. She heard a twig break on the forest floor and she got a creepy feeling—as if she was being watched. She turned around and saw the man. He was trying to hide from her, but now he knew she had seen him. He looked at her and didn't move. He just watched her and smiled his evil smile. He flashed the blade of a buck knife. It glinted in the sunlight.

Jeanette pretended not to see him, but her heart was filled with terror. She turned around and ran as fast as she could, but he chased her.

Natasha had an idea of what Lucas Phillip Renard had done even before she continued reading.

She shook her head and continued. The article said that Lucas Phillip Renard had disfigured and raped her. He had carved the number 666 into her chest. Natasha went into her vision again. She could see what the sheriff hadn't shared with the newspaper. She saw Jeanette running from him frantically and screaming out, "Jesus, help me! Jesus, help me!"

He pounced on her like a wild cougar. He pinned her body to the ground, removed a nylon cord from his pocket, and tied her arms securely to her side. He rolled her over, put his rough, dirty hand over her mouth, and held her head down.

Jeannette looked up at him frightened and crying.

He cut out her vocal chords with his buck knife.

Jeanette's eyeballs rolled and darted in terrified panic—but to her horror, when the man lifted his hand from her mouth, the only sound she could make was a gurgling noise.

Natasha snapped back to reality and recoiled from her vision. *Unbelievable. How horrible.*

She typed in "Lucas Phillip Renard" and twenty-nine articles appeared to be specifically related the killer. She clicked the third one down. The headline read, "Satanic Killer Explains."

Her eyes zeroed in on his photo. He was as she imagined. Under his photo was a quote in bold italic lettering:

> When my victims cry out to Jesus for help, I think it's amusing. Lucifer charged me to kill in order to test me and to prove to me that he is the one who saves, and not the man Jesus.

Natasha felt a chill go down her spine. She shook her head and couldn't read anymore.

When Natasha looked out the window again, the snow seemed less pure. She picked up the phone and dialed Jim's house. No answer. *He's probably with Deputy Green. It's noon and he hasn't even called. That's strange. For sure he should have called by now.*

Natasha walked to the kitchen and pulled Deputy Green's card out of her junk drawer. Tom was still watching the aftermath of the ferry attack. "How's it going, honey?" she asked loudly.

"Well, you haven't missed out on much in here. What have you been up to?"

"I came across some pretty creepy history from Mason County, just like Jim mentioned. The funny thing is that I was expecting to hear from him by now. I just called his house and no one answered. I think I'm just going to go ahead and call Deputy Green."

Natasha sat down on the couch next to Tom, and watched

the coverage of the ferry tragedy as she dialed. No one answered. She held the line and waited for it to ring more. Still no answer. She pushed the flash button and dialed Jim again. No answer. She pushed flash again and dialed Deputy Green's number. She heard the line click.

"Sheriff Green here."

"Sheriff, thank goodness you answered. I was starting to worry."

"About what?"

"Have you heard from Jim since last night?"

"Well, I know he tried to call me late last night. I saw his number on my caller ID and tried to called him back this morning. No one answered, so I just figured he'd call me back when he got a chance. It's been a busy morning for me. Douglas Blair from the governor's office called me this morning and appointed me as acting sheriff. I updated him on my investigation into Father Elijah's death."

"What did you tell him?"

"Just that it was a suicide."

"Did you tell him about the possibility that he might have been killed?"

"You and Jim are on the same page—but you're both wrong. I know all about this stuff and just because you guys didn't see it coming, doesn't mean he didn't do it. Besides, who would want to kill Father Elijah anyway?"

Natasha couldn't think of what to say.

"Now, Natasha, I know you're a writer, which means you get paid for having an over active imagination—and Jim's an old man who's full of conspiracy theories and fortune cookie sayings. Listen to me good here. I'm gonna say this as nice as I can. This is my investigation. Sheriff Darwood already ruled it a suicide. I'm doing my own investigation and I have to agree with the late sheriff Darwood at this time. Now this is important. Governor Jaimeson has just been elected president. Any reckless rumors about supposed murders on the island could really draw a spotlight—a spotlight that we don't want."

Natasha remembered the feeling in her gut from this morning and worried that maybe it wasn't just about the ferry. Maybe something had happened to Jim.

"Deputy, I mean, Sheriff. Jim was supposed to contact you and persuade you to let him look at the scene where Father Elijah was found. We made a plan. He was supposed to call and check in."

"Don't worry. He's okay."

"I am worried. I have a really bad feeling."

Tom motioned to Natasha to give him the phone. She did.

"Sheriff Green. This is Tom. We had Jim over for dinner last night. I have to say I'm a bit alarmed—come to think about it—that Jim hasn't checked in with us yet. Can you meet us over at his house?"

Natasha figured Sheriff Green was probably leaning back in his chair with his waffle boots propped up on the desk and looking around at his office walls made from faux timber beams in log cabin style.

"Yeah, Tom. I have to admit. It doesn't sound right. It's probably nothing. But I'll meet you over at Jim's place in say, fifteen minutes.

"We'll be right there."

"See you there," Sheriff Green said as he slammed the telephone headset down on the receiver.

Natasha and Tom hopped into the Subaru and drove to Jim's place. They walked up to his front porch and heard the Buick running. They could smell the fumes. They rang the bell, but no one answered.

"Why don't you go ahead and wait in the car until Green gets here, honey."

Green arrived and hastily parked close to the garage. He got out and slammed his door shut.

"Sheriff," Tom said. "We just got here. No one answers the door, but Jim's Buick is running."

Green nodded. He stood on his tiptoes and looked into the window of the garage door.

"No! What the heck is going on around here? Now Jim's committed suicide, too!"

Natasha turned to Tom and began to sob. She felt like she was going insane. Green snatched his radio from its belt clip.

"Dispatch, this is Sheriff Green. Over."

"This is dispatch. Go ahead."

"Code 1028. Send an ambulance to 211 Robin Road, Jerrell's Cove, right away. Over."

"Roger. Ambulance on its way. Over."

Green grasped the handle of the garage door and tried to open it, but it was locked.

"Jim! Jim! Are you still alive? Jim? Jim. I'm sorry I didn't call you back."

He kicked the door, clenched his fists, and looked up at the sky.

"Tom, I'm going to go around the back and break in. You and Natasha stay here or go home if you choose."

"We'll stay for now."

"Suit yourself. I don't know how much more of this she can take."

"I don't know how much more of this *any* of us can take."

Natasha wiped her eyes with her sleeves as Sheriff Green disappeared behind the house. Suddenly they heard a gunshot.

"Whoo!" Tom exclaimed. "Get back to the car!"

She was about to, but then the front door opened. It was Sheriff Green with a shotgun hole through his chest. Lucas Phillip Renard stood behind him with his evil smile.

"Ah, Satan sees Natasha," he hissed.

Natasha closed her eyes tightly, shook her head, and looked back at *Green*.

"Sorry if I scared you," he said. "Shooting the sliding glass door was the fastest way to break in."

Natasha shook her head again and checked again to make sure Lucas Phillip Renard was not there. He wasn't.

Her knees buckled and she fainted.

Luckily for Natasha, Tom was right there to catch her. He and Green pulled her in and laid her down on Jim's rusty colored velvet sofa.

Tom kneeled down next to her and petted her forehead.

"She'll be okay. Go to Jim! Maybe he can still be saved."

Green went into the garage. He turned the engine off and opened the garage door. It was obvious that Jim had been dead for several hours. He looked at the dashboard, and decided it was best to keep Tom and Natasha away. *In girum imus nocte et consumimur igni* was writ in blood across the front dash. *Sometimes suicides did occur in groups. This weird Latin phrase though—it just fuels conspiracy theories.*

He went back into the living room to check on Tom and Natasha. Natasha was conscious. Tom was sitting next to her, holding her up.

"Tom and Natasha," Green addressed them solemnly. "Jim's been dead for several hours. I need you two to go on home. The rest of this is police business."

"Come on, Tom. Let's go. I just want to go home. Call us later on and give us an update will you."

"I will. Tom, take her home now—and no more of these wild murder accusations. Maybe you need to take her on a vacation and just get out of here for a few days. The funerals might be too much to handle."

"That might not be a bad idea."

He thought of maybe taking Natasha to Mexico.

As Tom drove the last block, and turned into their driveway, neither he nor Natasha noticed the strangers in the sedan parked on Firecrest.

Natasha was strong again—or the piercing look in her eyes was a look of determination or seriousness. She was deep in thought and silent. She slammed the car door and ran straight to the bedroom. Tom went to the computer to shop for last minute, all-inclusive vacations in Mexico.

A few minutes later, he heard her down in the basement, beating the stuffing out of the boxing bag. He could hear her scream as she exhaled and performed a powerful roundhouse kick. The chain holding it to the ceiling chimed. . Puh-puh-puh-puh in rapid succession as she pummeled the bag with her fists. Puh, puh, chime, chime. Her strikes against the bag became rhythmic and therapeutic.

Tom listened to her fight her emotions out. The noises she made sounded wild and primal. He had to fight an urge to visit the website that featured the sexy jungle warrior women. He stayed focused on booking a vacation.

Three weeks in the Mexican Riviera would be perfect. He became engrossed in reading online hotel testimonials and comparing rates. His mind escaped from the death and despair of the recent days and imagined crystal-clear tropical waters and never-ending fountains of Corona.

An hour later, Natasha was showering and Tom had already pulled out their passports and was packing. They still used the highly coveted black diplomatic passports. Their flight would leave SeaTac 12:45 AM. It was from Seattle to Miami with a connecting flight to Cancun.

I don't wanna be around for the rest of the week of nothing but funerals and terror news!

"This was a great idea you had, Tom! Christmas and New Year's in Playa Del Carmen. What a great idea. You're just full of surprises!"

Suddenly, Natasha remembered the gift from Father Elijah she had carried home from the Christmas party. It was the only gift under the tree. She went out to the living room and looked at it. It was wrapped in red foil paper and a green ribbon. She sat down on the floor in front of the tree Eastern style. She picked up the gift and shook it to feel its weight and guess what might be inside. She wasn't supposed to open it until Christmas. *I think I should open it. He would want me to, I think.*

She looked down at the package and tore off the wrapping. Inside the box was a handsomely customized computer memory stick. Its exterior casing was polished cherry wood with gold trimming. He wrote a note in calligraphy. It read:

> Dear Natasha,
> Merry Christmas! From one writer to another, I know how great these little gadgets are. I hope you enjoy yours as much as I enjoy mine. Don't forget Jesus is the reason for the season!
> With Love in Christ,
> Father Elijah Alexander

Natasha momentarily reflected that Easter owed its roots to the Roman fertility goddess, Estar. She bitterly remembered how, after several years of unanswered prayers, while dyeing eggs for Easter Sunday, she had dunked an egg and made a wish for a baby—as if the egg was a shooting star or a coin thrown into a fountain. She had known for years that Easter eggs and bunny rabbits had nothing to do with Christ, but were actually symbols of fertility.

She still loved Christmastime. This gift from Father Elijah was very special. Included with the memory stick was a well-coordinated leather travel chain made to be worn around the neck and secured to the memory stick.

I'll keep it close to my heart. She snapped the chain onto the stick and placed it on her neck.

Natasha stood up and walked back to the bedroom. "Look what Father Elijah gave me for Christmas."

"Oh. That's cool. Let me see that."

Natasha disconnected it and handed it to Tom. It reminded Tom of a fancy pocketknife.

"He should have given this to me."

"Too bad for you." Natasha said. "I'm gonna transfer my stuff to it right now."

"Natasha, I'm already done packing and you haven't even begun.

So hurry up. We have to be at the airport by eleven, which means we have to leave here by nine-thirty."

Natasha looked at her wrist to see the time. She forgot that she had taken her watch off in the workout room.

"What time is it?"

"It's already three."

"Okay. I'll hurry."

Natasha ran across the hall to the office, sat down at the computer, and connected her old and new memory sticks. She began transferring her files when the phone rang.

She answered. There was just phone line static, and crackling. "Hello?" she said. Just static. She hung up.

She thought about something she had read called electronic voice phenomenon. She wondered if she recorded the static and played it back slowly, if there would be a message from Elijah or Jim. More likely, it was an automated telemarketing machine probing to see if anyone was home.

She looked down at her computer and resumed dragging files into her new memory stick. As she moved the mouse arrow to the next file, the arrow momentarily took off into its own direction. It was ever so slight. Natasha froze and just watched it. It moved again, ever so slightly. She looked down at her modem. The activity lights were blinking even though she wasn't using the Internet. Somebody else had hacked into her computer. "Oh I caught you whoever you are," she said under her breath. She pulled her memory sticks out and launched her anti-spyware program. The program would send Trojan Horse viruses back to the hackers and also identify approximately where in the world the hackers were operating from. "Gotcha!" She pounded the enter button and watched the trace program.

The program traced the hacking to Maryland. That was as specific as it got. *Hmm.*

The doorbell rang. Natasha walked into the entry as Tom answered the door.

The two men at the front door were wearing suits. "Thomas Azshatan?" the one with the short brown hair asked.

"Yes."

Natasha put her arm around his waist and stood at his side.

"Mr. Azshatan. I'm Agent Beck and this is Agent Matthews. We're with the United States Secret Service."

They held up their ID wallets to Tom and Natasha.

"How can I help you?" Tom asked.

"Sir, this is a Federal warrant, which commands us to arrest you on the charges of espionage and high treason."

"What?" Tom exclaimed. "This is a mistake. I've never done anything of the sort. I just retired from the Foreign Service."

Agent Beck interrupted, "If you're innocent as you say, then there's nothing to worry about. But for right now, you'll have to come with us."

"This is preposterous!" Natasha exclaimed. "This is crazy!"

"Don't worry. This will all be okay."

"Get dressed!" Beck commanded.

Tom grabbed his coat off the hook and put on his shoes.

"Up against the wall. Put your hands on the wall above your head."

Agent Beck pulled out his cuffs and slapped them on Tom wrists. Natasha gasped.

"That's not necessary," Tom said. "I'll come peacefully."

"It is necessary. And I know you'll come peacefully."

Beck frisked Tom for weapons.

"Tom Azshatan, you are being arrested on the charges of high treason and acts of espionage. You have the right to remain silent."

Agent Matthews pulled on Tom's cuffs, herding him toward the unmarked sedan.

"You have the right to an attorney."

Tom kissed Natasha.

"Don't worry honey. This will all get straightened out. Call Jerry right away."

"This is crazy!" Natasha cried. "You guys are making a mistake."

"If you cannot afford an attorney, the court will appoint one for you free of charge."

Natasha kissed Tom.

"Don't worry, honey. I'll take care of this. I love you."

"I love you, too. Don't worry. I'll be okay. Just call Jerry right away."

Agent Matthews opened the back door and protected Tom's head as he guided him in. Agent Beck followed. As they drove off, Tom turned his head to keep his eyes on Natasha. Natasha stood at the door a moment more trying to comprehend what had just happened. She looked down at the arrest warrant in her hands. *This is scary shit.*

She closed the door and went back to the office to call their attorney. It was four already. With any luck, he would still be in his office.

Jeremy Benton's voicemail greeted her.

"Hi, Jerry. Listen! This is Natasha Azshatan. I really need you to call me right away."

Natasha felt queasy and weak again. *Oh no. What am I gonna do?* She staggered back to the bedroom, flopped on the bed, pulled the covers up around her head, and passed out.

~

Natasha dreamt that she was scuba diving with Tom in the Mediterranean. Father Elijah was guiding them. They were looking at the exotic, colorful wildlife, but Natasha suddenly realized that Father Elijah was leading them to a secret place under water.

A Plexiglas-encased artifact seemed to be pulling him through the tropical waters. Natasha noticed that he was looking at a glowing treasure map on the reverse side of the artifact.

Tom was struggling with his buoyancy control. Natasha was afraid for him. If he ascended out of control toward the surface, his lungs would explode. Natasha reached up, grabbed Tom's leg, and tried to pull him back down. When she started to float up too, panic surged through her. She exhaled all of the air in her lungs and pressed the release button on her BCD vest, but the more they floated, the more buoyant they became. She remembered her SCUBA certification— Always Be Breathing. Suddenly, she felt a grasp on her calf. It was Father Elijah. He pulled them back down to safety. He held up two fingers. He pointed to his eyes and pointed into the distance.

Natasha looked and recognized the hazy outline of an ancient cityscape of medieval towers, and domed mega-structures. As they swam closer, she could make out the shapes and colors. *What was this place? Atlantis?* She could make out the letters on one of the buildings as they drew closer. "C o v r t H o v s e" was spelled in ancient tradition as on the front of all old courthouses.

Father Elijah pointed to his eyes again and then pointed to the map on the artifact. It was acting like a homing device. A circular track shape was glowing yellow and blinking. The map also had a glowing red indicator that looked similar to cell phone reception bars. The bars pulsated with an underwater alarm.

Natasha looked up. They were being circled by a school of vicious barracuda. The barracuda bared their razor sharp teeth and tightened their circle, their silvery scales reflecting violet from the pulsating light. The alarm on the map continued to pulsate.

Suddenly, Natasha was awakened by the realization that her cell phone was ringing. Her mind felt broken and her eyes felt glued shut. She answered the phone.

"Hello?" Natasha answered anxiously. She still felt disoriented from being ripped out of her dream.

"Is this Natasha Azshatan?"

"Yes."

"This is the Vatican switchboard operator. Please hold the line for His Eminence Cardinal Secretary of State Francis Charles."

"Guess who?" Francis asked.

"I don't know. Could it be 'His Eminence the Secretary of State Francis Charles'?"

"Ah. You got me."

"Yeah. You've got quite the introduction service."

"I can assure you. It's not that at all. All of my outbound international calls go through the switchboard."

"It's okay, Francis. I'm very proud of you. It's nice to get a call from such an *important* person."

"Natasha, what do you think could cause me to call you at five am my time?" Francis looked out his window. Only the hint of a sunrise to illuminate St. Peter's Square.

"I don't know. Were you able to come up with anything?"

"Well. I didn't have a lot of time yesterday. I had to make diplomatic calls to President Elect Jaimeson and the President. I didn't have any time for the type of in-depth research I know you'd expect of me."

"That's okay. Of course. You must have been very busy."

"But not too busy to think critically about your situation. Natasha. At first I thought the message, *We circle in the night, or we wander in the darkness, and are consumed by fire*, might be referring to the movement of the planets or perhaps rogue satellites falling back into the atmosphere, but none of that makes sense in the context. But then I thought again about your theory that the priest may have been murdered and also the note left by the killer."

"Yes," Natasha said. "Maybe it's a clue to the killer's identity."

Francis ignored Natasha's comment, and continued. "So I kept thinking. And do you know what else circles in the darkness and is then consumed by fire?"

"What?"

"The ordinary—or should I say the *extraordinary*—firefly. At night, it will circle around a campfire. It will fly closer and closer—attracted to the light.—until, finally, it flies too close to the fire and is consumed by the flames."

Natasha was fully awake now. Francis had paused, waiting for her reaction.

"That's true," Natasha said. "It fits the behavior of a firefly rather well."

"Natasha," Francis said seriously. "I don't think this is a clue to the killer's identity. I think it's a deadly warning."

"A warning to whom?"

"A warning to you—and to anyone else who shares your circumstances. For example, able to translate Latin and acquainted with the deceased."

"I see. Kind of like don't get too close to the fire or you might get burned."

"Or curiosity killed the cat."

"Oh my Go—, (Natasha switched her wording midstream) goodness!"

Jim fit the criteria, too. Natasha rubbed her eyes.

"Francis, today has been an absolute nightmare. When I researched the history of the area on a lead that father Elijah's death might be occult-related, I uncovered a creepy history of local devil worshippers. Then we discovered Deacon Jim Worley dead of an apparent suicide. When we got home, I noticed my computer was being hacked from Maryland and, a moment later, the Secret Service showed up at the doorstep with an arrest warrant for Tom, ludicrously accusing him of espionage."

"This is indeed a bad situation. Another church member is dead? Are you telling me that you are there all alone?"

"Yes—and Deacon Worley had theorized last night that the father might have been assassinated over secret knowledge he may have uncovered in the Apocalypse."

Francis stood at his window. He clasped his hands at his back and looked intently into the distance. His eyes squinted in concentration.

"Natasha, if these deaths are the result of foul play, then you could be on a very short list of who might be the next likely victim. There are not many more scholars like you on that island, I would think. I fear you are in mortal danger. "

"That might be, but I'm not worried about myself. I'm worried about Tom."

"Natasha, Tom is safe for right now. You are alone, but Tom's situation adds to your vulnerability. Not only does it leave you alone, but I'll bet that an order to freeze your bank accounts is already in the works."

Natasha's eyes widened. She wasn't worried about the money. It was just that the seriousness of the situation sank in deeper.

The line clicked. "Hello. Are you there?" Francis asked.

"Yes. I was just thinking about what you said."

"Natasha. Withdraw as much cash as you can from your ATM And catch the first flight to Rome. You'll be safe here as my guest at the Vatican. We can work together to help Tom. But it's imperative you leave right away."

Natasha thought of Tom alone in a jail cell. "But I would feel like I was abandoning him."

"No. Not at all. Trust me. He's worried about you. He'll be overjoyed at the news. We'll get this all squared away from here."

"Okay," Natasha said. "I'll call you as soon as I know my flight plan."

"Excellent. See you here."

" Okay, bye."

She hung up the phone.

~

Natasha looked at her wrist again for her watch. "Ah," she hissed at herself.

She recalled fighting the bag earlier and Handel's Hallelujah Chorus played in her mind as she jaunted down the stairway to the basement.

Natasha flipped the light switch when she reached the bottom, but the lights didn't turn on. The room was dark. She could see her watch on the other side of the basement. It glimmered in the moonlight shining in from the windows high up on the wall. She was about to continue into the darkness, when she remembered the note.

She sensed an evil presence. She quickly shut the door to the basement and locked it. As she did, she shot a lightning fast glance at the windows. Just as she feared. The latch on the window closest to the corner was unlocked—unnerving since she was sure it was locked earlier in the day.

Natasha ran up the stairs nearly petrified and shaking. She had never felt or been so close to such an intense aura of evil.

In less than sixty seconds, she dressed, grabbed her purse, and loaded it with her keys, passport, cell phone, pepper spray, and memory stick.

She was about to exit into the garage on the way to the car, but she stopped again. She remembered Jim. Killed in his garage. *What if the killer was hiding in there or hiding in the back of her car?* She tried to clear her mind of fear and use her senses. She felt like the car was a bad idea. The garage was a bad idea.

An image of her snowmobile floated to the top of her mind. It felt right. An image of Jim's boat with his keys on the captain's chair floated to her consciousness. She felt the influence of a helping spirit. She sensed it was Jim. He was trying to tell her to escape with his boat.

"But why Jim? Give me a reason to believe this is not a crazy idea," she asked Jim telepathically.

The answer came as a new thought floated in. *Not safe. Killer expects you will attempt flee by car.* Whether it was her own thought or Jim's was indistinguishable. For all Natasha knew, her mind was making up the answers to her own questions.

Natasha grabbed her purse and turned the TV on with the volume a little higher than usual. She exited quietly through the sliding glass door on the back deck. Her heart was pounding as she jumped on the snowmobile. *What if it won't start?* She slid in the key and pushed the start switch.

The snowmobile started right up. Natasha immediately squeezed the throttle and raced out from the back property and into the trailheads that led to the marina. She flew through the dark forest trails. Her path barely lit from the headlights of the snowmobile and whatever moonlight managed to shine through the forest and reflect off the snow.

Natasha couldn't look behind, but she could sense the evil chasing her. She raced down hill through that last dangerous curve. *Almost there. When you get there, be careful. If you twist your ankle, you're dead meat.*

She parked the snowmobile as close as she could to the marina entrance. She looked around. It was completely deserted. She listened, but didn't hear anything. *That was smart.* Maybe it was Jim telling her she had bought herself some time.

Natasha made each step deliberately and carefully, but also quickly on her way to Foresta. She climbed in and untied the boat. Natasha pushed the throttle lever all the way forward and cruised out of Jerrell's Cove. Downtown Seattle was the only place she could think of to sail to. It would be all lit up so she could easily find it.

When I get there, I can take a taxi the rest of the way to SeaTac airport. She was out in the open water now. The waves were choppy. She looked up and saw the moon rise over the cascade mountains. It was beautiful. Natasha sighed. She no longer sensed the evil perusing her. She steered Foresta and watched as the awesome Seattle skyline grew larger and brighter.

~

Francis closed the Bible on his desk and stood up. He clasped his hands behind his back and paced back and forth in front of the window. The sun was set in Vatican City. Large, fluffy snowflakes floated like feathers down to the cobblestone streets. The sky was pink and the edges of the clouds appeared to be glazed in gold.

He stood and watched the sunset. He looked out into the distance and thought about Natasha. *How strange it was that she had gotten herself mixed up in all this business on Governor Jaimeson's Island.* And now she was on her way to be his guest. She hoped that he, the "High and Mighty" Francis Charles, would be able to help her husband escape from charges of espionage and high treason.

Francis performed an "about-face" and considered the suitability of his home to accommodate Natasha. The apartment could more accurately be described as a palace. The ceilings were twenty feet tall. The outside wall was floor-to-ceiling windows, which looked out to St. Peter's Square. In the middle of the wall of windows, enormous double French doors opened from the formal living room onto his private terrace.

Adjacent to the formal living room was Francis' private library and home office. It also had a view and an access door to the terrace. His library was rich with his private collection of books. His desk was oversized and made from a beautiful cherry wood. The wall opposite the windows displayed a set of three separate paintings, which put together depicted one scene. It was a snapshot of the moments when the followers of Christ were carrying his tortured body down from the cross. The figures were shown dressed in the flowing fashions of the Renaissance. Mary, the mother of Christ, and Mary Magdalene stood by as the men carried his body. The men were perhaps Joseph of Arimathea and James, the brother of Jesus. The painting was done all in one color. The artist had used a reddish-brown color and had painted the scene as if it were a black and white photo. Only instead of black and white it was the sandy colored paper and various shades of the red-brown color.

A fourth work of art punctuated the set of three paintings. It matched the style and color of the other three. "The Five Wounds of Christ" was written in reddish-brown print across the top of this forth work. Below this title, and printed in giant reddish-brown letters, were the legendary names of each of the five wounds.

The Five Wounds of Christ

SATOR

AREPO

TENET

OPERA

ROTAS

Francis walked across his office over to the wet bar and poured himself a glass of whiskey. His face was red from the years of his occasional glass. His cheeks were marked with whiskey-stained blood vessels, which webbed out like the veins on the underside of a leaf.

Francis consumed his glass and poured another. He walked over to the grand piano in his main entrance room, sat down, and began to play dramatic and melancholy chords. He played hard; eventually his playing calmed to a soothing rhythm. He played four of the same chord, elevating to the next chord, and then back to the first chord another four times.

He sang the words and felt like he had written them a thousand years ago. He could hardly remember how the song went.

> In Rome, it's a cold and lonely night
> And the moonlight isn't shining very bright
> Friends aren't really friends, they just pretend
> And love's not really love, it's a dead end.
> An-nd-d-d I-I-I-I-I'm a lonely man
> The pain I'm goin' through, no one understands.
> An-nd-d-d I-I-I-I-I'm a lonely man
> If she can't love me, I think no one can.

The chords continued. His right hand flew up to the higher notes. Francis continued playing. He could feel the whiskey in his cheeks now. His music thundered through his palace of marble floors and high ceilings.

Francis got up from the piano and walked back to his office. His desk was equipped with a large flat screen LCD monitor and a wireless telephone headset. He put on the headset and dialed zero for the switchboard operator.

"This is Secretary of State Charles. Please connect me with the United States Attorney General."

He stood at his window again with his hands clasped behind his back. The Christmas lights of the Vatican shined magnificently. Three minutes passed before the operator came back.

"Your Eminence, the U.S. Attorney General is on the line. Please hold."

"Mr. Attorney General, thank you for taking my call."

"Not at all. It's a pleasure. What can I do for you?"

"I know the wheels of justice are spinning, but I just felt the need to call you and let you know personally that I support you in your work to bring Tom Azshatan to justice. I have the Vatican security surveillance photos your office has requested of Tom Azshatan meeting with KGB agent Alexei Kirov. But before I make them available, I want your personal assurance that Natasha Azshatan will be left alone in this matter."

"You have my word, Your Eminence. Thank you for your cooperation thus far."

"Do you know why Tom Azshatan wasn't arrested back then?" the Attorney General asked.

"Tom Azshatan was not prosecuted at that time because no one wanted to tip off the Soviets—and our alliance was secret from the public. Diplomatic relations between the Vatican and the U.S. government were young. I hope you know how important it is to us that he is vigorously prosecuted."

"I couldn't agree with you more, Your Eminence. This is a very important case to the Justice Department as well. He will be prosecuted to the full extent of the law."

"Thank you, Mr. Attorney General. Please keep me informed, if you will, on any progress you can report."

"Certainly, Your Eminence."

"May the Lord bless you. Go in peace, my son."

"Thank you, Your Eminence."

Francis pushed the "end call" button on his headset.

A small white jeweler's box rested on the corner of his desk. He picked it up and flipped it open. It held a gold watch that he planned to give to Natasha when she arrived. He had it inscribed with a Latin proverb, which was more fitting than she could imagine.

Roma tibi subito motibus ibit amor—"By me, you arrive to Rome, the love of your travels."

Francis handled the watch and read aloud the inscription. He smiled, and put the watch back in its case.

~

Governor Jaimeson's situation room was a beehive. Ceiling-mounted projectors showcased three separate news channels. The ferry disaster was one of the most deadly single terrorist attacks in US history. At least 915 people were confirmed dead.

An enormous round conference table stood in the center of the room. It was made from a beautiful reddish polished wood. In the center of the table, the Jaimeson family crest was artfully inlaid. The conference table stood at approximately bar height. Barstools were situated around the perimeter of the table, but they were rarely used.

People standing up around the bar created more energy than if they were sitting. They would reach across, walk around, and could more easily come and go.

Around the table was a who's who of the Washington State executive branch. William and Meredith Jaimeson, Douglas Blair, Lieutenant Governor Richard Winslow, General Alfonzo Perez of the State National Guard, and Admiral Justin Baker of the State Coast Guard.

Janice walked up to the Governor's right side and spoke softly in his ear. "Governor Jaimeson, sir. Darrel Burns from Homeland Security has just arrived by helicopter. He'll be escorted to the situation room momentarily."

"Good," Will said.

Janice returned to her station outside the situation room and Will turned to Meredith.

"I'll be interested in hearing what he's got to say."

"Governor," Douglas Blair said. "Darrel Burns just finished a live interview on KOJO in which he basically blamed our administration for not appointing enough State Patrol officers on the ferry system. I'm not sure I trust him in your situation room, sir."

"Noted, Douglas. Everyone," Will looked around at his people. "Today is a test for us. Douglas has brought up an important point. There's no escaping it. Accusations will fly, fingers will be pointed, and our political rivals will use this disaster for their own purposes. We must not fall into that trap."

"We must rise above it. Today, more than 900 peeople were murdered by a diabolical madman. Our mission is to stay focused! We must work together. Leadership is not about how well one can work with friends, but how well one can work with one's adversaries!

"We will not play the blame game. Let us not forget. Let us never forget that this disaster is the work of a terrorist. From what I know so far, there may be more attacks in the works. Whether they be in the Washington or elsewhere. We must all come together and cooperate. We must learn everything we can from each other."

Automatic glass doors slid open and Darrel Burns entered.

"Governor, First Lady, Gentlemen. Let me start by apologizing. My words came out wrong on the KOJO interview. As you can imagine, it has been a horrible and difficult day. I did the best I could during the interview."

"Apology accepted, Mr. Burns. We were just discussing your comments and we know you meant to communicate that the persons responsible are the members of the A.I.M. We must all work together and learn from one another. Finger pointing and blame games are not appropriate and the public will see through such rhetoric for what it is. Political games. The citizens of Washington know that my administration has worked tirelessly and diligently on counter terrorist measures. They also know that the Republican-controlled State House of Representatives voted down my proposal for increased spending on State Patrol. And they also know that there was no heightened alert status from the Federal Government.

"Yes, Governor," Burns responded. "With a humble spirit, I agree with you—and I am here to help. Here is what we know so far. The NSA has intercepted chatter. They are expecting a secondary event, but we do not know where or when. We also have intel that suggests that the explosion on the ferry was consistent with an explosion one might expect from a truck full of fertilizer chemicals. Satellite surveillance shows the explosion was massive."

The glass doors opened again. Press Secretary Pete Thomas approached the Governor and spoke softly in his ear.

"Sir, I've finished fine-tuning your speech. It has everything in it you wanted. Your press conference is scheduled in thirty minutes."

"Thank you, Pete. That's excellent. Gentlemen, continue to work together. I must prepare my remarks for the press conference, which will begin in less than thirty minutes. When I return, I want specific proposals on three things.

1. How can we best help the families of the victims?

2. What do we need to do to get the ferry system running again?

3. A list of likely next targets and what we can do immediately to thwart attacks on such targets."

Governor Jaimeson walked toward the exit. The glass doors slid open; he passed through them and turned right on his way to his private study. Pete Thomas followed him.

Jaimeson's cell rang. He flipped it open and put it to his ear.

"Governor Jaimeson?"

"Yes, this is he."

"This is the switchboard operator at the Vatican Embassy. Please hold for Secretary of State Francis Charles."

Francis Charles stood in front of the giant window at his Vatican apartment. He watched the snowflakes in Saint Peter's square as he held the line. The view reminded him of the souvenir snow globes that were commonly sold in tourist shops.

"Your Eminence, please hold. Governor Jaimeson is standing by for your call."

"Will, this is Francis. I know you must be busy, but I felt impressed by the spirit to call you."

"Thank you, Cardinal. I need all the help I can get right now, but I need to let you know that I am time pressured at the moment."

"All right. I'll be quick about it. Just two quick things I have been impressed to communicate to you. First of all. My prayers are with you—and the Vatican supports you. I feel impressed to advise you to speak strongly against and act strongly against the Islamic radicals. This is no time for political correctness. It is a time for decisive and honest leadership. Which I know you epitomize—but I felt impressed to share this with you in case your press people have advised you otherwise.

"Second is an amazing coincidence. I have two very old and dear friends who also live on Jerrell's Cove. We served together here in Vatican City twenty years ago. Natasha and Tom Azshatan. Natasha called me this morning and told me what happened to the village Orthodox priest. She thinks he may have been murdered.

"I mention this because I think it might be possible that members of the press may bring it up during any potential press conference. Since we spoke the day of his death, I know you were on your boat alone and in close proximity to the location he was found. You need to be prepared for any such questions."

"As always, Cardinal Francis, you are a wise and scholarly advisor and a trusted friend. I'm just now headed to my study to read over the final draft of my prepared remarks. Your call could not have been more timely. As far as the second thing goes, I appreciate your input on that, too. Although I feel comfortable it won't come up. I will follow your advice and consider ahead of time how to best react to such questions if they may arise. Please keep me in your prayers."

"I always do. Keep me in yours as well. May the Lord bless you, Will. Go in peace."

"Thank you, Cardinal. You are always in our prayers too. I'll call you as soon as I can. Good-bye."

"Good-bye, Will. Go in peace."

Will opened the door to his study. He slapped the speech down on his desk as he sat down. Pete sat down across from the Governor. Jaimeson read through the speech as Pete watched silently awaiting his reaction.

"Terrific work, Pete. Just one thing. I feel I need to come out with some stronger language concerning the Islamic radicals and how they are responsible. Please leave me to make those changes and bring the speech back to me in ten minutes. Janice, I'll need to be undisturbed for the next ten minutes."

"Yes, sir."

"Thank you."

Pete got up right away.

"Thank you, sir. I'll be right back with the stronger language revision, sir."

Pete exited and shut the door with care. Will closed his eyes and cleared his mind.

"That's right, honey." He heard his mother's voice in his head. "The people need you to be strong. They need you to give them hope."

~

Natasha exited the airplane in Rome and immediately noticed a limousine driver holding a sign with her name on it.

"I'm Natasha Azshatan," she said as she walked up to him.

"Pleasure to meet you, madam. No baggage?"

"No," Natasha laughed. "Not one bag. Just me and my purse."

She laughed again and followed the driver. Her face was puffy from sleeping on the plane. The driver opened the door and Francis Charles took her hand to help her inside. Her first impression was that he had hardly aged. Golden, square-rimmed glasses accented his penetrating dark brown eyes, his brow pointed as if he was a Vulcan/human hybrid and his full head of coarse black hair crowned his prominent forehead.

"Francis!"

Natasha gave him a joyous hug and he kissed her on the cheek.

"Good to see you, Natasha. I've missed you more than you know. So good to see you. Where is your luggage?"

"Francis, you were right. As soon as I got off the phone with you, I sensed an evil presence in my home. I noticed one of the basement windows had been opened and I followed my instincts, grabbed my purse, and got the heck out of there."

"Thank God, Natasha. You don't know how worried I was for you. I sensed it too. I felt you were in danger, but now you're safe." Francis reached out and caressed the side of her head. "And look at you. You must be so tired from travel, but you're as beautiful as ever."

"Thank you, Francis. You look great too. And I'm so proud of you."

"Natasha, if it's okay, my assistant is awaiting my call. She will procure you some fresh clothes. Francis dialed and handed the phone to Natasha. "Just tell her your measurements."

Natasha took the phone from him and relished speaking Italian again. As she gave the girl her measurements, she smiled and watched as the Italian countryside flew by at 100 kilometers per hour. They passed tomato fields and white farmhouses.

Natasha felt excited to be back in Rome. The sights and smells triggered her memories and made her forget the trauma and fatigue of recent days. All the excitement of her younger years rushed back into her blood. It was invigorating. Rome was so beautiful. A city full of trees, parks, Old World architecture, and Old World charm.

"*Gratsi*," she told the girl, flipped the phone shut, and handed it back to Francis.

"Francis. Were you able to find out anything about Tom? Is there anything you can do to help?"

"As a matter of fact, while you were on your way, I placed a call to the American Attorney General and spoke to him personally."

"What? You are kidding me? What?"

Natasha smiled at her old friend in admiration.

"What did you tell him? What did he say?"

"Put it this way," Francis said. "I very diplomatically expressed to the Attorney General my belief that Tom is completely innocent of the charges. And I personally asked him to look into the matter for me."

"What did he say?"

"He was polite. He said that he would look into it for me. He's a good Roman Catholic and I think this craziness will get all cleared up very quickly. I'd be surprised if we didn't hear some good news by tonight. I take it you have a good attorney as well?"

"Jeremy Benton. Of course I'm sure he's never had a case like this. Nevertheless, he is a very competent attorney. I spoke with him during my layover in Miami and he said Tom's arraignment won't be until Monday morning. Can you believe that?"

"That does seem like an awfully long time. Don't worry, my dear! Everything will be fine."

He caressed her cheek again.

"You'll see. Believe me. The best thing you can do for Tom's sake is to relax and rest. He'll be so happy and relieved to know that you are safe here at the Vatican. I'll try to arrange a call to him today. You'll see."

Natasha nodded her head and smiled. She felt the slightest bit of discomfort with this second caress from Francis. *He sure is touchy feely.* Mostly she was thankful that he had actually spoken to the Attorney General on Tom's behalf. She felt guilty to even think that something could be wrong with this wonderful man giving her a comforting caress. *He really does care. He really cares about people.*

She leaned over to Francis and kissed his cheek.

"Thank you, Francis."

Natasha looked out the windows again and could see they were closer. The scenery was getting a little more industrial. Her eyes felt heavy and she yawned.

"Wait until you sink into your bed," Francis said. "It's fit for a queen. You may never want to leave it."

"I slept on the plane, but I'm still a little sleepy."

The limo approached Vatican City and stopped at the VIP entrance gate. Natasha was awestruck. A Vatican Swiss Guard checked the undercarriage and a second Swiss Guard walked a bomb-sniffing dog around the vehicle. They gave the driver a nod and the gates opened. A few moments later they were home.

"Natasha, Nicholas will show you to your quarters. I'm very sorry, but I must continue on to a breakfast meeting. Please make yourself at home and I'll check in on you later."

"Thanks. I plan on showering and then sleeping half the day. I'll see you later."

Nicholas opened the door and took her hand to help her out.

"Bye! See you later!"

She smiled and turned toward the palace apartment. The limo

driver pushed the accelerator and whisked Francis off to his meeting with the Holy Father.

~

Natasha awoke to the sound of gentle piano music that flowed down the halls and into her suite. She was sunk deep into the soft bed. She got up and dressed in the simple clean clothes that were hung neatly in her closet. Her new undergarments and pajamas had been laid out on the bed for her. The clothes she had been wearing were taken to the laundry. The young woman who worked for Francis had done a good job. She had procured two light gray pairs of thick wool trousers and a snow-white wool sweater.

She smiled as she followed the source of the music back to the main entrance hall. Sunshine beamed in diagonally from huge windows in front of the terrace. The beams of light stretched across the marble floor and seemed to reach toward Francis like a spotlight. He was singing softly.

> I've seen a mother's prayers be answered
> When life's struggles got too rough.
> I've seen an old man healed of cancer
> I've seen a lonely man find love!

He intensified his playing with this last part and smiled up at Natasha as he played into the chorus.

> And ... I've seen the light of God shine through
> I've seen his promise of new life come true
> I've experienced His joy and hope
> And I know that you can too
> I've seen the light of God shine through.

Francis slowed back down, and sang softly again for the second verse.

> I've seen a child kneel beside her bed
> I've seen her Mommy change her ways
> I've seen a homeless person being fed
> You see what happens when we pray.

Once again, he intensified his playing as he led back into the chorus. He finished with soft charismatic splendor as his fingers danced into the higher notes and then back down again for the final rich chord.

Natasha was standing in the curve of the piano with her hands on her hips, watching in admiration.

"*Bravo! Bravo! Bravissimo! Bravissimo!*"

Francis stood up and took a bow to his audience of one. "You must be starving!"

Natasha nodded and smiled.

"Well, then come with me. I hope we have what you're hungry for. I had Maria fix up a few things."

Natasha marveled at the kitchen. It was the size of suburban three-car garage. There was a breakfast nook area near the windows and off from the side of the nook, another set of double doors leading onto the terrace.

"If it weren't so cold, we could have coffee and breakfast out there."

Francis gestured at the terrace with both palms up.

Natasha looked at the island bar. It was laid out with two catering style hotplates. One had scrambled eggs; the other had a potato skillet dish. To the side of those, a bowl of sliced fruit offered apples, grapes, peaches, slices of mango, kiwi, and cantaloupe. Another plate offered a pyramid of croissants.

Natasha popped the croissant into the toaster oven and turned it on. She dished up some eggs and potatoes, but mainly the fruit salad. She grabbed the croissant and sat down at the table. Francis was right behind her. He went heavy on the eggs and potatoes and light on the fruit salad.

"Natasha, you won't believe it. The Holy Father and I have been prayerfully drafting an announcement of one of the greatest church reforms in modern history. Have you ever noticed that while the Roman Catholic Church suffered from a plague of pedophilia in the priesthood, that one never hears of such problems in the Orthodox Church? Why do you think that is?"

Natasha thought for a moment. She took a sip of coffee and looked sideways out the window.

"Do you think it's because Orthodox Priests can marry and have families?" Natasha asked.

"Precisely."

"Among other things, the new reforms I'm working on will lay aside doctrine that denies the servants of God the opportunity to have families of their own." Francis' eyes welled up in tears.

"Oh my goodness, Francis! That's the most sweeping reform in a millennium."

"You have no idea the hurt and the sacrifice that doctrine causes," Francis continued. "You have no idea the sacrifices I have had to make to get where I am today. And even in all of this—even as much as I have achieved—how empty it feels to have no one to share it with. I feel hollow!"

Francis pounded his chest with his fist. His eyes were still wet.

Natasha went to him. She knelt in front of him and embraced him. She felt so ashamed that she had been irritated earlier. She was ashamed that she had a fear he might misinterpret her affection. She was teary-eyed now. She lifted her head from his chest and looked him in the eyes.

"Of course you're lonely, Francis. I'm so sorry I haven't done a better job at staying in touch. But I'm here with you right now."

"Thank you, Natasha. Please forgive me for getting emotional. This particular reform is too close to my heart." He lifted the sides of her shoulders to urge her up.

Natasha went back to her chair.

"I know a little of what you are saying. Since I cannot have children—and all the money in the world can't dull the pain of being barren—Tom is all I have. And we love our life. But sometimes when I see a beautiful innocent baby smile up at her mother, it really hurts. It's a dull pain in my heart and stomach. It's the pain of a broken heart."

"Yes. At least you have each other."

Francis forced a smile—and then smiled more genuinely as he remembered his gift for Natasha.

"I almost forgot. I have a surprise for you. Wait right here. I'll be right back."

Francis hurried to his office and returned with a gift box for Natasha.

"I hope you don't mind."

"Francis! You didn't have to."

"Tom's all you've got. But *you're* all I've got. I couldn't resist. Please open it."

Natasha smiled her you-shouldn't-have smile and ripped off the paper.

"It's beautiful!" she exclaimed as she pulled the watch out and checked if it was set to the right time.

"I have one other for you, but you'll have to wait until Christmas Eve."

Natasha read the inscription aloud.

"Wonderful, Francis! And thank you so much. For this and your hospitality. You're a great friend."

"I'm glad you like it."

He looked satisfied. They both turned back to their food and finished dining.

"That was good," Francis said as he slapped his thin belly. "Find out as much as you can about Tom today. This evening, we'll make some calls."

"You have a deal."

"All right then. See you tonight. Don't lift a finger. And Nicholas will drive you anywhere you want to go or fetch anything you need. Don't hesitate to call."

"Thanks. I won't. See you tonight."

"Have fun, Natasha. It's Christmas and you are in Rome!"

~

Tom leaned back against the cold prison wall. He was sitting on his bunk and looking up at the television. The news channel was still reporting nonstop about the ferry attack. Sound bites from Governor Jaimeson's now famous "Freedom From Terror" speech were playing again.

> Dear Citizens. In the wake of one of the single most deadly terror attacks in U.S. history, we find ourselves at a crossroads. Shall we continue the battles for peace and stability in foreign lands? Or shall we fight for the peace and stability of our own land? For too long we have focused on one and not the other. It is time we remember the inheritance from our forefathers. They sacrificed to give the citizens of our nation the promise of Life, Liberty, and the Pursuit of Happiness. These are the ideals worth fighting for. These are the ideals worth dying for. And in the defense of the lives of our innocent citizens, yes, these are the ideals worth killing for.

Governor Jaimeson's speech reminded Tom of his new home. He wondered how Natasha was doing. Jeremy Benton had told him that she had traveled to the Vatican upon the invitation of Francis Charles. Tom's mind thought back to the afternoon he had been arrested. *It doesn't look good. The fact that I was planning to fly to Mexico that night. A prosecutor could twist that into evidence that I was planning to flee the country.*

Tom flipped the channel. Governor Jaimeson was in the middle of answering a question when Tom started listening to him.

"We must cast aside political correctness and adopt a realistic approach. It is clear who our enemies are. They are men of Middle Eastern decent who have adopted the perverted worldview of radical fundamentalist Islam. These men are not in a foreign country—they are here among us. They are in our cities and towns."

"Yes, Governor Jaimeson," the interviewer probed. "But what are you proposing as a solution?"

"Here's one example," the Governor answered. "Middle Eastern men who apply for a visa to visit our country must pay a fee that will cover the cost for a Department of Homeland Security background check.

"Middle Eastern men who are already in our country must be evaluated with fair and honest criteria. I believe a litmus test of societal integration should be applied to help the Department of Homeland Security to zero in on individuals of interest."

"What is a 'litmus test of societal integration'?"

"It means a person of Middle Eastern decent who chooses to not socially integrate into our society is a person that Homeland Security should have an interest in. That's all."

The interviewer looked into the camera.

"And we'll be right back with President-elect and Governor William Jaimeson after these messages."

Tom turned the TV off. He folded his hands over his stomach and looked up at the ceiling, thinking about his predicament.

I'll bet this is about Alexei Kirov. They had met three days before Alexei had been arrested in 1989. Alexei had seemed paranoid. He was sweating profusely, and his eyes were darting all over.

"They're after me," Alexei had said.

"Who?" Tom had asked.

Alexei rattled his head in irritation. I don't have time to explain—and even if I did, you'd think I was crazy. Thanks for your help, Tom. I have to go. Alexei stood up from the table, took the file in his left hand, and held it close to his body.

The file Tom gave to Alexei contained ten copies of an "apartment for rent" advertisement flyer. Alexei needed to leave suddenly and had asked Tom for help in making the flyers in order to help his landlord lease the flat out quickly.

Tom stood up and offered his hand. "How will I reach you?"

"I have friends in Istanbul. Seek wisdom there."

"Good-bye then."

"*Dos Vedanya.*"

Tom cracked his knuckles as he remembered that final handshake with Kirov. He stared up at the ceiling. *What did he mean by that anyway?*

~

Natasha went back to her suite. She walked over to the window and moved the drapes aside to look down into the busy streets. Christmas shoppers and tourists went hither and thither. Some rode in horse drawn carriages. *That would be nice.* She made a mental note to ask Nicholas about arranging such a ride.

Natasha picked her cell off the desk and dialed her voicemail. It was still the middle of the night in the States, but she hoped that, by some miracle, Tom might have been able to call her. She had one new message.

"Natasha, I've been concerned about you darling." She recognized the rich tone of voice and the crisp British accent. "I happened to be in the Seattle area yesterday and stopped over to give you a surprise visit; however, you and Tom were not to be found. I know something is wrong. Give me a ring, my dear. Day or night it doesn't matter. Right away—it is important."

Grant Nuby had to be the most amazing psychic medium she had ever known. Natasha's gift was more of a gift that came and went. It was spontaneous and unreliable. Except in matters of personal guidance, it was almost useless.

Grant Nuby, however, was skilled. His abilities were more like carefully focused powers. They were at his will. He could control them. He could harness his power and direct it.

And if he's concerned… She didn't want to even think. She knew Grant had been scientifically verified to be 85 percent accurate under carefully controlled experiments. *If he's concerned too, that is not a good sign.*

Natasha's eyes widened in an expression of self-congratulatory epiphany. *Eureka! Grant may be able to help Tom.*

Last year, Grant had gotten quite a bit of press when he used his powers to *will* a kidnapper to release a boy in North Carolina. The kidnapper had not only released the boy, but he had surrendered to the police. He claimed that he had suffered from insomnia and a voice inside his brain had kept telling him to "release the boy, turn yourself in, and then you will sleep."

Maybe Grant could *will* the Justice Department to abandon their ridiculous charges against Tom. It was worth a try. She dialed Grant's number and he answered right away.

"Natasha, darling. I'm so glad you rang. I didn't think you would take me seriously when I told you to ring day or night. But I'm elated that you did."

"Thanks, Grant. I really appreciate your concern. You were right. My whole world's been turned upside down since Sunday."

"Natasha. I've seen the dream with Lucas Phillip Renard. He says. 'Ah, Satan sees Natasha.' Correct?"

"That's incredible, Grant! He said those very words to me in a snapshot vision I had after I was startled at Jim's house. I fainted afterward. What do you think it means?"

"I hate to say, darling, however I believe an evil spirit is after you. I think it is the same spirit that possessed Lucas Phillip Renard. You probably couldn't be in a better or safer place than the Vatican. Under the circumstance, I am considerably relieved that you are there."

"But why would it be after me?"

"Because, my dear, you're a threat to its agenda somehow. At least that is what I'm sensing."

"I've been racking my mind to figure out what's been going on. How is it all connected? Why him? And why me?"

"Natasha darling, you'll need to meditate. The answers will come. Pay attention to clues in your dreams."

"If I can figure out what some of this is about, then maybe I can get the upper hand. I'll be in a position of strength."

"You know the proverb—knowing is half the battle."

"Yes. The other half is following your instincts."

"Natasha, my dear. Please listen to me carefully. I have some important tips for you to stay hidden from this evil spirit. It's very important for you to remember them."

Grant paused to make sure Natasha was giving her undivided attention. He had correctly perceived that Natasha's mind was still thinking about all the matters that she had told him about. He wanted to make sure that she was truly listening.

"Remember that negative thoughts and emotions are like a scent trail to these spirits. It's a path in which they can find you. If you're putting out signals of fear, anxiety, or sadness, they can tune into you. It is much like a metal detector finding a coin in the dirt. Once they lock onto your signal, they can track you. So stay positive."

"What else?"

"You may not exactly believe the Gospel, but one thing is for certain. In the spirit realm, there is no more powerful spirit than that of Jesus. Pray to Jesus. There is no one like him. Whether by accident, fate, or destiny, He is the one being who has lived and died—and attained such a following in the spirit realm."

"Yeah, but doesn't that make him too busy for me?"

"Who do you want to pray to? Perhaps some poor soul who doesn't really have the power or influence to affect anything?"

"I always commune with the people whom I've known and loved," Natasha answered.

"That's not enough, my dear. They alone don't have the power to hold back the force that is against you. You need a powerful spirit to work your cause. Always start at the top. Think of it from the point of view of the Lord Jesus. There are so many other people praying for his help. How can he turn away from them to help you, if you haven't even asked him for his help? That's what intercessory prayer is all about. We must reach out. Pray earnestly. Pray unceasingly. Listen mentally for the guidance."

"Thank you, Grant. I will."

"Excellent, darling. And I will pray for intersession on your and Tom's behalf. All right, then. Call me with updates."

"I will."

"Good-bye, darling. Take care."

Natasha sat down Eastern meditation style. She closed her eyes, and exhaled, and cleared her mind. She breathed deeply and concentrated on keeping her mind blank. She wanted to start a conversation with Jesus, but she felt awkward doing so. She would go to open her mouth and speak a prayer to address him, but she closed her lips and breathed deeply again. It was like initiating a conversation with a long-time estranged acquaintance. She couldn't do it. It was as if her throat was locked shut and her stomach was full of butterflies. She tried not to think about anything and strained to perceive anything at all.

She went into a deep trance. She felt warm all over and very relaxed. *Dear Jesus. She* couldn't think of what to say. A teardrop escaped her right eye and traveled down her cheek. She thought of Tom.

Please help us. Please. Please Jesus. Help us. When she opened her eyes, she felt like a weight had been lifted. It wasn't an eloquent prayer, but she had reached out for the help of Jesus. That was the first step anyway.

She stood up, picked up the desk phone's receiver, and dialed Nicholas' extension.

"Hello?"

"Nicholas. Hi, this is Natasha."

"Hello, madam. I'm at your service."

"Would you care to escort me on a horse-drawn carriage ride?"

"For certain. What time would you like?"

"Can we go right now?"

"Your wish is my command," he declared in good humor. "I'll meet you in the main entrance hall. The carriage will be waiting for us down at the street."

Natasha smiled and bunny hopped with joy. She felt excited and looked forward to the excursion with great anticipation as she readied herself.

In the main entrance hall of Francis' apartment, a narrow Christmas tree rose to the height of the ceiling. A large rectangular gift box lay under it for Natasha. It was about the size of two briefcases put side to side.

Francis sat at his piano playing another one of his self-composed pieces. He sang a soft, twinkly, kind of dreamy Christmas song in a slow soft voice.

> A snowy winter's night
> A man walks alone on the street
> He looks around at the Christmas lights
> And remembers the people he's loved in his life

He remembers festive gatherings
and the sound
Of people laughing and talking.
And love filled the air all around

Francis intensified the tempo as he played into the chorus.

'Twas was the season of hope
'Twas the season of joy and gifts
and peace could always be found.
It was the time of Christmas cheer.

Natasha emerged from her hallways with a bright smile as Francis repeated the chorus. He hastened to finish with his usual flourish.

"That was wonderful," Natasha exclaimed.

"I haven't finished it yet. Maybe today's excursion will give me the inspiration I need."

"I thought you were working?"

Francis pulled his hands down from the piano keys and stood up. "I was, but then I got to thinking. How often do I have such a special guest as you? Nicholas informed me of your request and I just had to come home early."

"Are you sure?" Natasha teased. "You won't get bored while I'm trying on clothes."

"Don't worry. I'll give you your space."

Francis Charles bent over and plucked Natasha's gift out from under the tree. He held it up to her.

"Surprise."

"I feel bad. I don't have anything for you."

"No worries," he answered in an Australian accent. "I can wait until Christmas day."

Natasha sat down on the piano bench and placed the box on her lap. She pulled the ribbon loose and opened it. It was a luxurious silver and white fur coat. Natasha had never owned one before. They were taboo in the States, but very much still in style throughout Europe.

Natasha gasped, "Oh my goodness!"

She felt awkward accepting this extravagant, guilt-laden gift, but she was overwhelmed at the gesture and she knew Francis was lonely and had a need to give nice gifts to someone.

She radiated pure delight to show Francis how overwhelmed she was by his special gift.

Francis reciprocated a slightly self-conscious smile.

"It's cold out on the street and I really wanted to make sure you enjoy yourself. Here let me help you."

Francis pulled the fur up her arms and wrapped it around her shoulders. He was wearing a gray pinstriped suit. He pulled his matching gray cashmere overcoat from out of the coat closet and put it on.

He held out his arm to Natasha, bent at the elbow.

"Shall we?"

"We shall."

Snow fell lightly as they sat back in the carriage and rode through the narrow cobblestone streets. Francis held his arm around her back as they rode in a sideways embrace.

Natasha was beginning to feel more awkward. He was squeezing her waist in the carriage. *Is he putting the moves on me?* She tried to push the thought away. *That's absurd. He hasn't tried to kiss me. He's just being a gentleman.*

It was dusk when the carriage stopped at St. Andrews Village Square. Their last stop before heading back.

"Francis, why don't you go along to some of the shops you like apart from me? I still need to find something a little special for you."

"All right then. Why don't we meet at the corner in say sixty minutes?"

"That should be enough time."

Once Francis had disappeared out of view, Natasha briskly walked to the Internet café she had noticed.

She sat down and logged into her e-mail account. She opened an e-mail from Jeremy Benton.

> Dear Natasha,
>
> Tom says there's a man who may be connected to the conspiracy against him. He says the man may be able to shed some light on the matter. There's just one problem. Tom says he's a fugitive. Interpol has been on the lookout for him since 1990. Tom says the only way to find him is to go to Istanbul and "search for wisdom" from a man known as "the priest." He suggests hiring a private investigator to find this man, and interview him for information that may help.
>
> Other than that, nothing new. Tom sends his love. He's doing fine. He seems to be in good spirits. Mainly concerned about you.
>
> I'll e-mail you an update on Monday afternoon.
>
> Best regards,
> Jeremy Benton

Natasha remembered the Eastern Archeological Society in Istanbul. Natasha's eyes widened. Father Elijah had a file on Aya Sophia on the memory stick. It was the Church of Holy Wisdom and those Greek proverbs found at Aya Sophia and the Basilica Cistern beneath. They were all in Istanbul, but something was nagging at her. There was something else.

Grant had told her to pay attention to the clues in her dreams. She had dreamed of an ancient cityscape in the Mediterranean, hadn't she? The cityscape she remembered had vast domed buildings and Medieval-styled towers. *That was Istanbul, too.* Natasha ran her hand up her forehead, and combed her fingers through her hair and down the back of her head to the side of her neck.

I'm in the wrong city.

She pulled up and printed more info on this trend of thought, Aya

Sophia, the Eastern Archeological Society, and the Library of Istanbul. The library was one of the oldest and greatest on earth.

Natasha looked at her watch. *Time to go meet up with Francis.* She walked out of the storefront and stood at the corner. No sign of Francis or the carriage. She turned and looked up the street. It was dazzling with all the little white lights. But still no Francis. She stuck her hands in her fur coat and enjoyed its warmth.

Suddenly, someone from behind shot their arms through the loops between Natasha's armpits and where her wrists entered the pockets of her fur. The hands interlaced fingers at the point of Natasha's abdomen, and pulled her close. For a moment she was shocked, but then she realized it was Francis surprising her with a hug. He held her tight, put his jaw over her shoulder, and whispered, "Merry Christmas!"

Natasha put her hand on her chest and said, "Francis, you startled me."

"Oh. I beg your pardon. I am sorry. I just couldn't resist. I haven't held a woman in a fur coat since I—" He didn't finish.

Natasha thought to ask him if he remembered that she was a married woman, but then bit her lip. *Everything he had done was so innocent. If I say anything right now, he can just say he's lonely and in need of a little human contact and affection. I would be stuck looking hypersensitive—and then everything would be uncomfortable.* She shook it off. *Don't burn a bridge, Natasha. He may very well be able to help Tom get out of this mess. So, you play along with his little games as long as it gets you Tom.*

"Here's the carriage now," Francis announced. He gave Natasha his hand to escort her up into the seats.

As the carriage slowly pulled them through the ancient streets, Natasha was silent. Francis did not have his arm around her. Perhaps he had begun to sense her discomfort.

"After dinner, we'll make those calls for Tom," he said. "I would have called sooner today of course, but the time difference must be accounted for. Can't really get a hold of anyone until 7:00 a.m. Eastern."

Natasha stared out with a look of indifference. This last bit really made her feel uncomfortable.

~

Later that same night, tensions continued to build as Natasha reminded Francis about his promise to help her husband. Eventually, Francis could not stand any further mention of Tom. He clenched his teeth and lowered his eyelids.

"What?" Natasha asked. "What was that expression?"

Francis stood up, and walked to the far side of the kitchen island. He turned around and put his hands on the countertop. He locked his elbows, leaned on them as if they were two kickstands holding up a bike, and lowered his head.

"There was a reason I was playing for you a song about the light of God shining through. Even in the darkest times, God's love finds a way to illuminate our lives and to show us our way. I mention this to offer solace in the wake of bad news regarding Tom's situation."

"What? What did you find out?"

"I'm very sorry, Natasha. I didn't want to discuss this with you while we were eating. But now that we are."

"What?"

"Natasha, this is hard for me. I can't just blurt out information. Please try to understand that in my role as a government official, I'm privileged with classified information. I was provided some of such information regarding Tom—and all I can tell you is that I believe Tom is in quite a bit of real trouble. I believe the U.S. Justice Department is very serious about their case against him."

Natasha sat speechless.

"Natasha, I'm reasonably certain—based on the classified information which was shared with me—that Tom is not innocent in the matters against him."

Natasha burst into tears.

"I know he's innocent! He's my husband!" Natasha screeched. "Whatever information you saw is wrong. Tom is 100 percent innocent. You, of all people, should know that. You married us for God's sake."

I have the power to annul your marriage. Natasha sensed he was thinking, the idea had flashed out of his eyes. He composed himself.

"Natasha!" he pleaded. "Don't you understand? Tom's guilty. It will take all my influence to keep him from being hanged. Life in prison is the best we can hope for."

Natasha froze. Francis put his hands on her shoulders and looked down at her.

"Tom is gone, Natasha. He'll never be with you again. I know it's hard for you to accept, but he would want you to continue your life. Why not continue it with me—*here*. I love you. I always have." Francis reached out to wipe a tear from her cheek.

Natasha deflected his gesture.

"I am a married woman—and shame on you for attempting to take advantage of my vulnerable situation."

Natasha slapped him across his cheek. She ran to her suite and locked the door behind her as she packed her things to travel to Turkey.

⌐

Natasha walked along a crowded marketplace in Istanbul. The merchants called out to her. She walked past a young man selling marble souvenirs—ashtrays, square block paperweights, and small animal sculptures.

"American lady. Look, look over here. I have what you are looking for. Name your price."

Natasha smiled, shook her head no, and continued to walk. The young man followed her, calling out to her persistently.

"How much you want to give? You name the price."

Natasha stopped and looked at him. He was thin, but he smiled big. He held up the small marble keepsake box that Natasha had browsed momentarily. Natasha took it out of his hands and looked at it more carefully. It was mainly white, but it had shades of blue marbled through it.

"Five dollars," Natasha said.

"Please, my lady. It is worth more. Fifteen dollars and it is yours."

Natasha handed it back to him, but he wouldn't let her give it back.

"Ten dollars."

Natasha was satisfied. She thought that maybe she could have gotten it for five, but she could tell he wasn't getting rich.

"How'd you know I was American?"

"Your smile. It was your beautiful smile, my lady."

Natasha blushed a little and smiled.

"What's your name?"

"My name? My name is Ishamel."

"Ishmael?"

"No No. Ish-amel. Ish-amel."

"You speak good English."

"Yes, I learn from American, too."

"Thanks."

She paid him the ten dollars and continued on her way.

"Make my day," Ishamel said. "Thank you. Come to me if you need anything else. I can give you guide. I can show you city."

"Thank you, but I must go now," Natasha answered, waving at him as she continued walking.

She wanted to give him more money, but to do so would not be wise. Her years in the Foreign Service had conditioned her to be extra cautious. Flashing large amounts of cash in a public marketplace such as this one was not wise. Despite good intentions, it could draw the attention of thieves and conmen.

The marketplace was full of all sorts of smells and noise. People called out to her and some of the men whistled at her. She was glad to emerge from the alley. As she did, she enjoyed the music of a group of Peruvian musicians playing wooden flutes and guitars. She crossed the busy street and entered the grounds of Aya Sophia. With the acres of gardens surrounding the temple and its accompanying structures, it took a while for her to finally reach the church.

Natasha looked down at the historical note that was monumentalized just before the entrance. It was titled, "Aya Sophia, Church of Holy Wisdom." Among other details, it stated the temple was built by the direction of the Roman Emperor Justinian in AD 537.

Aya Sophia was one of the grandest Christian temples of all time. It was unrivaled in its scale for more than one thousand years. It was, in fact, one of the largest domed structures of all time.

Natasha walked to the prayer area, put a donation in the collection box, and took a candle. Natasha reverently made her way forward. She lit her candle with another candle's flame and placed it in the sand and stood in front of it. She cleared her mind and bowed her head in meditation.

She sensed a man standing behind her. She could smell his aftershave—a spicy, clean scent. She opened her eyes and turned around to confirm her suspicion. The man before her was slender and European. His dark hair was parted to the side. He was wearing a custom-tailored French-cuffed white shirt and black Armani trousers. It was Grant Nuby.

"Grant! What a surprise!" she whispered. "What are you doing here?"

"Natasha, darling."

He kissed her cheek.

"I've always wanted to visit Turkey—and I thought you could use some company. Viola! Simple as a plane ticket."

"How'd you know where to find me?"

"I didn't for sure. But I had strong influences that made me believe you'd be here."

"Wow. You're good."

She glimpsed an old priest entering the confessional booth across the room behind Grant.

"Grant, I'm sorry. Wait for me here. I'll be right back."

He noticed her attention to the confessional booths behind him.

"Have you been naughty?"

"All right. I'll be right back."

Natasha walked to the special little dark corner of the confessional booths. She entered the booth and closed the door. She sat quietly for a moment—not completely sure of what to say. Then she just went for it.

"My name is Natasha Azshatan. I am the wife of Thomas Azshatan. I'm looking for a particular man here. He's known as 'The Priest.' Can you help me?"

"You'll have to tell me your whole story."

She told the same one that she had told Francis Charles and Grant Nuby.

"I don't believe I can help you, my dear."

"No. Please. I know you know something. From the questions you asked me, you must know something."

"As I was about to say, I believe the man you seek is actually the priest librarian. He is known as a holder of secret knowledge."

" Okay, then. Please tell me. How do I find this man?"

"Go to the Library of Istanbul. Request a copy of the 1599 Geneva Commentary Bible. Then take it to the first floor reading area. Sit in the rear corner table and read the second half of the Apocalypse. Once you have done this, the priest librarian will find you."

"When? When should I do this?"

"Today. 4:00 p.m."

"Thank you."

"Go in peace, child."

Natasha exited the booth and looked around for Grant. He was leaning forward on a bench with his head down. He looked up, saw Natasha, and smiled.

Grant stood up and walked toward Natasha.

"Looks like we have a lead," she said.

"Like what?"

"I don't know for sure. We have to go the library at 4:00 to find out."

"Good. So we have time to take the tour."

"The tour?"

"Yes. Look over there."

Grant pointed to a small group of people gathering near the entrance. Natasha and Grant joined the group and leisurely walked as the tour guide revealed the secrets of Aya Sophia. Originally constructed by the orders of Justinian I in AD 537, its interior was so elaborately decorated that Justinian had declared, "Solomon, I have surpassed you."

The walls were inlaid with white, green, and purple marble; they were richly covered with gold mosaics.

The entrance was covered by a separate dome and the eastern section was used for the orthodox services. An enormous central dome—thirty-one meters in diameter and fifty-six meters in height—connected the two sides. The support beams ribbed the interior of the dome like the inside of an umbrella. *Large enough that it could accommodate the Seattle Space Needle.* The tour guide took them outside and stopped in front of the famous Fountain of Sophia. Natasha recognized the inscription from Elijah's file.

νιψον ανομη ματα μη μοναν οψιν

The tour guide translated it into English. *Nipson anome mata me monan opsin*—wash your lawlessness, not only your face.

Natasha stared at it. *I'm missing something.* She couldn't shake the idea.

The tour group approached an outbuilding, which was the entrance to the Basilica Cistern—an enormous underground structure built for the sole purpose of holding and protecting the water for Constantinople.

As they approached the entrance, Natasha recognized another inscription from Elijah's file. The inscription over the entrance read:

νομον ο κιονοσ εξε σον οικονομον—"Whoever you are, let the law be your guide."

Natasha took a picture of the inscription with her cell phone. They followed the group down narrow stairs. Haunting music echoed and colored lights theatrically illuminated the amazing chamber. They reached an area near the water level. A walking bridge crisscrossed the cistern above a gigantic lake. Hundreds of huge marble columns emerged from the water and towered to the ceiling. There was enough space between the columns that small boats could sail through them.

Natasha thought about the reference in the inscription to "law." *Justinian was known to be the father of modern law, but what did law have to do with this place? What did allowing the law to be one's guide have to do with anything down here?* She pulled out her phone and typed herself a reminder to think about this later.

At 5:00, Natasha and Grant sat at a reading table inside the library. Natasha looked around at the incredible maze of enormous bookshelves. Light poured in from high windows and a slight mildew odor affected

the air. Ancient manuscripts, loose-leaf writings, and modern volumes all shared the massive shelf space.

Just as the old priest prescribed, Natasha and Grant read the last half of the Apocalypse. Natasha was eager to make connections now with the Apocalypse because it lined up with Jim Worley's speculation that Father Elijah had come across secret knowledge within its pages. It was those very secrets that may have killed him.

A man wearing the robe of an Orthodox priest approached the table and sat down. He was an older gentleman, perhaps sixty years of age. He wore rounded spectacles and a short white beard. He carried a tattered black briefcase with him and placed it on the large table.

"Dr. Azshatan," the priest librarian addressed her with a Russian accent. "Nice to meet you."

He substituted a handshake with a partial bow, his hands at his chest in a prayer position.

"I will be to show you truth about most amazing mystery in human history. First part of mystery may be to shocking to you—but *not* to too many others because is known for well over one thousand years. Before I say more, I must say something first. Let me make sometzing very clear."

The priest librarian paused and cleared his throat. He looked up as he searched for the right words.

"Pretend I am a Muslim. What does it mean about me if Antichrist turns out to be Muslim? Does it means that I am evil? What about the Antichrist himself? Must he to be an evil man? Or could he be misguided, but with good intentions? Perhaps he leads world astray thinking zat he is doing good?"

Natasha and Grant were silent. She was curious where this man was leading them.

"You see. Demonizing and name-calling is because fundamental misinterpretation of the Apocalypse. I will to prove my point. I to say a word, commonly associated with Apocalypse, and you tell me what you to think. Agreed?"

"Yes."

"Good. The first word. *Antichrist*."

"Evil world dictator," Natasha stated.

"Satanic ruler," Grant said.

"Why?" the priest librarian asked.

"*Anti* means *against*," Natasha said. "The title itself is self-explanatory. Christ stands for all things good and pure and the Antichrist is the opposite."

"Wrong," the priest librarian declared bluntly.

Natasha was startled to be declared wrong in this matter. "What do you mean?"

"You are conditioned to read modern use of this word, despite the fact that it has another meaning."

Natasha looked at the priest librarian.

"This most common mistake. No shame. No one remembers everything from university."

Natasha shook her head doubtfully.

"As far as I have ever known, the definition of *anti* is the English word *against*."

"You just forget other meaning is all," he dismissed her rebuttal and continued. "To properly understand meaning of word Antichrist, one must look to its meaning in its original context. The word originated and is found only four times in original Greek manuscripts of Judeo-Christian scriptures.

"In any dictionary of Biblical Greek, word *anti* does not have meaning of *against*. The exact translation of Biblical Greek *anti* is English word *instead*. The title of Antichrist literally means *instead* of Christ, not *against* Christ."

Natasha didn't know what to say. In all the years she had studied Greek and Latin, she had never come across this.

"Well, I would like to see for myself that the Greek word *anti* means *instead*, rather than *against*."

"I thought you might."

The Librarian pulled a dictionary of New Testament Greek from out of his briefcase and handed it to Natasha. She flipped through till she came to the word *anti*.

> anti - (an-tee) prep.
> 1. for, instead of, in place of (something) 2. on behalf of something 3. substitution

The definition was in fact the English word *instead*. Natasha shook her head in disbelief.

"I know. I know," the priest said slowly as he empathized. "It is an amazingly simple truth and so few people have ever noticed it. It is context."

"I guess you're right," Natasha agreed. "Context is everything."

She knew where her mistake was now. It lay within the subtle differences of what is known as Attic Greek, such as the writings of Plato, versus the Biblical Greek.

Grant sat quietly with his hand on his mouth, staring out in deep thought.

"So you see; Antichrist is not necessarily evil at all. For example, Pope's official title actually means exact same thing. His official title is a Latin title. It is *Vicarius Christi*. It exactly translates 'Vicar of Christ.' But what does this word *vicar*, with Latin root of vicarious, mean?"

"Vicarious has the meaning of being unrestrained," Natasha answered.

"Once again your translation is more modern."

Grant raised his eyebrows and looked at Natasha.

"I thought this type of subject matter is your expertise?"

Natasha shook her head defensively.

"I'm an expert on handwriting and authentication—not necessarily translation. Translation is a part of it for sure, but there's a lot I don't know."

The priest librarian continued, "I will to show you what the dictionary actually says." He pulled an English dictionary out of his briefcase, flipped to the word vicar, and showed them the definition:

Vic-ar – (vik-er) - noun. 1. A person who acts in place of another. A substitute. 2. A person who is authorized to perform the functions of another; deputy: God's vicar on earth.

"Or for even more clarification look at the next word down."

Vi-car-i-ous (vahy-kair-ee-uhs) – adjective. 1. Performed, exercised, received, or suffered in place of another: vicarious punishment. 2. Taking the place of another; acting or serving as a substitute.

"We all know that through history there have been both Godly as well as ungodly popes. But they have all had essentially same official title: *Vicarius Christi* simply means 'instead of Christ' or, once again in Greek, Antichrist. Understand? I will to show you more. In the context of Apocalypse, what does word *beast* mean?"

"The devil," Grant said.

"You probably are going to say it's wrong," Natasha added. "But I'll say evil empire."

"You are partially right," the priest librarian encouraged. "A beast in Bible prophecy is a symbol of a nation or an empire—or a *political* power. However, a beast is not, *in and of itself*, evil. We do same thing today. Eagle represents whom?"

"America," Grant answered.

"Bear represents whom?"

"Russia," Natasha answered.

"Lion represents whom?"

"Great Britain," they answered together.

"And so it is simple. Beasts in Apocalypse are simply symbols that represent world powers. They are not necessarily evil or good. Each beast is different and the characteristics attributed to *beast* help us figure out which world power is being represented."

"Understand?" the priest asked. "What about word *woman*?"

Grant and Natasha looked at each other.

"I will to help you. Do you remember reading about woman who sits on beast? Do you remember part where 'voice from heaven' said, 'Come out of her, my people?' So obviously woman is not a real woman. God's people are not inside of a real woman. No. Where are God's people?"

"Church," Natasha said thoughtfully. "Christ often is said to have referred to his church as a bride. She was the bride and he was the bridegroom."

"Yes," the priest librarian continued. "It is very well established that a woman in prophecy represents a church. A pure woman would represent a pure church. An impure woman would represent an impure church."

"So when 'voice from heaven' says, 'Come out of her, my people,'— what is meant by this? You see? You understand? The 'Great Schism' was actually foretold in Apocalypse."

"What's the 'Great Schism'?" Grant asked.

Natasha answered, "It's the point in history in which the Eastern Orthodox Church broke away from the Roman Catholic Church over theological issues."

The priest librarian continued the explanation. "Many differences festered for several hundred years until finally in eleventh century, Great Schism. Apostle Paul also foretold such a fate, referring to the church as a woman, he wrote this."

The priest opened the Geneva Bible and read aloud:

> For I am jealous over you with godly jealousy: for I have espoused you to one husband, that I may present you as a chaste virgin to Christ. But I fear, lest by any means, as the serpent beguiled Eve through his subtlety, so your minds should be corrupted from the simplicity that is in Christ....
>
> For such are false apostles, deceitful workers, transforming themselves into the apostles of Christ. And no marvel; for Satan himself is transformed into an angel of light.
>
> Therefore it is no great thing if his ministers also be transformed as the ministers of righteousness; whose end shall be according to their works.

The priest librarian looked up and said, "And this knowledge is not new by any means. The Orthodox Church has always known this interpretation and, later, the reformers.

I will continue so as not to leave any doubt. There are several more clues to identity of this woman and beast she sits on, which make it clear that the woman here known as Whore of Babylon is actually Christian Church, gone astray."

The old priest opened up his briefcase and pulled out a stack of papers and booklets. It was a messy stack with layers of various thicknesses and coloration of papers. He pulled a cheat sheet from it, and began to go through the bullet points.

"Clue number one:

> And the woman was arrayed
> in purple and scarlet color.

He pulled out a color photo that pictured the Papal Coronation ceremony of Pope Paul VI. The photo showed hundreds of cardinals and bishops gathered at the coronation ceremony. They were all clothed in scarlet and purple.

"Roman Church is a woman clothed in purple and scarlet."

He pulled out several other photos that showed the cardinals and bishops in purple and scarlet attire.

"Tradition of the purple and scarlet dress code goes all the way back at least to Donation of Constantine."

Natasha interjected, "But the Donation of Constantine was determined to be a forgery."

"A forgery based on an original," the priest answered.

"I've heard that too. But no one has ever seen the evidence for that."

"Evidence is all around us," the priest answered. "There was obviously a transfer of power. And the fact that Donation of Constantine was a forgery doesn't change fact that the Papacy used it for over eight hundred years to legitimize her power in secular political matters."

Natasha bit her lip. The priest's argument made sense to her.

The priest librarian smiled and continued, "In Donation of Constantine it was written that 'Princes' of the church should be adorned in purple and scarlet.

"And next:

And in her was found the blood of prophets, and of saints.

"This is an easy one. As a result of veneration of the saints, church actually does keep pieces of the remains of saints: pieces of bone, strands of hair, and blood itself."

Natasha's mind raced. She surprised both men with her observation.

"The Apocalypse says, 'She was *drunk* with the blood of the saints' and he 'marveled at her.' Most people would probably incorrectly draw from this language a vision of an evil woman drinking blood like a vampire, but actually the opposite is true. The keyword here being *drunk*, not *drank*."

"I don't understand," Grant said.

The priest nodded. He was excited as he anticipated what Natasha would say.

"What do we say when someone has been driving drunk?" Natasha asked rhetorically. "We say they have been driving under the *influence*. Yes? The word *drunk* here is code for *influenced*.

"John marveled as he saw the future persecution of the church," Natasha explained. "And he marveled as he saw that the church was *influenced* by the blood of the saints. Do you understand? She was a victim."

"Yes," the priest librarian affirmed. "Blood of saints persuaded her into compromising with Roman paganism. She did this in desperation to escape ruthless persecution. You understand me?" he asked, insecure about his own language skills. "All right."

The priest sat back in his chair. He took his glasses off and rubbed his eyes.

Natasha didn't exactly know where he was going with all of this. It was very interesting to speculate and to ponder the possibilities.

The priest librarian put his glasses back on and stroked his beard.

"So to summarize." the Priest librarian announced. "First part of the mystery is this: The mystery of Whore of Babylon.

A. I believe that theWhore of Babylon is a symbol of the medieval Christian Church -gone astray, but not in a name-calling sense. It is in sense of real life. A woman forced into prostitution in order to survive poverty and violence. In a sense, she is a victim.

B. I believe the Beast that she rode is a symbol for the medieval Vatican.

C. I believe the official Latin title *Vicarious Christi* literally can be translated as *Antichrist* in Greek language.

"Are you ready to hear second part?"

"Yes," Natasha said.

"Good. Because this is part that is really inconceivable," he said as if he was a Russian scientist who had made a mind-blowing discovery. He put his hands around his head and burst them out into the air. "And I believe with your unique expertise, Dr. Azshatan, you will quite enjoy it."

"Second part of the mystery is Mystery of 666 and of mark of the beast. In order to understand beast, its mark, and its number, we must first identify beast. Do you understand?" he asked again self-consciously. "All right. The beast in question makes his appearance in thirteenth chapter of Apocalypse. Please turn to that right now if you would please."

Natasha flipped back a few pages to the thirteenth chapter.

"Good." The priest said. "Please read me first few verses and pay close attention to description of this beast."

Natasha read it aloud.

Then I stood on the sand of the sea. And I saw a beast rising up out of the sea, having seven heads and ten horns, and on his horns ten crowns… Now the beast, which I saw, was like a leopard, his feet were like the feet of a bear, and his mouth like the mouth of a lion. The dragon gave him his power, his throne, and great authority. And I saw one of his heads as if it had been mortally wounded, and his deadly wound was healed. And … he was given authority to continue for forty-two months.

"Very good," the priest librarian assured. "Now let us to visualize this beast. It is a leopard-like beast with seven heads and ten horns. Yes? Hmm. Does that sound familiar?" he asked.

"Yes, it does," Natasha answered.

"Did you catch it? That this is the same beast that carries the Whore of Babylon. I believe this beast represents the geo-political aspect of the Vatican. Now let us look at other details, and clues. First, *Power was given unto it to rule for 42 months, or 1,260 days.* In Bible prophecy, that means 1,260 years—remember this."

Natasha knew the priest was correct on this issue. There were many instances in the Judeo-Christian scriptures, in which an angel or some other spokesperson for God had interpreted that a day in this or that prophecy actually equaled a year. It was known as the "a day is as a year" principle of Biblical prophetic interpretation.

"After completing construction of Aya Sophia and dedicating it December 27, AD 537, Roman Emperor Justinian appointed his own pope. In AD 538, he sent this pope to Rome with his own army. They besieged Rome and took the rightful pope prisoner, where he died one year later. Justinian's Pope Vigilius I took power of Vatican in AD 538. It was a point in history that marked the beginning of Vatican as an arm of Roman Empire. The Vatican ruled with supreme authority as the former Roman Empire fizzled away. In 1798, 1,260 years later, French General Berthier conquered the Vatican, and took the pope prisoner, thus bringing an end to prophetic 1,260 years."

The priest librarian scribbled notes on a blank piece of paper as he explained the timeline, periodically tapping his pointer finger at the notes. He pointed at the Bible verse. "Notice how beginning and end of this period was predicted in next clue in Revelation:

> He who leads into captivity,
> shall be led into captivity.
> He who lives by the sword,
> shall die by the sword.

"Remember what Paul wrote when he referred to those whom might corrupt the chaste virgin? That their 'ends would be according to their works.' 'He who lives by the sword, shall die by the sword' is just another way of saying same thing, yes? Whose end shall be according to their works? John's language is a concealed reference to Paul's warning of a possible future apostasy."

The priest pointed back to his notes.

"So back to timeline. For more than one hundred years, the Vatican remained poor and powerless—until 1935, when Mussolini restored to her papal states, and returned to her the right to exist as a sovereign nation. Slowly and surely, she has recovered. Until now, she has almost completely recovered. That brings us to yet another clue:

> And I saw one of his heads as if it had been mortally wounded,
> and his deadly wound was healed.

"Now power of the Vatican is once again vast and global. Truly her mortal wound has been healed."

The priest pointed again to the Bible.

"And here. Another clue:

> All the world worshipped the beast.

"Once again, indicating a religious aspect to this political power. And once again indicating global power."

"Let me ask you a question," the priest asked Natasha. "Do you remember your Roman Numerals?"

"Yes. Of course. V equals five. I equals one."

Grant nodded that he also knew them.

"Yes. Good."

The priest librarian turned to Grant.

"Now let me ask another question. How often in your life have you ever *needed* to know them?"

Grant answered, "Almost never."

"Do you think it is strange then, that practically every person in world with a third-level education knows Roman numerals? Why do you think that would be? I mean, they are so useless right?"

Natasha tried to think of an answer. None came.

"Maybe it is because God wanted every man, woman, and child on earth to be able to do this:"

He excitedly pulled out a blank piece of paper.

"I told you before that pope's official title is Latin. What I did not tell you was that title may not have always been *Vicarious Christi*. The pope's title—*Vicarious Christi*—may have had its beginning in document we discussed earlier—the Donation of Constantine. It named Peter and his successors, *Vicarious Filii Dei*—which translates to Vicar of the Son of God. Thus, the beginnings of pope's Title Vicar of the Son of God. But how and why did the title change from *Vicar of the Son of God* to its present version—*Vicar of Christ*? They both essentially mean same thing. The word Christ essentially means the same thing as the words *Son of God*. So why switch?"

Natasha and Grant leaned over spellbound, anticipating what the priest would say next.

"You said you remember your Roman numerals. Now you have a chance to prove it. Decode this if you will." The priest wrote out the title vertically.

Natasha took the paper and the pencil from the priest.

"V equals five. I equals one. C equals one hundred."

She skipped over A and R.

"A has no value. R has no value. I equals one. U has no value."

"Not so fast," the priest corrected. "U is a relatively modern invention in language."

"Of course," Natasha remembered. "That's right. Up until Benjamin Franklin's alphabet reform, the letter U was simply the lowercase version of the letter V. They were considered to be the same letter." She turned to Grant. "If you look at the writing on any old building of significance, you'll see that our modern day U is actually a V. The easiest examples are on old courthouses."

Natasha remembered her dream and a chill went down her spine.

"Yes," the priest said. "And even look at letter in your alphabet known as W."

He wrote a W, demonstrating that a W was actually two V's put together. It is actually a double V. V+ V = VV.

"Therefore U has same value as a V. Please continue," the priest prodded.

Natasha wrote a value of five next to the U and continued.

"S has no value; F has no value. I is one. L is 50. I is one; I is one; and D is 500. E has no value and I has the value of one."

Natasha added them up. She knew where it was leading, but to see it add up was astonishing.

"The values of the letters in this title add up to six hundred and sixty-six," she said solemnly.

"Yes," the priest said. "And look here at end of the chapter that mentions the number 666. It says it will be:

The number of a man, the number of his name.

V	5
I	1
C	100
A	NA
R	NA
I	1
U	5—prior to alphabet reform, U was lower case of V
S	NA
F	NA
I	1
L	50
I	1
I	1
D	500
E	NA
I	1

TOTAL	666

The priest librarian continued his explanation.

"If the Pope's title was ever in fact Vicarious Filii Dei, then we could understand why the Vatican might have changed it to its present version. If this were the case, then in changing title away from a title that spells 666, they inadvertently would have changed it to a title that exactly translates as Antichrist. Yes. You understand? Now let us look even further."

He turned back to the thirteenth chapter.

"Look here," he said and read aloud:

And all the world worshipped the beast, and he caused all to receive a mark on their foreheads or on their right hand. And no one could buy or sell less they have the mark of the beast, or the number of his name. Here is wisdom. Let him who hath understanding calculate the number of the beast. For it is the number of a man. It is the number of his name. And his number is 666.

"All right. Important thing to notice here is that mark of the beast is not number 666. The number is simply number of his name. Mark of the beast is a different thing."

"Yes," Natasha said. "The mark of the beast is given on the right hand because that represents our actions and on the forehead because that represents our thoughts."

The priest nodded affirmatively and tapped at the Bible again with his finger.

"Yes. So when beast forces all to receive this mark, it means he is forcing world to act and think as it commands."

The priest paused for a moment and observed Natasha and Grant.

He cleared his throat and continued, "The mystery of the beast and of its mark is this—there is a possible future of a coming one-world government. This New World Order will endeavor to dominate thoughts and actions of every person on earth."

Natasha scratched her head and ran her fingers through her hair. She pointed back down to the Bible.

"So what does all of this have to do with us? If all of this has been known for centuries, then what's it have to do with people I know getting killed and imprisoned."

"It has everything to do with them, but that is third and final part of mystery. It is part of which I know only partially and rest we will have to figure out. I believe the reason for the assassinations is to protect the well-laid plans of the biggest power grab of all time. You see? Do you remember immediate times after America was attacked on 9/11? Remember how easily Americans gave up their freedoms in exchange for promise of security? It will be same—only a hundred times worse. There is a well-laid plan that involves something fearsome. A catastrophe of such horrible scope that it will cause all of mankind to give up their national identities and individual rights and drive entire world to unite under leadership of first one-world government. Democracy will be exchanged for a global theocracy. All for promise of peace and safety. You, me, and everyone else who knows truth is a threat to those well-laid plans. However, Elijah and Jim Worley and others perhaps had even more specific knowledge. I don't know. As far as Tom is concerned, I think only reason he is in prison is because Francis wants you for himself."

"This is probably the only reason you're still alive," Grant added.

The priest continued. "Natasha, your connection to Elijah and Jim Worley and Francis Charles—it cannot be simply a coincidence. You were put in this position for a reason. It must be because Francis Charles is a one who is to fulfill this prophecy."

He slowly raised up his withered hand and pointed at Natasha. You have a destiny to fulfill, too. You may be only one who can stop whatever diabolical plan Francis Charles is setting into motion. You must go back to Vatican and try to uncover whatever it is that he is planning."

Natasha looked over at Grant to see what he had to say. His elbows were on the table and his hands covered his face as if in prayer.

"Grant. Are you okay?" she asked. "Grant."

She pulled his hands down from his face. Grant was in a trance. His eyes were shiny black.

"*In girum imus nocte et consumimur igni,*" he hissed like a king cobra about to strike.

Natasha recoiled.

"It's you. Who are you?"

The priest librarian jumped across the table at Grant. Grant easily deflected him and flung him across the room into a bookshelf, which came crashing down on top of him.

"Daughter of Eve. You must be destroyed!" he hissed and lunged at her.

"Awwwwwwweeeee!" Natasha screamed. "Noooooooooohah!"

Natasha fell backward onto the ground as she panicked to escape the demonic monster. She was terrified beyond terror, knowing this was the same evil being that had possessed Lucas Phillip Renard.

He jumped on top of her and pinned her to the ground. She struggled and fought with her hands. He gripped her neck with both hands and began to strangle her. Her face turned red and her eyes bulged. She couldn't scream. He was so incredibly strong and his grip was inescapable. He leaned forward and his eyes rolled up in ecstasy as he prepared to inhale her soul.

The priest librarian came from behind and smashed a chair across the side of Grant's face.

"In a name of Jesus Christ, leave this man!" the priest shouted.

"He is ours!" the demon hissed.

The demon had momentarily lost his grip on Natasha's neck. She inhaled. She remembered the news clip and Lucas Phillip Renard's words.

> When my victims would cry out to Jesus for help, I would laugh. For it is Lucifer who has the power to save, and not the man Jesus.

The demon ignored the priest, and turned its attention back to Natasha. She fought him as he grasped at her neck.

"In the name of Lucy Fur," she shouted. "I command you to release me and let me alone!"

The demon recoiled, stunned.

"You do not have the power to call on the name of Lucifer. You do not serve him!" he hissed.

"Oh no?" Natasha shouted. "Lucy Fur, I call on you to rebuke this demon. My body is to be kept for Lilith. The master has plans for me that you know not of."

The demon inside Grant studied Natasha. He shifted his weight from side to side.

"In the name of Lucy Fur, I command you to release me and let me alone!" she shouted again with even more determination.

The demon became aware of the priest standing next to him chanting exorcism prayers.

"I'll leave you for now, Daughter of Eve, but you wait right here!" he hissed.

The demon whipped around and thrust his arms at the priest with an explosive burst of power. The priest flew across the room again and crumbled to the floor.

"You cannot call upon Lucifer for help, can you, priest?"

The demon marched over to where the priest lay on the floor, dazed and mumbling prayers. He kneeled over the priest and smacked the rosary beads out of his hands.

"Priest," the demon hissed. "I will take your soul now."

The demon grasped the priest's neck and strangled him. The priest kicked and flailed, but could not move the demon. He clenched his teeth and tightened his neck muscles to resist the stranglehold. The priest's eyes bulged out and he began to see darkness envelope his vision.

The demon shook his neck and squeezed harder.

"Die! Give. Me. Your. Soul."

The demon could sense the man's spirit departing. He leaned closer and opened his mouth to inhale the priest's soul. He closed his eyes and began a deep sharp inhalation.

Natasha, thinking quickly, quietly approached the transfixed demon. As he began his deep soul-sucking breath, Natasha shot a stream of pepper spray directly into its mouth.

The demon recoiled in shock. He stood up disoriented, his lungs burning. Natasha followed up with an earth-moving roundhouse kick to Grant's abdomen.

"Εκ βαλλετο κακασ πνευματασ. *Ek balleto kakas pneumatas!*" Natasha screamed as she kicked.

"Huuuuuhh!"

Grant breathlessly collapsed to the floor. He huddled over and heaved, trying to catch his breath as his diaphragm convulsed in shock. The demon was gone. Natasha quickly went to the unconscious priest librarian. She put her cheek next to his lips to check if he was breathing. He wasn't.

Natasha pinched his nose and tilted his head back. She sealed her lips around his mouth and filled his lungs with air. The priest coughed and inhaled. His eyes opened. He stared up at Natasha and gathered his thoughts.

"You called upon name of Lucifer?" he whispered with concern.

"No," Natasha corrected. "I called upon my long-dead college roommate Lucile Fur. I simply had to distract the demon by fooling him. Then I had to figure out how to save you from his evil clutches."

"My angel," he marveled at her. "How did you do that?"

"I just thought that, in the original Greek scriptures, when Jesus cast the demon out of the possessed man, he said, *Ek balleto kakas pneumatas*, which is usually translated 'Cast out your evil spirit.' But "*ek balleto kakas pneumatas*" can also be translated as 'Expel your bad air.'

Anyway. It just felt like the right thing to do."

She laughed as she remembered the shocked, disgusted look on the demon's face.

"What happened?" Grant managed to finally ask in a hoarse, cracked voice. He looked up with a bewildered expression. Mucus poured out of his nose and his eyes were puffed out and bloodshot.

It wasn't funny, but Natasha and the priest librarian looked at each other and busted out into a fit of laughter that was so severe, it caused them to shed tears and hyperventilate.

After the laughter subsided, the priest shot a serious look at Natasha. She knew he was concerned about what to do with Grant.

"Grant, do you know what just happened?"

Grant was still a little disoriented and quiet.

"No. I must have blacked out. One moment, I was listening to the priest explaining the Apocalypse—and the next moment, I remember waking up to you guys over there on the floor laughing."

"Grant, you almost killed us. You were possessed by the same evil spirit that killed Father Elijah."

"How do you know?"

"It used the same phrase. *In girum imus nocte et consumimer igni.*"

Natasha looked at the priest.

"Now at least we know what that's all about. We wander in darkness and are consumed in fire is akin to the demon that identified himself to Christ as 'Legion. For we are many.' Grant, the demon told the priest 'you are theirs.' Like you are their property."

Grant put his face in the palms of his hands. He looked up sorrowfully.

"I'm so sorry, Natasha. I am cursed. I am dammed. There's a reason why your powers are so random and why mine are so precise. It's because yours are natural and mine have been paid for. Bought—and at a horrible price."

"Did you sell your soul to Lucifer?" the priest asked.

"To my everlasting damnation. Yes. I did. Now I can be possessed by any demon that needs a body. They use me. I don't know what for, but they use me. It's one of the reasons I came here to Istanbul. I am also seeking help. Priest, is there anything you know of that can break Lucifer's control of me."

"Grant," Natasha looked at him sternly. "Was it you that killed father Elijah and Jim?"

"I don't know. Truly, I can't remember anything of the sort."

"But you admitted to me that you were at Jerrell's Cove the day before I arrived at the Vatican. That was the day Jim was found dead. Did you kill Jim?"

"If I did, it wasn't me. I swear to God. It wasn't me!"

The priest librarian interrupted, "All we know right now for sure is that you are definitely a demon-possessed man. I must do everything possible to cast demons out of you and undo your curse. I must warn you that I cannot promise you anything. You may not even survive. Are you prepared to risk your life?"

"Yes," Grant answered. "I'll do anything."

"Natasha, we will have to keep Mr. Nuby locked up at the monastery. Grant, if you survive your cure—and that is a big if—you will then need to turn yourself in as a person of interest in the deaths of Elijah and Jim. Agreed?"

"Yes! I'm so sorry. I'll do anything."

The priest turned again to Natasha.

"We will have to act quickly and get him under lock and key right away. We cannot afford another appearance by you-know-who."

Natasha looked around the library.

"We need something strong to bind him."

She couldn't see anything readily available, but she realized that the leather shoulder strap of her purse would work perfectly. She unclipped it and held it up to Grant and the priest.

"Do you know any demon-proof knots?" Grant asked the priest.

"I will do my best."

The priest walked around the table and stood next to Grant and Natasha. Grant stood up. The priest took the leather strap from Natasha. Grant held his hand out in front to be tied.

"I am sorry, son. I need your hands behind your back."

Grant complied.

"I have to tie your wrists up back here very tight. Do you understand it is for your own good?"

Grant nodded. The priest gave Natasha a nod as he finished the knot.

"Good," the priest librarian announced. "Natasha, Mr. Nuby is under my care for now. We will go back to the monastery and we will do what we can for him. Now I have my mission and you have yours. Go. Hurry. Get out of here. Do not forget this evil demon will be after you."

"And don't forget what I told you before," Grant said. "What I told you was the truth. Remember the tips I gave you. Stay positive. Pay attention to the clues in your dreams—and pray to Jesus."

The priest was on his cell speaking Russian. "*Edee Sudah. Saychass*! Reinforcements are on their way. We will be without problems."

"Well, if it's all the same, I'll see you off," Natasha said.

"Grant, it'll be all right."

She hugged him and kissed him on the cheek.

"At least you won't be a tool of evil no matter what happens."

"Yes, Natasha. Please. If I don't survive, please remember me rightly. Please remember me. That I was not an evil man."

The reinforcements arrived just then.

"Thank you, priest."

"Keep safe, Natasha. I will be praying for you."

He performed the sign of the cross over her.

"Godspeed."

He turned and followed the group of four men who were already leading Grant out of the library. Natasha watched them leave. She looked around at the great library. Something was nagging at her. She wasn't ready to leave yet.

~

Natasha hailed a cab outside the library to take her back to her hotel room. She pulled an apple out of her purse and ate it along the way.

When she arrived at the hotel, she checked her voicemail. She had two messages. One of them was from Jeremy Benton and the other from Francis Charles. Jeremy Benton had bad news. Since Tom was planning to fly to Mexico the day he was arrested, the judge decreed that he was a flight risk and denied bail. Francis Charles had left a message begging her to come back to the Vatican. He was worried about her and Tom and he was still trying to save Tom's life.

The phone was still drawing her attention. It chimed that she had an unheard message. She flipped open the phone and listened. Once again, Francis was pleading with her to call him back and return back to the Vatican, where he could protect her. He also had a bad feeling about her—the same as the night she'd fled Jerrell's Cove.

Natasha knew she needed to go back to try to find out more of what he was up to—and also persuade him to help Tom's situation.

She dialed Francis' number. He answered.

"Natasha! Thank you for calling me back. I'm so sorry, Natasha. I only meant good. Please come back to the Vatican. I'm trying to help Tom. Against all odds, I'm trying. Please. Just come back here. I'm worried about you."

"I've been thinking about things, too," she said. "Francis, I do love you—but it's agape love. Do you understand? I'm a married woman and I love my husband with all my heart. You have to respect that. Do you understand?"

"Of course I do, Natasha. Please forgive me. I don't know what I was thinking."

"Okay. I have to say I can understand that after all those years of celibacy, the hope of companionship must be very special for you."

"Yes. That's it, Natasha. How could you blame me? You are an amazing woman. I was just not thinking straight. Please come back. I promise I'll behave myself."

"All right, Francis. I'll come back."

"I can't wait. So you'll be here on Christmas Day?"

"That's the plan. I'll call you with my flight info later. All right?"

"Good. Thank you, Natasha."

"You're welcome. Good night."

She pushed the end call button.

The next morning she stopped by the marketplace, and paid a visit to Ishamel.

When he saw her, he smiled. "American lady. You're back. Nice to see you.

"Nice to see you too, Ishamel."

He smiled again. "You remembered?"

"Ishamel. Do you know where I can find a chess set with hand-carved pieces?

"*Chass?*"

"You know—the game. You know—checkmate. It's a game."

She gestured as if she was playing, but he wasn't understanding. She remembered the Russian word for chess. Natasha knew perfectly well that she was in Turkey, not Russia, but she also knew that Russian was to Turkey what English is to Mexico.

"*Shock-ma-ti,*" she said.

"*Shock-ma-ti,*" he repeated. "Yes. Follow me."

Ishamel led her through a short set of turns within the marketplace. They arrived at a kiosk that sold chess sets. Natasha zeroed in on a set that had hand-carved wooden pieces. It was the Ottoman versus the Christians Medieval crusades-styled set. She bought two sets. One for Tom and the other for Francis Charles. They both loved to play chess. She took off her backpack and put the chessboards inside. Then she walked the remaining two blocks back to the hotel.

The security and customs officials didn't give her any trouble at the airport. She flashed her black passport to the security personal, passed her backpack around the metal detector, and walked through it. She picked up her backpack and simply boarded her flight as usual with just her boarding pass.

Natasha felt nervous as the limo neared the home of Francis Charles. *There's nothing to be nervous about.* Natasha thought about the idea that Francis Charles could be the Antichrist, but it didn't seem likely. *Was he really ambitious for more power? He always seemed so happy to serve at whatever position. He's just lonely and maybe a little egocentric.*

After the limo pulled up, Nicholas got out of the driver's seat and opened the door for Natasha. A cold wind blew and snow pelted Natasha as she made her way from the car to the entry. She was wearing the fur that Francis had given her.

Francis was playing his music when Natasha entered. A large glass of wine sat atop of the piano.

> Tis the season of hope.
> Tis the season of gifts and joy.
> And peace can always be found.
> It's the time of Christmas cheer.

"Natasha! Welcome back."

He embraced her unselfconsciously. She felt him smooth his hands over her fur as he withdrew.

She smiled and said, "Merry Christmas, Francis. Wait until you see what I got for you. I'll just go to my room to freshen up. Then I'll put your gift under the tree."

"Have you eaten yet?"

"No. I'm starved."

"You'll enjoy dinner then. Maria made the most amazing Chicken Marsalis."

"Sounds great."

Natasha smiled and turned toward her room. Francis went back to playing his song. While she walked back to her room, she continued to fight with herself as to why she was really there. She felt conflicted.

Was Francis Charles an ambitious, egomaniacal madman, suffering from delusions of grandeur and a bad case of coveting another man's wife?

Had he played a part in the conspiracy against Tom? Could he really be planning a deadly event in order to seize world power?

Or was Francis Charles just an old friend who had found out that it's lonely at the top? An old friend who is sincerely trying to help Tom's situation, but… and who also loves me? She felt like a betrayer. *Of course you feel that way. Alexei Kirov sent you back here to spy on him. To use his love for you against him. You're about to embark on a spying mission against a head of state. Well, practically a head of state. He's the Secretary of State.*

She remembered her own advice. *Test all things. Does it harmonize with known science? Does it harmonize with personal experience? Does it harmonize with other known truths?*

Natasha put the backpack in her closet. She opened her suitcase and pulled out one of the chessboards for Francis' gift. Then she picked up the phone and dialed Nicholas.

"Could you bring me some wrapping paper, scissors, and cellophane tape?"

"Right away, madam."

She hung up the phone and turned on her bath water.

This idea that Francis Charles could be an up-and-coming Antichrist didn't pass her test. Does it harmonize with science? No. Prophecy has never been proven by the scientific method. Does it harmonize with my personal experience?

She had to think about this one. The idea of foretelling the future harmonized with her experience, but the real question was more about the true identity of Francis Charles. The idea that he's the up-and-coming Antichrist that's planning a deadly event didn't harmonize with her personal experience of the man.

But then again. You don't really know him. You have hardly seen him the last ten years.

Nicholas knocked at the door. Natasha opened it and thanked him for the gift-wrap supplies from him.

"For certain, madam," he answered and turned to go.

Natasha shut the door and went back to her thoughts as she wrapped the gift.

Does it harmonize with other known truths? Good question. There were quite a lot of little evidences that seemed to support the idea, but he's also ambitious. That's a truth. He's also very political too. Hmmm.

Natasha finished wrapping, undressed, and slipped into her bath. She decided to meditate. She cleared her mind and tried to distinguish if there was any guidance.

IN GIRUM IMUS NOCTE ET CONSUMIMUR IGNI

The words floated to her mind's eye and startled her out of her meditation.

"*Eureka!*" she whispered to herself. "It's a palindrome!"

She got out of the tub, threw on a bathrobe, accessed the Internet on her cell phone, and searched for Latin palindromes. Natasha waited anxiously for the results. The page loaded up to show several results for her search. The the first choice had the phrase "Latin palindromes" in its URL address, which seemed promising. The site had a whole page dedicated to a long list of Latin palindromes. Everything from small words to complex sentences. "*In girum imus nocte et consumimur igni*" was on the list. It was apparently known as the "Devil's Verse." She clicked on it and read.

Natasha thought for a moment. *This is well known to scholars, I'll bet. It's hard to believe that Francis wouldn't have known about this, yet he pretended he didn't know what it was.* He was like an encyclopedia. She thought about all the languages he knew.

Could he have just simply not known about this one? Natasha found her answer. One of the longer palindromes was at the bottom of the page. It was the proverb that Francis had inscribed on her watch. It was a palindrome too. She saw another familiar item.

The Five Wounds of Christ. "*Rotas arepo tenet opera sator*" was also a palindrome. One of the greatest palindromes of all time, in fact. She saw it in her mind's eye incorporated as a piece of art, which was displayed prominently in Francis' office.

Palindromes are some kind of hobby of his. There's no way in the world that he could have possibly been unfamiliar with the Devil's Verse. Why did he pretend otherwise? Did he have something to hide?

Natasha finished dressing for dinner. She decided to see if Kirov was correct. She would spy on Francis Charles.

~

Francis Charles was still playing when Natasha came down and gently placed his present under the tree.

"You can't open it until at least tomorrow."

She shook her finger at Francis and he stopped his performance.

"But that's not fair. I let you open yours early."

"Not until tomorrow," Natasha teased.

They walked into the kitchen and dished up the dinner that Maria had left on the island in heated catering trays. They sat down and Francis poured very generous portions of Italian red wine.

"Natasha, I have a plan to help Tom. Of course, as I have told you, I've been pushing for the Attorney General's office to drop the charges. I don't think they're going to. However, if a good attorney fails to defend Tom and he is convicted, then I have a very good plan B."

"What is it?"

"A presidential pardon."

"How can you guarantee a pardon?"

"There are no guarantees, of course. But definitely good probabilities. You'd be surprised at what we know about the lives of just about every president. The ordinance of confession, you know. Of course we can never reveal, but they know that we know. And sometimes they think we know even things that we have no idea of. We can almost always rely on a favor from the White House. Of course, there's our friend from Washington, William Jaimeson. He's do to be sworn in as the new president next month."

"Sounds like you're gonna take care of us, Francis. Thank you."

"Stick with me kid."

He winked at her.

"You can count on me to help you get Tom free."

"In the meantime, I can just stay here as your guest in these luxurious accommodations?" Natasha took a bite of the chicken and smiled as she chewed.

"As long as you like. By the way, how was Turkey?"

"It was amazing! I loved it. I had never visited the Basilica Cistern until this trip. I don't know why. Well, you know how it is when you're in the State Department."

"Yes. I have known some diplomats who would never leave the walls of the embassy compound."

"Anyway. Turkey was amazing. I spent a lot of time exploring and, as you could probably tell from my bulging bags, I did tons of shopping. By the way, I saw a painting a lot like the one in your office. Maybe it was painted by the same artist."

"You mean the *Five Wounds of Christ*?

"Yeah."

"Well, I doubt it was the same artist. I painted that one myself."

"Wow. I had no idea. You are such a Renaissance man. You never cease to impress me."

Natasha leaned back in her chair. She held up her wineglass.

"A toast," she said. "To the most gifted man I know—Francis Charles."

They clinked glasses and drank.

"Let's go look at it."

Francis got up and led the way.

"I finished the last piece just two years ago. I have a studio upstairs that I rarely get a chance to play in these days."

They entered the study and Francis flipped on the lights.

"Yes. *The Five Wounds of Christ.*" He named them and pointed to the corresponding part of the body of Christ as he did so. "*Rotas, arepo, tenet, opera, sator.* The tradition of these being the names of Christ's wounds dates back as early as AD 79, where there are records that it was known to the Ethiopian Christians."

"Isn't that something? But it's in Latin."

"Yes. The Ethiopian's version varied slightly, but one can tell it was the same. They had transliterated it into their own phonetics. Look at how each word is five letters—and it all spells forward and backward the same. It's what mathematicians call a magic square."

He looked away from the painting for a moment and stared seriously at Natasha.

"It was used in Medieval times as a prayer to ward off evil spirits and down through the ages as a charm to heal. During the time of the plague, people would chant it over and over again with the hope it would ward of the plague."

"Fascinating," Natasha stated.

They sipped their drinks. Natasha sat down leisurely on the sofa. She curled her feet to her side and leaned against the arm. Francis sat down kitty-corner to her in the easy chair and put his feet up on the ottoman.

"Mind if I smoke?" he asked.

"Go ahead."

Francis got up and walked around to his desk. He opened the drawer and pulled out a fancy cigarette case. He clicked it open and offered her the first cigarette.

Natasha waved at it dismissively.

"I'll be fine with secondhand smoke."

"Thought I'd offer."

The cigarettes had no filters, but the clove tobacco burned smoothly.

"I rarely smoke, but when I do, these are what I like. They're French."

Natasha looked up again at the painting and then over at the desk. She could imagine that when Francis sat behind the desk, the paintings would be directly in front of him. She had a feeling that his password had something to do with those five wounds. She felt strongly about it. Almost the way that a gambler can feel so sure that they are about to win the lottery. Only in Natasha's case, her strong feelings usually ended up bearing fruit of some kind.

Natasha took a sip of her wine. *Another good source to figure out his password might be his Bible.*

"You know, Francis. Just because I don't believe the Gospel exactly, it doesn't mean that I don't like to read the Bible. Did you not leave a Bible in my suite on purpose?"

"No. Not at all. I guess I just supposed that most my guests have their own Bibles if they like."

"Maybe you can loan me yours. Sometimes I like to read it late at night if I have trouble sleeping."

"Go ahead."

Francis leaned over to his desk, grasped the Bible, and handed it to Natasha.

"I've been thinking lately about the story of Noah and the Ark," he said and took a drag on his cigarette.

"Why is that?" Natasha asked.

"Um. I don't know. I guess it's just interesting how God chose to deal with mankind at that point in time. They had become so evil that he just gave up on them. He decided to wash the earth clean and start all over again."

Natasha put her wineglass down on the corner table.

"Seems like I remember a Bible verse somewhere where it says something like, 'So as in the days of Noah, so it will be in the time of the end'—or something like that."

"Yes. You're quite right. It does say that," Francis affirmed.

"So what do you think that means?"

"What do *you* think it means?"

Francis left the room and came back with the wine bottle. He filled their glasses and sat down again. Natasha grasped her wineglass again and took another sip.

"Kind of scary, don't you think? That global genocide can be so easily rationalized and justified. I mean, let's just say for example that the story is really true. Do you think that everyone who perished in the deluge was evil? What about the children? What about the babies?"

Francis looked upward. His eyes followed his bookcase all the way to the top of the high ceiling.

"The innocent perished with the wicked, but it was for the greater good. And so it will be in our times," he stated coldly. "Innocent will perish along with the wicked, but once again it will be for the greater good."

Natasha shook her head vigorously.

"See I don't believe that, Francis. Don't you see how twisted that is? It's the same logic used by Islamic radical terrorists and suicide bombers. I think it's really misguided how supposedly spiritual people can talk about the story of Noah and the flood and teach it to their children, all the while romantically glossing over the fact that a global genocide occurred—a religiously motivated global genocide."

Natasha leaned forward and put her glass down again. Francis listened to her, seemingly indifferent to her argument.

"I talk about this in my book," Natasha continued.

"Well, anyway," Francis responded. "I'd stay out of the Middle East if I were you. Revelations says a third of mankind will perish, and I wouldn't be surprised if that third turned out to be the Islamic third."

An awkward silence manifested. They sat for a moment while Francis extinguished his cigarette.

"I think I'm ready to retire for the evening, Francis. That was a very nice dinner."

"The pleasure was all mine, Natasha. I'm so glad to have you."

He stood up and they hugged goodnight. Natasha took the Bible with her as she walked back to her suite. Francis sat back down and lit another cigarette.

~

Natasha was very disturbed by Francis' comments about the great deluge. It seemed more likely to her that he could possibly somehow be involved in the planning of a deadly event. *A deadly event in which Muslims would be the victims.*

She felt an urge to read Revelations again. Something about the phrase drew her attention:

He who lives by the sword,

shall die by the sword.

She sat down at the desk next to the window and opened Francis' Bible and found the phrase she was looking for:

He who lives by the sword

Shall die by the sword.

He that leadeth into captivity

Shall be taken into captivity

Then I saw a second beast come up out of the earth.

It had two horns like a lamb.

And it spoke like a dragon.

Natasha was surprised to see the mention of a second beast. She, like most people, had pretty much always gone under the assumption that there was only one beast.

Hmm. It's not just one world power—it's two world powers working together. There's the leopard-like beast, which Kirov identifies as the Vatican. There's also the lamb-like beast. If I can identify the lamb-like beast, it may help me to figure out who Francis is allied with. It could be the key to stopping the deadly event.

She opened the desk drawer, and pulled out a note pad and pencil. She wrote on the top:

Clues to the Second Beast
A. Come up out of the earth
B. Has two horns like a lamb
C. Speaks like a dragon

Natasha stared down at her list and tapped the pencil. *The word "then" was used. "Then I saw a second Beast coming up out of the earth."* Natasha stared at the words and contemplated. *The word "then" indicates a timeline. He who leads into captivity shall go into captivity. According to Kirov, that part was fulfilled when the Pope was taken prisoner in 1798. So this other beast rises up after 1798. It comes up out of the earth. The first beast came up out of the water. The Apocalypse says:*

The waters where the beast sits are
people, nations, multitudes.

Water represents a populated place—the "earth" would seemingly represent an unpopulated place. The second beast rose up out of the wilderness sometime around 1798.

Natasha's eyes widened and her mouth opened.

Does this text actually predict the rise of America? Was there any other power that could possibly fit the clues? Was there any other world power that was born around the time of the fall of the Vatican in 1798? And it was a lamb-like beast. Could that be a clue that it would be considered a Christian nation? What else? What about the phrase "it speaks as a dragon"?

If a world power is speaking, that means it's legislating. According to Kirov, the Dragon power was the ancient Roman Empire. The Apocalypse says it gave the first beast "its power, its seat, and its great authority." That certainly happened in the case of Rome. It pretty much withered away and transferred all of her powers to the Vatican around 538 A.D.—it's a Christian nation that is also a nation based on Roman law. It comes into being around the end of the eighteenth century.

Natasha looked down at the text.

It brings fire down from

heaven in the sight of men.

Could that be alluding to a ballistic missile-delivered nuclear explosion? Or satellites being brought back down into the atmosphere via remote control? She shook her head.

If this prophecy is real, then this has to be the United States. If this prophecy is real, then it is predicting an end time alliance of the Vatican and the US to obtain and maintain global power.

Natasha remembered Kirov pointing at her.

"You may be the only one who can save the world from whatever deadly event is being planned," he had said. "I have *my* mission—and you have *yours.*"

I have to figure out Francis' password. She wrote down the five wounds of Christ.

$$
\begin{array}{ccccc}
\text{S} & \text{A} & \textbf{T} & \text{O} & \text{R} \\
\text{A} & \text{R} & \textbf{E} & \text{P} & \text{O} \\
\textbf{T} & \textbf{E} & \textbf{N} & \textbf{E} & \textbf{T} \\
\text{O} & \text{P} & \textbf{E} & \text{R} & \text{A} \\
\text{R} & \text{O} & \textbf{T} & \text{A} & \text{S} \\
\end{array}
$$

Natasha noticed that the word TENET crisscrossed itself in the sign of the cross. On top of everything else amazing about this magic square, that fact seemed significant. Her feeling was strong. She felt certain that she was on the right track. *I feel drawn to the feeling that the N in the center is important. Like it's a starting point.* She wrote the letter N.

Now what. So what's the pattern? The pattern is in the sign of the cross. The paatttterrrnn. She saw something. *This thought about the pattern. Paatterrnn. Pahhhttterrrnnnnnnnosssssterrr.* It was the phrase "Paternoster,"—"Our Father" in Latin. *The title of the "Lord's Prayer" in Latin. The famous street in England mentioned by Benjamin Franklin in his autobiography. They were all known as the "Paternoster."*

"Whoo!" she whispered to herself as she wrote it out.

A

P
A
T
E
R
A   PATER   N   OSTER   O
O
S
T
E
R

O

The only remaining letters were the Latin equivalent of the Greek alphas and omegas. She added those to the end of each point on the cross.

Using each letter from the five wounds magic square, the double "Paternoster" could only be formed one way—in the sign of the cross. Because each word had to share the only N.

That's got to be it!

Natasha got up from the desk and stretched. She looked over at the window, but couldn't see outside because of the desk light reflection. She turned it off and stared out the window. Large fluffy snowflakes fell through beams of light emanating from the myriad street lamps. In the background, she could ever so slightly hear the music of Handel's Hallelujah Chorus.

> King of Kings. Forever, and ever
> Lord of Lords. Forever and ever

Hallelujah, Hallelujah

Natasha thought about what to do next. She thought about the possibility of sneaking into Francis' office right now. *He's had a lot to drink. He's probably passed out by now. What if he walks in on you while you're at his computer? I'll just tell him I needed to use the Internet. What if he asks how I figured out his password? Then I'll just chastise him to not be so foolish as to leave clues of his password hanging on the wall. I'll tell him it was easy for me to guess it. Maybe my intuitive gifts helped. Lucky guess. Who knows?*

Natasha made up her mind. She would do it now and get the heck out of there. She quietly tiptoed back to the study. She didn't make a single sound as her feet moved smoothly across the marble floors.

Natasha opened the enormous door to the study. It moaned a low squeak as it swung open. Natasha stopped and waited to see if anyone had heard the door. Then she thought about how when she was in her room, she couldn't hear anything else in the entire apartment. *There was no way anyone heard that door. I can do this quickly. I know exactly what to do.*

She sat down at the desk without turning on the lights and turned the computer on. The computer booted up and prompted her for a password. *Hope this works.* She typed "paternoster." "Invalid password." The computer replied. Natasha pressed the caps lock button and retyped "PATERNOSTER." It worked. "Valid password." The computer replied.

Natasha plugged her memory stick into the USB slot, and began transferring files immediately. She tried to distinguish files of interest from files that weren't relevant at all. She had three specific objectives in his computer.

    A. Copy all of his favorites
    B. Copy all of his saved web pages
    C. Copy all of his saved documents

As she transferred, she noticed some files that caught her attention.

One file had population maps of the Middle East. Another file had all kinds of data about UFO sightings and the conspiracy theories that America is hiding the truth about what happened in Roswell, New Mexico. Another file had to do with the top-secret military base known as Area 51. Francis had biographical files on the outgoing U.S. President Jackson and his cabinet and the presidential candidates—including William Jaimeson. He also had biographical files of several prominent senators and on a multitude of highly influential Roman Catholics. Lots of the files didn't have any title at all, just numbers. Some of the files had titles, but Natasha couldn't tell of anything significant about them.

Natasha transferred the last file and pulled her memory stick out. It was warm from all the action. She snapped it on to her special neck chain and turned off the computer, standing up to go.

"You're a treasonous swine—just like your husband," the stern voice of Francis Charles startled Natasha intensely.

She froze in mid-step, her arms flailed, and her heart pounded with fear.

"How dare you?" she sputtered. "I was just trying to use the internet. You must be out of your mind to say something horrible like that to me."

She tried to walk around him and out the door, but Francis stepped in her path and blocked her. She tried to push him aside.

"Let me out of here."

She pushed at his chest.

"You're lying."

Francis slapped Natasha across the face so hard that she fell to the ground. He slowly walked over to her, bent over, and yanked her head back with his left hand clutched around her hair. With his right hand, he ripped the memory stick from her bosom.

"Did you think you were just going to walk out of here with my files?"

He pushed her head back with a jerk and walked around her in a circle.

"We've caught you on video, Natasha."

He pointed up at the far corners of the ceiling where two small video cameras were installed.

"I am the Cardinal Secretary of State of Vatican City, a sovereign nation, and you have just been caught stealing classified documents from my computer."

Natasha stood up. Her face was flushed with rage.

"We have a special punishment for people like you."

"It couldn't be any worse than listening to your pathetic music."

She spat blood on his face and Francis wiped it off his cheek.

"I'll remember that. I'll make sure to have my songs played for you over and over again while you spend the rest of your life in a damp, cold, solitary dungeon."

The Swiss Guards entered the room.

"Guards, arrest this woman on charges of espionage!"

"Stop!" Natasha shouted.

She pulled out her diplomatic passport and showed it to the guards.

"I am a United States diplomat. Any attempt to arrest me is a violation of international law. Besides, Francis, you wouldn't want the content of these files to become evidence in a court of law, would you?"

The guards backed off because they knew she was right. Natasha snatched her memory stick.

"I noticed the file you have on the Attorney General."

Natasha let the power of her statement take its effect on Francis. She pushed through them and walked briskly to her suite to retrieve her backpack. Francis stood speechless. He watched her walk down the hallway.

"Don't just stand there—arrest her!"

"I'm sorry, sir. We cannot. But we will stay at your side until she is gone."

Francis curled his fists in frustration.

"Natasha. Natasha, Natasha. Wait. I'm so sorry. How did you expect me to react? Please! Please, Natasha."

She came out of her suite wearing her backpack and toting a small piece of luggage. Nicholas appeared and Natasha turned to him.

"Nicholas, please help me with my things. We're leaving for the airport right away."

Nicholas turned to Francis for authorization. Natasha turned to Francis and shot him a stern look. He nodded to Nicholas to take her.

"Please, Natasha. Let's pretend this didn't happen. Tomorrow is Christmas Eve."

He looked at his watch.

"Actually it's today already."

Natasha and Nicholas made their way down the hallway with her luggage. As they passed near the Christmas tree, Francis pleaded again.

"Please, Natasha. Please, it's Christmas."

"You did this to yourself, Francis."

"Look. I'm opening your present to me. Ah. It's a beautiful chess set. That's so thoughtful, Natasha. It's the nicest present anyone has ever given me."

"Francis," she said.

She looked at him seriously. He dropped his smile and waited for what she would say.

"What?"

"Checkmate! Game over! You lose!"

Natasha walked out the door and Francis stood defeated next to the tree.

"This is not a checkmate, Natasha. The game's not over! If anything, it's a stalemate."

~

Once at the airport, Natasha bought a first-class ticket to Istanbul. The flight would leave at 7:00 a.m. and would arrive in Istanbul at 1:00 p.m. Natasha made her way to the terminal and immediately went to the Internet booth. She sent a copy of everything on her memory stick to Jeremy Benton—along with instructions on what to do with the information, should anything happen to her.

She also sent an e-mail to Francis Charles reminding him to make the arrangements for Tom's release and warning him of the safeguards she had put into place.

Time passed slowly as she waited to board her plane. Natasha used the time to think about everything and to attempt to make sense of it all.

She remembered Kirov's words. "And what about the Antichrist himself? Would he have to be an evil man? Or could he be misguided, but with good intentions? Leading the world astray thinking all the way that he is doing good?"

Natasha thought the answer to that question would be the latter. "Misguided, yet with good intentions." She thought that Francis Charles played that role rather convincingly. He was a trusted spiritual counselor and advisor to William Jaimeson. It wasn't hard to see how easily the whole Apocalyptic scenario could fall into place.

What are his good intentions? What are his motives? He thinks he will save the world by somehow ridding the world of Islam once and for all. Even if it means the murder of millions of innocent people. She remembered how callously he spoke of the death of innocent people in the Biblical story.

Could all of this really be true? Can Tom and I ever be safe again? Can I simply go back to Jerrell's Cove and enjoy a peaceful life of fishing, sailing, and writing books?

Natasha looked up. There were a few others at her gate and a boarding pass agent was behind the counter. She looked down at the watch that Francis Charles had given to her and saw that it was 6:00 a.m. She remembered how he had slapped her so hard and she felt repulsed that she was even wearing the watch.

She boarded the plane and tried unsuccessfully to fall asleep. The flight was turbulent. She stood up to walk to the restroom and was overcome by a sick feeling in her stomach. She continued briskly to the restroom and shut herself inside just in time to vomit into the sink. *Oh no. I hope to God Tom is safe.*

Natasha rinsed her mouth and looked in the mirror. Cosmetics disguised the bruising on her left cheek, but they couldn't hide the cut on her lip. Natasha felt completely enraged. She unclasped the watch and threw it in the garbage.

~

Grant lay on his bunk, sweating while he slept. His eyes moved rapidly back and forth as he dreamt. "Natasha!" he shouted and awoke abruptly. He was shaking.

Grant looked around his room. It was simple hardwood. The window was protected with iron bars. The solid wooden door was outfitted with an iron lock. Locked from the outside, Grant knew. The locking mechanism was loud and clunky as the key turned inside the door.

Grant hadn't eaten since the lunch he had shared with Natasha after they toured the Basilica Cistern. The priest's first exorcism treatment was a prescription of fasting in combination with a rigorous bowel cleansing. He was instructed to chant the phrase "Cast out the evil spirit" in Latin, Greek, and Aramaic during each session he spent on the commode. This latter part was an experiment on the part of the priest librarian inspired by Natasha's method of exorcism, which had clearly worked.

Grant was weak and his muscles trembled as he made his way to the door. He leaned against the door and hollered to the priest with painstaking effort. Grant knocked on the door with his knuckles.

"Get me the priest. I have seen a vision that he must know about immediately. Tell him it's about Natasha. Tell him she's in danger!"

~

Alexei sat at the controls of a closed-circuit security camera room. His monastery was locked up tight and the guards were notified to be on a high alert.

Alexei noticed movement in Grant's room. Earlier, he had been frail and weak. This time Grant stood with strength and confidence. Alexei zoomed the camera in closer. It appeared that Grant was examining his whereabouts for the first time. Alexei looked to make sure the computer was recording. It was.

The room Grant was locked in was very small. He moved in a circle as if he was trying to videotape a 360-degree view of his room with his own eyes.

It looked like he might be either sleepwalking or possessed again. Grant stood straight and tall and faced the window. He clasped his hands behind his back and stared out the window with concentrated effort.

The gesture caught Alexei's attention immediately. It was a distinctive gesture. It was a gesture particular to none other than Francis Charles.

"Shok-ma-ti!" Alexei uttered under his breath.

He picked up his phone. "Euvgeny! *Bistra! Eedee sudah!* Hurry! Come here! *Eta ocheen vazshna!* It's very important!"

Euvgeny, a small, middle-aged Ukrainian man with sandy brown hair, showed up a minute later. His eyes were bloodshot and his face was still sleepy.

"What is it?"

"Something is going on with Mr. Nuby. Watch this."

Alexei played back a looped recording of the gesture.

"Does his gesture remind you of anyone?"

Euvgeny shook his head.

"No. What about it?"

"I have seen Francis Charles use this body language many times. His mannerism is almost exactly the same."

"What does it mean, master?"

"We are all pawns, Euvgeny. We are all pawns. The question is who the master is. I believe that Francis Charles may be practicing a well-honed ability of remote viewing. Look at the way he moves in a circle. It is as if he has never been in that room before."

"Why would he be interested in Mr. Nuby's room?"

"He is trying to figure out where Mr. Nuby is at this very moment, so that he might know how best to use him as he goes forward with his deadly plans."

They studied the monitor in silence for a moment.

"You see, Euvgeny, Mr. Nuby is a pawn on his game board."

Natasha was met at Istanbul International by Alexei. Once on the street, his driver pulled up. Alexei opened the door and put Natasha's backpack on the back seat. The car drove off leaving them at the curb. Alexei hailed a taxi, opened the door for Natasha, and followed into the back seat beside her. Alexei leaned forward, spoke to the cab driver, and they drove off in a different direction from the car that had her backpack. Natasha was wondering what was going on. Why was the car with her backpack being taken on a different route?

"We are being followed," Alexei whispered sideways to Natasha. "I sent my driver without us as a decoy, but I can see they are still following."

"But why did you send him away with my backpack?"

"Because we need to make sure it hasn't been compromised with a homing beacon. It is so easy to slip one on to a person's backpack—that it is one of the most common methods."

He leaned forward and spoke to the driver in Turkish.

"We obviously do not want anyone to follow us, so I have a plan."

The taxi made a right turn at the next street. Natasha looked out the window and could see the Black Sea. The taxi continued to drive closer to the sea until it stopped by a marina. Alexei and Natasha got out of the cab.

"Hurry. We need as much time as possible."

Natasha was amazed at how physically fit Alexei was—even in his old age. At the docks, Alexei hastily walked up to a shack and spoke with the attendant. Alexei gave the man a rather sizeable wad of cash and the man handed him a set of keys, pointing Alexei where to go. Alexei briskly walked back to Natasha and whispered to her hoarsely.

"We just bought ourselves a jet ski."

He kept walking, and Natasha turned around and followed him. They jogged just a few moments to the Ski-Doo.

Alexei and Natasha ripped out of the marina. Alexei drove and Natasha clanged to his waste. They went airborne as he accelerated full throttle over the choppy waters.

Their pursuer and his partner hurried into their sedan and followed as far as they could up to the marina.

"They're headed to the marina. We will pursue on foot. Over. Bring in the helicopter. We'll rendezvous at the marina. Over."

"Affirmative," the voice on the radio answered. "You are authorized to use lethal force. Over."

Ahead of the marina, they rocketed almost out of sight. Alexei rode close to shore and curved around a bend of shoreline to the next little marina. They tied up to the dock and Alexei helped Natasha off.

"We need to switch our transportation. We will need to borrow one of these boats. But which one?"

"We don't have much time. Do you know how to hotwire a boat?" Natasha asked.

"I have absolutely no idea. We must have to find one with the keys in it."

The dock was slippery. They looked around again.

"Use your intuition. Do you have any idea which boat we should try first?"

"It depends," Natasha answered.

She strained to perceive any clues. She heard the faint noise of scuba tanks being tested.

"Come on. Give me your gun."

Alexei pulled the handgun out of his pocket and gave it to her. They ran down the dock.

"What are you doing?" Alexei yelled.

"We don't have time to find a boat with keys waiting for us in the ignition. The solution is clear. We're going to have to hijack one."

They arrived at the boat. Two scuba divers were standing on the deck checking their equipment. They looked up to see Alexei and Natasha. Natasha jumped on the boat immediately.

"Sorry about this, guys, but we need your boat. It's an emergency."

Alexei climbed in and translated. The scuba divers looked at each other with stunned faces. Natasha looked and saw the keys were in the ignition.

"Untie the boat and get off!"

The scuba divers just looked at Alexei until Natasha pulled out her gun and screamed.

"Now!"

The divers jumped off the boat and untied it.

"Full throttle! Get us out of here, Alexei."

"Where to?"

"Out of here and back to the city."

Natasha took a defensive position in the rear and scanned for their pursuers. The divers were running to the marina clubhouse. One of their pursuers arrived at the new marina and scanned for motion. Natasha knew that he had made them. The boat was now just barely out of the marina. Alexei hit the lever full throttle and the boat made its way out and turned the corner out of sight.

"Scuba diving in Turkey is best this time of year!" Natasha yelled over her shoulder as she scanned for danger. "I had a dream that we were scuba diving in a life-threatening situation. And here we are."

"But we are *not* scuba diving."

"We're on a scuba boat. Same difference. It's close enough!"

"So what is the plan?" he asked her.

Suddenly, the fearsome sound of a military helicopter hummed in the distance. Natasha looked at Alexei.

"We're out of time."

Francis Charles climbed a narrow, steep staircase in his palace. It led to a secret chamber room, which lay hidden behind his art studio. It was a small, plush room. Around its perimeter's edge lay dozens of silk and velvet pillows. The pillows were various shapes and sizes and colored in bright shades of red, purple, and pearl.

The ceiling was curved into a dome and, along the walls, a display nook displayed a secret collection of treasured antiquities. Francis reverently approached a tiara. He held it in his hands and enjoyed its heavy feel. He closed his eyes and raised his brow in pleasure as he placed the tiara on his own head. He inhaled a breath of satisfaction and exhaled slowly.

Francis relished the feel of his triple crown. His mental powers were magnified by the tiara. It was like an antenna booster, catching brainwaves like tinfoil on rabbit ears.

A unique golden chess-like game board was centered on the main table. On the surface was an old world map of the earth. The intersecting longitude and latitude lines created the checkerboard pattern. Instead of traditional chess pieces, Francis had hand-carved his own personal set. They were meticulously carved to resemble as much as possible the person they represented. He had a Natasha the Empress, William Jaimeson the President, and Grant Nuby the Seer. There were many other such pieces, which covered the space of his special game.

The helicopter flew up over the rocky hilled peninsula that protected Natasha and Alexei from sight. The pilot scanned the waters below for the boat. It was further away than he had expected. The pilot pushed a control and tilted the craft forward to accelerate toward Alexei and Natasha.

"Target is in sight," the pilot reported.

"Excellent," a voice in his headphones affirmed. "Blow them out of the water."

"Missile is locked onto target."

"You are go for missile launch."

The pilot pulled the trigger and a missile bulleted toward Alexei and Natasha faster than the speed of sound. It shot out of the helicopter with a muffled boom and then swerved to exactly target the boat.

Within a moment, the missile reached its target. The boat exploded into a fireball. Thousands of fragments and jagged splinters burst out in all directions.

"Target vaporized," the pilot reported.

"Excellent."

Natasha and Alexei survived the missile attack by diving into the Black Sea with partial scuba gear. The bubbles flowed out of Natasha's mouthpiece and up through the water as she handed the secondary breathing apparatus to Alexei. He purged it as he placed it into his mouth and inhaled deeply. He looked at Natasha. She was beautiful with her hair swirling in the blue abyss. They heard the chopper come close and then the boom of the missile launch. The boat exploded into flames. Fuel sprayed out across the water's surface and burned overhead. They looked at each other with wide-open expressions of amazement.

Natasha pointed to Alexei with two fingers. Alexei acknowledged that he understood, but then he patted his back and reminded Natasha that he didn't have his own tank. Natasha nodded. She knew that. She just wanted to tell him.

"I know where we need to go. Follow my lead."

They surfaced carefully onto the high bank waterfront. There was a small dock and a steep set of stairs affixed to the cliff. They shed their weights, Natasha shed her tank and vest, and they carefully made their way.

"We are safe for now, Natasha. They think we are dead. Do you still have the gun?"

Natasha patted herself and pulled the gun out of her front pocket.

"Do you still have your cell?" she asked.

He patted himself, pulled his cell from his pocket, and flipped it open. Water drained out of its inside casing.

"I still have it, but it is only a paperweight now. What about yours?"

"Mine's in my backpack."

"Then it is safe at least."

At the top of the stairs, they stood near a busy roadway and thought for a moment. Alexei turned right and pointed down the road.

"There is a phone that direction we can use to call my driver. It will be just a short walk."

A few minutes later, they arrived at the phone. Alexei pulled damp coins out of his pocket, pushed them into the slot, and dialed. Natasha looked around, still being vigilant, scanning for signs of danger, while Alexei spoke with his driver.

After ten minutes of waiting, the driver pulled up.

"It is a short drive, but you will need to put this on."

He handed her a blindfold.

Alexei led Natasha blindfolded into the heart of his monastery. Natasha couldn't see, but she perceived that they were in a large building. Maybe it was the groan of the front doors or the echo of their footsteps. Somehow she had a sense.

Natasha was brought into a room. The doors were shut and locked. She was seated at a rustic circular conference table and her blindfold was finally removed.

"Welcome," Alexei greeted her. "We are inside what the CIA refers to as a bubble room."

Natasha looked around. She was relieved to see her pack set neatly against the wall. She walked over to it and took it back. They were in what appeared to be a large circular library. Tall bookcases lined the walls and soared high until the walls began their arched transition into a domed ceiling.

"What's a bubble room?" Natasha asked.

"It is a room that is insulated from all sides to block any electronic signals. No signals can get in and no signals can get out," Alexei answered.

Other than the bookcases, the walls appeared to be made entirely of wood. There was no sheetrock and no paint. It felt like a mixture of cedar lodge and a castle.

"We have a problem to solve," Alexei said.

He produced a flask and two shot glasses. Natasha thought about the shot glass puzzle Santa had showed Tom the night Father Elijah had been murdered. Alexei poured the vodka into each glass. He raised his glass into the air.

"Let us drink to the success of our sacred mission."

Natasha consumed the vodka with the ease of a seasoned diplomat. The alcohol took its medicinal effect, helping to calm her nerves. Alexei opened a laptop computer and turned it around for Natasha. He played the film loop that he had showed to Euvgeny.

"As you can see, that is Mr. Nuby in his quarters here at my monastery. Please watch his body language and tell me if it means anything to you."

Natasha watched. Grant Nuby arose from his bed. He stood in the center of the room and rotated clockwise 360 degrees. He stopped and stood straight as a soldier. He clasped his hands behind his back and spied out his window with concentrated effort.

Natasha recognized it right away.

"That reminds me of Francis Charles."

"*Tochna!* Exactly! I saw it right away myself. Can you tell me what you think is happening here?"

Natasha waited for him to explain.

"I believe Francis Charles has mastered the skill of remote viewing.

These few moments, we have not been watching Mr. Nuby. We have been watching Francis Charles."

Natasha's mind made a startling connection. If this was Francis Charles acting remotely from inside Grant's body, then it could have been Francis Charles who killed Father Elijah. Remotely, of course.

The part of Natasha that was a handwriting expert pondered this thought. It had been Francis Charles who had sparked her interest in paleography when she had witnessed his everyday handwriting. It was an incredibly beautiful and distinctive calligraphy. She had never seen handwriting like it, ever. It was a perfect melding of ancient and modern styles that he had made his own. Of course she could never have made the connection before. She closed her eyes and focused on her memory—especially on the letter G, the letter S, and the letter U. She pictured them on the wall. Then she pictured the last note he had written to her. She remembered noting the very unique style Francis had of forming those particular letters. The bloody writing on the wall next to the body of Father Elijah was consistent with the distinctive and very rare writing of Francis Charles.

Natasha looked up.

"It was Francis Charles who wrote the Devil's Verse. It's so obvious to me now. I'm certain of it. He is a remote killer."

"Now do you understand the reason for the blindfolds?"

~

Natasha looked around at the book-lined walls of the room, searching her mind for the next step.

"We need to think about what we can possibly do," Natasha said.

"We need to get some kind of proof," Alexei answered. "From what you have told me thus far, information you pulled off of his computer doesn't prove Francis is planning a terrorist event."

"If we could just get some good evidence, we could show it to the Swiss Guard."

"I agree," Alexei said. "We need a proof of a plot."

"But how can we get more proof?"

There was silence again until Natasha spoke up.

"What if we can't find any proof that's good enough? We can't just let him go through with his plan. People's lives are in danger."

"So we must work on two goals simultaneously," Alexei said. "We must work to find and stop the deadly event and we must try to gather more evidence."

"But how?"

"We have to use our heads. We need to think about our next move carefully."

"So what can we do?" Natasha asked.

There was silence for a few moments.

"Alexei, can you get out some paper and pens. We need to brainstorm. The key is to not restrict our thinking. Write down every thought—no matter how crazy it may seem. Don't censor. Just write everything freely."

They looked down at their blank notepads for a long few moments before they suddenly broke loose, quickly jotting one idea after another and looking for connections.

Wait a second. Maybe there is something. Natasha bent over to the backpack at her feet and pulled out the Bible of Francis Charles. *Maybe there's a sample of his handwriting in his Bible. Then I can show how distinctive his writing actually is.*

She flipped through the Bible and it more or less fell open to a particular page. As if it had spent a lifetime opened to that page. Four words were outlined with a yellow marker—"You shall not die."

Interesting. Natasha continued to make notes as she brainstormed. A few minutes later, she looked up from her notes.

"Listen to this, Alexei. This is after King David has a man killed in order to steal his wife. The prophet Nathan comes to David to pronounce a curse on him."

Natasha looked down at the Bible and read the text.

> And Nathan said unto David,
> … thou shalt not die.

Natasha slid the Bible across the table to him.

"Look at the words he underlined."

"What are you getting at?" he asked.

"What I'm getting at is one of the most important questions. The question of who is Francis Charles. Who is he really?"

"Yes. I see where you are going. He is not just an ordinary person, is he?"

"No. I've never known anyone like him. Even twenty-five years ago, he seemed to have a vast super human knowledge of our world— philosophy, science, literature, history, culture, languages, art, music, calligraphy. He seemed to be a genius in every category."

"So what are you thinking, Natasha?"

"He wants to perpetrate genocide against the Muslims," Natasha answered. "He thinks he will save the world by doing so."

"Noted," Alexei responded. "But what does your Bible story have to do with it?"

"Well. As we were saying, the question of who is Francis Charles is an important one. Who is this man? Who is this brilliant, amazing person who among so many other talents has also demonstrated a skill for remote viewing?"

"The Chinese say it takes a lifetime of disciplined training even to cultivate the slightest skill at remote viewing. It is not something you can learn at university."

"Right. It's more like a skill one would develop after spending fifty years communing with mystical Chinese monks," Natasha finished.

"Who is this man who seems to be poised to take world power? We need to know if we plan to be successful in stopping his deadly plans."

"All right. I'm just floating this as a free idea. Remember brainstorming—no censoring, let everything flow."

"Yes. Yes," Alexei encouraged.

"Look at what Nathan tells David—'Ye shalt not die.' There it is—as plain as day. A curse of immortality. David was cursed that he shall not die!"

Alexei leaned forward. *What a bizarre and interesting idea.*

Natasha continued, "What if the man who is seeking world power through the vehicle of the Vatican government is a man who feels it's his for the taking? A man who knows that Jesus was his own descendant."

"This is an interesting idea," Alexei admitted. "Nobody has ever found the final resting place of King David. There is no tomb, no burial site. Nothing. Other than the pages of the Bible, there is almost no proof that he ever existed at all. It is as if the proof of his existence has been covered up."

"That's right. Archeological scholars actually debate whether he existed at all. Proof of King David is akin to proof of Noah's Ark."

"And, of course, that makes sense if he were immortal," Alexei said. "He would be forced to relocate every fifty years or so to keep people from growing suspicious. Not for fear of death, but for fear of imprisonment. The worst punishment for an immortal."

"Even King David in all his glory at some point in time would have had to worry as the years passed and as the people around him grew old and suspicious," Natasha said.

"He would have to worry about questions such as—"

Alexei paused for a moment to formulate the questions.

"He would have to ask himself: When will someone finally figure out that I'm immortal? When will they arrest me and try to kill me in every conceivable way? How many times and how many different ways will they try to kill me? Will they burn me alive? Will they cut me into pieces?"

Natasha continued, "And so, at the right time, when the arrangements had been made, King David escapes to the land of the Far East. Every fifty years or so, he will suddenly appear in a new town and assume a new identity—but with all of his knowledge, skill, and wealth, he must still always worry about that one horrible possibility. The possibility that forced him to run from his land of Israel. The horrible prospect of being tortured a thousand ways and then locked in a prison cell. It's a fate worse than death."

"That is why he aspires to be the unquestioned leader of the world," Alexei concluded.

"Yes," Natasha affirmed. "Not only does he see himself as uniquely qualified, and entitled, but it's the only way he can guarantee his own safety and well-being. It's his only possible escape from his 3,000 years of reinventing himself. It's a position that he feels he will finally be able to apply all of his vast knowledge, experience, and abilities to the good of human kind."

"How could you possibly know if you are right about this?"

"I can think of at least two separate ways to independently verify this hypothesis," Natasha answered. "But I'll need Mr. Nuby's assistance.

Red lights began to flash.

"It is the alarm!" Alexei announced.

There was a sound of the lock inside the door being rotated. The door swung opened and Euvgeny entered.

"Master, we are under attack."

"Attack? From whom?" Alexei demanded.

"From mercenaries, presumably."

"But how could they know our location?"

Natasha pointed to the laptop computer.

"You were paying attention to Mr. Nuby's body language. But were you paying attention to what he might have been able to see from out of his window?"

"Of course we thought of that. But there is nothing out there that could help Francis Charles know where we are."

"Nothing on the *ground*," Natasha stated. "He may have been able to see the planes landing and taking off. That would give Francis Charles our position relative to the airport."

"In any case, it doesn't matter. They found us now. We must bring Mr. Nuby here right away. It will take the mercenaries some time to break through our defenses and the bubble room is in the innermost secured area. We have a little bit of time, but we must hurry."

"Natasha, you stay here. Do not open the door for anyone except for me. Euvgeny and I will retrieve Mr. Nuby. You can monitor our progress by watching the video feeds from our security cameras."

Alexei pointed at the LCD screen that showcased twenty separate video feeds.

"Euvgeny, radio," Alexei demanded.

Euvgeny unclipped his radio and handed it to Natasha.

"Radio us if you see something we should know about."

Alexei opened a Velcro flap on his robe and handed her a pistol.

"Do not hesitate to use it, Natasha."

"Don't worry. I won't."

She took the gun from him and placed it on the table next to the laptop. Alexei and Euvgeny quickly shut and locked the door behind them. They ran down the corridors lit by flashing red bulbs. Natasha watched the video monitors. Video feeds 4, 8, 12, and 16 showed the perimeter areas. The mercenaries were preparing to blow the locks on the front door of the monastery. One of the mercenaries ran up and back. He had just placed the explosive. There was a flash and the mercenaries were in.

Natasha pressed the button on the hand radio.

"They've just blasted through the entry," she announced.

"Understood," Alexei answered back.

Natasha looked down at the video feeds. She was watching Grant Nuby's room. She saw the door open. Alexei and Euvgeny propped the weakened Grant Nuby onto his feet. They each took one of his arms over their shoulders. Alexei put the radio to his mouth.

"Is the corridor clear?"

"All clear," Natasha radioed back.

Natasha looked down and tried to see if any of the mercenaries would intercept them or discover them from behind. She pointed at one of the video screens to herself and grabbed the radio.

"Run!" she commanded. "They'll be on your rear end anytime."

Alexei and Euvgeny ran, dragging Mr. Nuby along between them.

"Get out of that hallway!" Natasha yelled.

The mercenaries turned the corner and saw Alexei, Euvgeny, and Grant at the far end of the corridor. They raised their guns to fire. In that instant, Alexei swung shut a steel door. The automatic gunfire ricocheted off in a deafening thunder.

Alexei put a huge key into the door and turned it with great effort to secure the lock. The three of them ran ahead to yet another steel door, locked it behind them, and then ran to another steel door.

A moment later, it was the lock on the enormous bubble room door being turned. Alexei, Euvgeny, and Grant Nuby rushed in. Alexei locked the door again.

"Try not to panic. We have time. We are at the inner most center of my compound. Underneath the wood façade, the doors and walls are impermeable steel."

"What about the Turkish police?" Natasha asked. "Won't they help?"

"If the mercenaries have come this far, it means the police have been bought and paid for."

Grant looked very bad. His eyes were sunken and they were ringed with dark circles. His hair was matted and stuck to his forehead with perspiration. Natasha hugged him, but he barely responded.

"I'm sorry," he said. "I'm not well."

"It's okay, Grant. We need your help. And we need it fast. Alexei, do you have any water for him?"

Euvgeny walked across the room and pushed on a cabinet door. It was a secret panel that hid the wet bar and mini fridge. He took a bottle, opened it for Grant, and handed it to him.

Grant grabbed the water and quickly drank the entire bottle.

"I'm weak because I'm fighting to stay in control," he stuttered. "I'm fighting off the control from another entity."

"That has to be Francis Charles," Natasha exclaimed. "We can use this to our advantage."

"How?" Euvgeny asked.

"Remember when the Russians stopped that shipment of typewriters that was on its way to the U.S. embassy? They planted bugs in them that would transmit the sound of the print ball spinning as it typed."

"Yes," Alexei answered.

Natasha turned to Euvgeny.

"It was ingenious. The Russians could listen to that ball spin and they could tell which letter was being typed. For years, they deciphered every document typed on embassy typewriters."

"When the CIA discovered one of the bugs, they used it as an opportunity to feed bad information back to the Russians—and, for years, the Americans were able to use the bugs for their own purposes."

"I understand what you are saying," Alexei said. "We use Mr. Nuby to send false data back to Francis."

"But wait," Natasha said. "This is a bubble room. I thought no signal could come in or out."

"That is right. I was going to do this anyway," Alexei said as he made his way to the other side of the room.

He turned a large wheel around and around. Above them, the large domed ceiling opened as if it were the electronic iris of a camera.

"Grant, it's Francis Charles trying to get inside your mind."

"How do you know it's not a demon?" he asked weakly.

"It's him, Grant. We have something that he wants."

"Grant, now that you know it's him, we need you to tap into whatever wavelength he's using and use it against him. Follow his signal back to his own head and tell us what you can find. Can you do that?"

"I can try."

"Must do better than try, Mr. Nuby. You must make atonement!"

Natasha put Francis' Bible in Grant's hands, so he could focus in on Francis more easily.

"Grant, we want to know more about who he really is. What are his fears and weaknesses? What are his deadly plans? Especially, we need to know about the attack he is planning."

Grant nodded his head.

"I will make atonement. Remember me well, Natasha. Remember that I am not an evil ma—."

"It looks like the signals are getting in now," Alexei announced.

Grant bared his teeth in effort and more beads of sweat appeared on his brow. Natasha put her hands on Mr. Nuby's shoulders and looked him in the eyes.

"Grant, we're going to blindfold you. Let Francis take you over. While he's staring at blackness through your eyes, you follow his signal back. Tap into it. I'll give you five minutes. After that, I'll electroshock Francis Charles out of your brain. Do you understand?"

"Yes."

Alexei put the blindfold on Grant and helped ease him into a chair at the round table. Euvgeny came back with the remains of what used to be a lamp cord. The positive and negative wires had been separated from each other and the plastic insulation stripped from their wires.

"The sensory deprivation will confuse Francis Charles. It may cause him to intensify his remote ability, which might make it easier for you to tap into it."

Natasha grabbed the earplugs and pushed them into Grant's ears. Grant relaxed his tense muscles and the room went silent.

~

"There is no time," Alexei whispered sharply. "We must prepare our escape simultaneously."

He hurried over to his control panel and began turning a hand crank in circles. Euvgeny lifted on the back of Grant's chair, and pulled him backward from the table. Two cylinders rose out of the center of the table like a bull's eye. The center cylinder pushed out first. It was an encasement for a tall thin compressed gas tank.—the type used for helium.

The second cylinder rose up around the compressed air encasement. Alexei finished turning the hand crank. He hurried back, jumped up on the table, and pushed a button on the air tank, igniting a flame.

He pulled blue nylon fabric from the cylinder that ringed around the center. The fabric came out like tissue. Alexei held it over the flame and pulled a drawstring closed. The fabric began to inflate and rise higher. It grew larger and taller as more fabric climbed out of the ringed container.

Alexei put his finger to his lips, signaling Euvgeny and Natasha not to utter a word about their escape vehicle. Natasha stood in awe as she watched the round conference table transform into a hot air balloon.

Euvgeny reached under the side of the table and unlatched something. It was the basket walls. They were folded in on the underside of the table. Euvgeny unlatched them, swung them into position, and locked them into place.

Now the tabletop was the floor of the balloon and chest-high walls were now in place along the circumference.

Alexei continued to feed the balloon additional fabric as it inflated. Euvgeny joined Natasha in watching the video feeds. The mercenaries easily blasted through the door that had previously deflected bullets.

There were only two doors left.

Natasha looked at her watch before she looked down at Grant.

Grant was moving his head around. His wrists pulled against his handcuffs. He caressed the cover of the Bible. He rubbed his finger over the gold-embossed name on the lower left corner and his eyebrows raised.

He held the Bible up to his nose with his cuffed hands and inhaled. A look of acknowledgement manifested itself on Grant's face.

Then he began to inhale again.

An alarming idea washed over Natasha. *This isn't just remote viewing. It's remote sensory. He's sniffing for info.* Natasha took the positive and negative ends of the lamp wire from Euvgeny. She pressed them onto Grant's chest. Grant seized in a tremendous spasm. His chest arced outward and his eyes rolled back into his skull.

He fell forward unconscious. Natasha checked his pulse. His heart was still beating. She shook his shoulders.

"Grant. *Grant*!"

Grant looked up and smiled.

"You won't believe what I just learned."

An explosion rattled the room.

"Quickly!" Alexei shouted. "The only door left for them to break through now is that one. Get in here now."

Alexei gave Natasha his hand and she pushed off against it as she climbed in. Euvgeny helped Grant inside and guided him to sit down with his back leaned against the wall. Euvgeny jumped in and Alexei unclipped the anchor lines.

A pile of rope spiraled out of the basket as they ascended. The end of the rope was attached to a lever that controlled the iris.

As the basket cleared the iris, an explosion shook the tower. The rope attached to the iris lever became taut and the balloon jerked to a stop. Alexei freed the rope's end from the balloon floor. He leaned over the edge and yanked on the line like a fisherman trying to free a snag.

"Help!" he yelled. "We must pull the lever to shut the iris. Otherwise they'll be able to shoot up at us through its opening!"

Natasha and Euvgeny pulled on the line too. Suddenly, the lever jerked and released; the iris began to close. Beneath them they could see the mercenaries rush into the room. One of them was directly below the iris. He fired his automatic weapon. The iris was closing. His bullets ricocheted off of the underside of the iris and the hot air balloon speedily ascended into Turkish airspace.

Natasha looked below. The buildings appeared smaller, and smaller. The mercenaries were scrambling out of the monastery like ants rushing out of a disturbed nest. They rushed out and tried to follow, but were thwarted by heavy rush hour traffic.

"Alexei, he sent a missile-armed helicopter after us."

"Hopefully that won't happen again."

"So what did you find out, Grant?"

"He's a powerful adversary. You already suspected it, didn't you? That's why you asked me to find out who he really is."

"Yes. Who is he?" Alexei asked.

"He's King David. He's Francis Charles. He's a hundred lives in between. When I entered his mind, I entered thousands of years of memories. They flashed at me one after another. Only the prominent ones of course—the battle with Goliath, the curse of the prophet, the death of his child, the fear of imprisonment, the fear of torture, his ambition to be emperor, his obsession for Natasha."

"And then I saw his plans. It will be an airplane. It will be hijacked and flown into the United Nations building."

"Oh my goodness! I've been having a reoccurring nightmare of that," Natasha exclaimed.

"I told you," Grant gloated. "Pay attention to clues in your dreams."

"It will happen January 1. The pope will be addressing the world from the United Nations podium."

"What plane? Which flight?"

"I don't know. All I know is that Francis leaked the pope's itinerary to the American Islamic Militia."

"How can we prove it? Where is there proof?"

"I don't know," Grant said. "I guess he more than leaked it. They have an agreement."

"Francis is too smart," Natasha remarked. "He's not going to leave us any proof of his involvement."

For a moment there was silence as the four crusaders floated through the skies.

"Where are you taking us?" Natasha asked.

"I have been trying to figure that one out."

"We have six days. Between now and then, we need try to find another way short of sending Grant to the airport with a set of witching sticks."

"True," Alexei agreed. "Are there any suggestions as to where we should land this balloon?"

Natasha stood up and leaned against the wall as she looked out into the skies. Grant stood up too. It was as if everyone was looking for shapes in the clouds to give clues on what to do next.

A friendly pigeon flew near. It made Natasha smile. The bird seemed to float and fly so effortlessly.

"When Paris was surrounded by the Prussians in 1870, all of the communications were cut off. The only way Paris could communicate with the outside world, was via pigeon mail," Natasha remarked.

"Pigeon mail?" Grant asked.

"Yes, pigeon mail," she continued. "In fact, they used hot air balloons to transport the pigeons safely over enemy lines."

"Interesting."

"Yes. Amazing, but true. They were also used in World War I and World War II. I read about one pigeon that was actually awarded a medal by the French government. Despite being shot, it delivered its message, which barely dangled from the poor bird's exposed tendon. The message saved more than two hundred American soldiers that were trapped by the Germans."

"Wasn't there also speculation that Osama Bin Laden at one time used pigeons to communicate?" Euvgeny asked.

"I think I once heard something about that too," Natasha remarked. "Either him or the Taliban. Something like that. There are still mountain villages in India in which the only means of communication is in fact pigeon mail."

Grant's eyes rolled as if he were using them to access a file in his brain.

"What?" Natasha asked.

"I'm just remembering some images from Francis Charles. I have memories of him handling mail pigeons going back almost one thousand years."

"How do you know how long ago?" Alexei asked.

"Just guessing based on clues from the images and impressions of the memory. Instinct. It's hard to explain."

"Of course," Natasha exclaimed. "That makes perfect sense. Of course he would be a master at pigeon mail."

Grant looked up at Natasha.

"He's using pigeons now, too."

"I'll bet that's how he's communicating to the Islamic radicals," Natasha speculated.

"You said it yourself," Alexei said. "You heard Osama Bin Laden and the Taliban used them."

"I sense that's correct," Grant said.

Natasha said, "I know that when the French used the pigeons, they would send as many as thirty of them with the same message to the same location to guarantee that the message would arrive. If Francis Charles is communicating with terrorists via pigeon mail, then his messages would have to be encrypted in some type of cipher code."

"That might be the proof we need," Alexei said.

They all looked at him.

"I will bet that right now we have two pieces of information that will get us the proper attention from the Swiss Guard," Alexei explained. "Number one. We tell them that we know the pope is planning to travel to the United Nations on January 1. I am sure that the pope's itinerary is top secret. That should get their attention. Number two. We can tell them that we know why they have been finding postal pigeons with indecipherable messages. If what you say is true about the need for multiple pigeons, then I will bet that a stray pigeon has found its way to the Swiss Guard office more than once."

"We have a way that may be able to prove our theory and also catch Francis Charles and the terrorist red-handed," Natasha added.

"That answers the question then," Alexei announced. "We go to Rome"

~

Several hours passed.

"The balloon is blue and white camouflage," Alexei remarked. "We are hard to see from the ground with just the naked eye."

Natasha looked out into the distance. Sunset transformed the skies into a beautiful collage of fiery clouds on a violet canvas. The setting sun stole the last remains of warmth. Natasha sat down and leaned against the basket wall. She crossed her arms around her drawn up knees. Alexei sat next to Grant. They were scrunched together as a family seated at a semicircle diner booth. The flames burned above them like a levitating campfire.

"There's something else I discovered," Natasha broke the silence. "I think I may have stumbled onto the third part of the mystery."

"What is it Natasha?" Alexei asked.

"When you talked to Grant and I about the beast of the Apocalypse—the one with seven heads that sits on the seven hills—you were very convincing. I believe you were right. That beast is the Vatican, but you never mentioned the second beast in that chapter. I suspect you read right past it like most people."

Natasha opened her backpack, pulled out the Bible, and re-read the passage.

"Notice that there are actually two beasts," Natasha said. "The second beast has two horns like a lamb and speaks as a dragon."

Euvgeny looked down to confirm that what she was saying was true.

"Remember that the first beast comes out of water and that the Apocalypse describes the symbolic meaning of water as 'peoples, nations, multitudes.' In other words 'a densely populated region.'

"But the second beast does not come out of water. It comes out of the symbolic opposite of water. It comes up out of the earth. Earth would then be symbolic of wilderness or a sparsely populated region."

"Hmm. Very good," Alexei encouraged.

"But look at this," Natasha continued. "You said that when France conquered the Vatican in 1798, it was the fulfillment of the prophecy in which the 1,260 years of power comes to an end and also that it fulfilled the part of the prophecy that states the beast would be mortally wounded. Last but not least. The conquering of the Vatican in 1798 was specifically marked in this prophecy by the words:

> He who leads into captivity shall go into captivity.
> He who kills by the sword will be killed by the sword.

Well. Look at the word that follows this line."

Natasha handed the Bible across to Alexei and continued her explanation.

"It's the word *then* that denotes a timeline. The beast is mortally wounded in 1798, but *then*..."

"But then what?" Euvgeny asked.

"But then look at the very next verse. No... the very next word, in fact. After the word *then*."

Alexei looked down and read aloud. Chill bumps ran down his arms as he read.

Then, I saw a second beast
coming up out of the earth.

"Unbelievable!" Alexei exclaimed in complete awe.

Natasha nodded as the idea sink into his mind.

She continued, "Name me one world power on the face of the entire planet that sprang into existence in a sparsely populated area in the world immediately after the period of 1798."

"Australia!" Euvgeny interjected.

"Australia has never been a global power," Alexei countered.

"But America wasn't founded in 1798," Grant argued.

"It wasn't founded in 1798, but in 1798 it was an infant. That's for sure," Natasha defended.

"It was coming up out of the earth so to speak in 1798," Alexei said.

Alexei used his cell phone to connect to Onlinecopedia. He read aloud:

1776—Declaration of Independence

1783—Great Britain officially recognized America as a sovereign nation.

1787—Constitutional Convention. Delaware, Pennsylvania, and Georgia become states.

1788—Connecticut, Massachusetts, Maryland, South Carolina, New Hampshire, Vermont, and New York become states.

1789—North Carolina

1790—Rhode Island

1791—The Bill of Rights. Vermont becomes a state.

1792—Kentucky

1796—Tennessee"

Natasha explained, "So, as one beast is going down, mortally wounded … *another* beast comes up. One goes down—the other comes up.

"Now look at the rest of the chapter. You see. It's the American beast that enforces the economic boycott amongst the inhabitants of the world. This chapter does not speak of one power. It speaks of two powers working together. It speaks of an alliance between two powers for the purpose of global control."

"*Shok-ma-ti!*" Alexei exclaimed. "Natasha, this is it. It is the missing piece. The lamb-like nation that will change into a nation that speaks like a dragon."

"Yes. But there is more."

"Now that we know who Francis' ally could be, we have some clues as to how he may proceed. Here is one possible scenario. I believe he is planning not one deadly event, but two. The first event will be to bring about its own power. The second event will be the most deadly event and will require his alliance with that second beast power. It will be the terrible and fearsome event that you spoke of.

"The newly elected Pope Francis Charles will remind the world that the Book of Revelation predicted that a third of the earth would be scorched and that a third of mankind would perish. He will quote scripture that states, 'As it was in the days of Noah, so it will be in the time of the end.'

"The horrible, crazy, and terrifying reality will unite the world under the dictatorship of Francis Charles. William Jaimeson would be his accomplice. We must find a way to save these two great powers from falling into the hands of these two men and this dark destiny."

The three men around her sat silently as they digested what Natasha just said. They looked at the flames. Natasha looked at Grant. She could tell that he was fighting his own mind as it thought about all of these things.

"We won't just be able to so easily land this balloon on the Vatican helipad," Natasha said. "We're going to have to call the Swiss Guard. We'll have to convince them."

"Yes. And we will need to make sure we are off of Francis' radar," Alexei answered.

They turned to look at Mr. Nuby. He had been sitting quietly, but suddenly he became a little bit twitchy.

"Grant, are you all right?" Natasha asked softly.

"I'm fighting the entity. He's trying to get into my head again."

"You mustn't let him in, Grant. Please fight him off."

"I know. I know," Grant answered.

Natasha remembered that earlier he had said that he had become weak from fighting off the entity.

"Alexei, you have survival food and water in here, right?"

"Not exactly water. It is a vitamin drink. Yes, I understand what you are saying."

Alexei opened up a box and handed out chocolate bars and plastic pouches of vitamin water. He gave Grant an extra granola bar.

"Please eat right away, Mr. Nuby. Do not allow your defenses to weaken. If Francis breaks into your mind, he will know our plans."

Grant sat silently, but Natasha knew that he could tell what they were thinking.

"Don't be afraid!" he said resolutely. "I will not fail. Francis Charles will be going to sleep himself soon. He'll become tired of his attempts at me."

"But what if he gets to you while you sleep?" Natasha asked.

"I can't allow myself to sleep. It's my burden. If you see me sleep, please wake me up—or kill me," Grant answered. "Throw me over like Jonah."

Natasha looked at his tired eyes and cried.

"You would give your life, wouldn't you?"

"I will do whatever it takes to help us save the world. It's my chance at redemption."

He shuddered with effort as he fought another wave of intrusive remote energy. It was as if he had a brief seizure and then he recovered.

~

Natasha awoke to the sense that someone was watching her. She looked up at Grant and smiled. This adventure was so radically different from the way they normally spent time together. She was used to seeing him as the celebrity that he was. Dressed like a million bucks and a powerful and charismatic presence. *He's never seen me like this either.* She shook her head.

"I know what you're thinking," Grant said.

"Well, I know what you're thinking, too," she whispered.

"What?"

"You're thinking that I can't tell you what you're thinking."

"Nice try, Natasha. But not quite."

"Then what?"

"Natasha, I need to go my own way. I'm not supposed to be here," he whispered.

Grant looked up into the dark sky. The moon was bright yellow. He rolled his eyes up again as he seemingly accessed information.

"It's not just me that's not supposed to be here. None of us are. That's why I feel uneasy."

"What?" Natasha questioned. "What's wrong?"

"We're not safe."

Natasha stood up and looked down. The ground below was dark. She knew they were over land, but that was it.

"Wake up, everyone! Grant senses danger and so do I."

Alexei and Euvgeny opened their eyes.

"Get up!" Natasha said. "Hurry."

"Alexei, do you know where we are?"

Alexei reached into his pocket and pulled out a handheld GPS monitor.

"We are currently sailing over the farmland of Romania."

Alexei looked over the side of the balloon to confirm.

"No lights, just farms."

Euvgeny looked over the side, too. He didn't say anything.

"Is there anyone here that feels safe right now?" Grant asked. "Because I'm sensing danger."

Alexei and Euvgeny looked at each other then at Grant. They stood quietly as they assessed how they felt.

Grant interrupted the silence.

"Alexei, what would be your plan of escape if you knew a Black Ops chopper was about to intercept us?"

"It would depend. How much time do we have?"

"Minutes," Grant answered.

"That would not be enough time to land. We are too high up," Alexei answered. "We have two choices. We can either try to ascend to where the air is too thin to support the helicopter or the four of us could tandem dive out of here using the two parachutes onboard."

"He is right, master," Euvgeny announced. "Radar indicates an aircraft closing in on our position rapidly."

"Natasha, do you wish to ascend higher or tandem dive?"

"We've seen what a helicopter can do. We will dive."

Alexei pulled out the parachute.

"Who is first?"

"Hurry!" Euvgeny shouted.

"Grant first," Natasha volunteered.

"Turn around."

Alexei secured the parachute onto Grant and then hooked Natasha in on Grant's front.

The sound of the helicopter manifested. He gave the radio to Natasha and the GPS to Grant.

"When you land, make your way south to the railroad, and then head west. I'll meet you in Rome."

He put the ripcord in Natasha's hand and swung open the gate. Natasha stepped over to the edge and looked down. Her nightmare flashed in front of her. She remembered screaming. *You're all going to die anyway. The chutes won't open. You're going to fall like little bombs.* She remembered as she had envisioned the people from the airplane falling to their deaths. *Their eyeballs shooting out of their sockets, their spines ejecting out of the tops of their skulls.* Natasha looked over the edge down at the blackness. The wind blew against her face. She was petrified. The sound of the chopper was getting louder.

Alexei performed the sign of the cross over them.

"Count to thirty, then pull the cord," Alexei yelled.

He put his foot on Grant's back and literally kicked them out. Natasha closed her eyes tight and locked every muscle in her body. The wind whipped furiously as they fell through the moonlit sky. The countdown seemed like an eternity and Natasha was terrified that they would impact the earth at the count of twenty-nine.

Natasha pulled the ripcord. The chute shot above them and opened. Natasha felt the jerk as air filled the chute and suddenly stopped their fall momentarily. Floating gracefully through the night sky, they heard the chopper above them. They looked up, but they could see nothing. Then a bright explosion filled the atmosphere. Natasha and Grant knew that possibly both of their friends had just perished. A moment later, they saw the earth coming at them quickly. Grant pulled down on his control cord to break the landing sideways as they neared earth.

They unclasped the chute harness and checked for their gear. Natasha still had the gun and the radio. Grant still had the GPS. He turned it on and they looked at the screen. They looked around. They were in the middle of a field. They immediately set out at a brisk pace headed due south.

~

The GPS device guided them to a small Romanian farming village. They didn't even know the name of the village, just that it had a train station. They arrived at the station exhausted, hungry, and freezing. Natasha immediately went to the large wall radiator heater. There was no food, but at least she could get warm. Grant approached the cashier to buy tickets. A few moments later, he returned.

"We have a problem," he said.

"Let me guess," Natasha answered. "They don't accept American Express."

"Or Visa or MasterCard, or debit, or out-of-state checks."

"So what do we do?

"The cashier pointed me north and said the word *bank*.

"We have to hurry because the train we need leaves in forty-five minutes."

Natasha looked up at Grant. "No problem. The bank can't be far. Let's go."

They went outside and looked up the street to see if the bank was immediately visible. It wasn't.

Grant stuck his hand out at passing cars. A car pulled over to the curb and rolled down the window and the driver asked Grant a question.

"Do you speak English?" Grant asked.

"Where?" the man asked.

"Bank," Grant answered.

"How much?"

"Ten dollars," Grant answered.

The man agreed and urged them into the car.

"My name Favro," he said.

Grant opened the back door and Natasha entered. Grant followed her in.

"Nice to meet you," Natasha said. "We need to go fast. Can you take us to the bank and then back to the train station?"

"No problem!" Favro exclaimed.

Just as they had hoped, an ATM machine was near the bank entrance. Grant put in the card and withdrew $500 in local currency from the machine.

Favro raced them back to the train station. They ran to the cashier and bought their tickets. Then they had to run out to the train's loading platform. They heard an announcement on the loudspeaker and were sure it was the last call.

They ran on a concrete pathway with trains parked on both sides. The smell of burning coal was in the air. The trains were green. They ran up along their train and finally reached the entrance cabin. A worker was there to check for their ticket. Natasha showed him her ticket and climbed the metal stairs leading into the train. She led the way for her and Grant. They had purchased a cabin for themselves that would actually accommodate up to four individuals.

They entered the train cabin as the train began to slowly disembark the station. They looked out the window and watched the train station and the train on the rail across from them slide out of view. A small table folded out from the wall just below the window. On either side of the table lay the narrow bunk beds.

There was a knock on the door.

"Who's there?" Grant asked.

From the other side of the door, they could hear an old Romanian woman, but the only word Natasha understood was the word "*te*." She jumped up.

"Tea, they offer tea," she told Grant and opened the door.

The hunchbacked woman held out an empty glass.

"*te?*"

"Si," Natasha answered before breaking off in Italian.

A few minutes later, she returned with a full teapot, sugar cubes, teaspoons, napkins, as well as an uncut loaf of French bread, a stick of kielbasa, and a sharp knife.

Soon the scene outside the window changed to small snow-covered village cottages, one after another. Grant and Natasha sat across from each other as they drank the tea and ate the bread and kielbasa. The simple food was extremely rewarding after their many miles of walking the Romanian countryside in the pre-dawn hours. They had been nearly frozen by the time they made it to the train station. Natasha put her feet up on the bunk and leaned back against the wall next to the window. The rhythm of the tracks underneath was calming. Grant lay on his back with his left arm extended underneath his head for a pillow. His eyes stared up at the bunk above him. Natasha closed her eyes. She could hear the voice of Francis Charles echo in her mind. "Go in peace child, go in peace."

She had only dozed off a few minutes when she heard a noise at the door. The doorknob was slowly being turned. Natasha shot forward alarmed. Who was breaking into their room? Natasha looked around, reached down into her jacket, and pulled out her pistol. She silently climbed up to the top bunk so that she would have high ground against the intruder. Grant had accidentally fallen asleep, but Natasha couldn't control that. She held her gun pointed from over the door and switched off the safety with the side of her thumb. The door slowly opened from the opposite of Natasha's position and a figure emerged into their room. Natasha recognized the gray hair and musty aroma right away. She let out a sigh of relief when she recognized Alexei.

"You could have knocked," she whispered harshly. "I was about to kill you."

Alexei smiled, seemingly amused.

"Mr. Nuby, you better say something before she kills me.

Grant was sitting up on the bunk underneath Natasha. He looked up sideways to see Natasha.

"What are you doing up there?" he asked.

"I was about to save us from an intruder, only it turned out to be Alexei. Here," she said and held the pistol out to him. "It's yours anyway."

"That is okay, Natasha. I am glad to see you will not let it go to waste. That is why I gave it to you in the first place. May I sit down?"

The scholar, the seer, and the priest talked and planned out their next moves.

⌒

Natasha couldn't shake the idea that if Francis Charles used pigeon mail, his messages certainly would have to be encoded with a cipher because of the high probability of one of the pigeons mis-delivering at one time or another. He wouldn't be able to write out anything as plain as *Dear Mr. Terrorist, This is Vatican Secretary of State Francis Charles. Please move forward with deadly event.*

No. If he were to use pigeon mail, for certain it would have to be written in a code.

Natasha disconnected from the conversation with Alexei and Grant. They were debating American history and playing their hands of obscure French-American Revolutionary War trivia, but Natasha felt compelled to continue on about pigeon mail code. She pulled her phone out of her jacket pocket, curled up on the opposite end of bunk above Alexei, and began to make notes.

First she thought that the interchangeability of the letters U and V may somehow be relevant. It was the key to properly decoding the "*Vicarius filii dei.*" She was also able to envision an interesting pattern.

Up until Benjamin Franklin's alphabet reform, the letters U and V were simply the upper and lowercase of the same letter and the ampersand symbol (&) was the English alphabet's twenty-seventh character.

Therefore, if U and V are interchangeable, then logically they would both have the Roman numeral value of five.

Then there is the letter VV. Literally two V's next to each other. Its numeric equivalent would be a "double five."

So if one writes the letters down in their alphabetical order—she typed the letters in on her handheld device.

S T U̲ V̲ V̲V̲ X Y Z &
5 5 5 5

Hmm, that's interesting. All fives, all right in a row. What happens if we build off of that pattern? The numeric pattern fits the alphabet perfectly.

She built on the pattern as she continued to make her notes.

A B C D   E F G H   I J K L   M N O P   Q R S T   U V W   X Y Z &
0 0 0 0   1 1 1 1   2 2 2 2   3 3 3 3   4 4 4 4   5 5 5 5   6 6 6 6

Natasha looked up and then continued her notes. *Isn't it also interesting that in this particular cipher, the last three letters are assigned the numeric value of 666. Is it just a coincidence?*

The cipher seemed more than her own invention. She felt like it was real. She decided to test it out a little.

How would "bomb" be written in the cipher?

B=0, O=3, M=3, B=0

So the word bomb would be written: 0330. So in order to decode it, one would have to first write a magic square of sorts and then connect the letters as in a word-search puzzle.

Natasha wrote it out.

0	3	3	0
A	M	M	A
B	N	N	B
C	O	O	C
D	P	P	D

Natasha raised her eyebrows. This box reminded her of the PATERNOSTER box. The exercise seemed similar to the one she had used when she deciphered the magic square to figure out that it hid the double Paternoster in it. Her heart pounded with excitement. *Eureka!* She looked down at her notes once again.

0	3	3	0
A	M	M	A
B	N	N	B
C	O	O	C
D	P	P	D

Reading from left to right, was "bomb" the only word? She scanned for other possibilities. *AMMA, ANOD, BOPA, COOC, CONA, COMA, BONA, BOND. Actually, the words "COMA" and "BOND" could also be spelled out. Part of the genius of the code actually. Almost impossible for a computer to break. It would take a human being to figure out the correct meaning by using context.*

"The XYZ Affair," she overheard Grant answer back to Alexei.

Natasha looked down at them.

"What did you say?"

Grant looked at Alexei and then back to Natasha.

"The XYZ affair," I said.

"Yes, what about it?"

"It's what was happening between the Americans and the French in 1798. Alexei asked me if I knew what was going on in American history at the time that France was overthrowing the Vatican. Of course it was the XYZ Affair," Grant answered.

"Natasha," Alexei said. "You have made some connection. What about it?"

"What if the XYZ Affair didn't just coincidentally occur during this timeframe? What if it was somehow linked to the overthrow of the Vatican? Look at this," she answered.

She climbed down and turned her handheld device to them.

"I extrapolated a pattern based on the significance of the interchangeability of U and V and its correlation to the Roman numeral V. I discovered a pattern that fit our American alphabet exactly. And when you build the pattern out and apply it to the whole alphabet, the last three letters—X, Y, and Z—have the number six assigned to them. Therefore, the phrase XYZ Affair, according to this cipher, could be translated the 666 Affair."

"XYZ is code for 666," Alexei said. "Not an insignificant thing when you consider many at the time saw the overthrow of the Vatican as a partial fulfillment of the Beast/666 prophecy of Revelation Chapter 13. I failed to mention it before, but there was actually dancing in the streets of Paris at the news of Pope Pius' arrest. The crowds came out in the bitter February cold and burned—" Alexei searched for the right word. "I forget how you say. They burned representations of the man—in celebration of his capture."

"Very interesting," Grant said. "Have either of you ever heard of the Society of Cincinnati?"

Natasha and Alexei shook their heads no.

"Most people haven't. It's one of the most powerful and secret of all societies—the most exclusive, too. Membership can only be passed down from father to firstborn son. That's it. You can't buy your way in or earn your way in. It's only from father to firstborn son. George Washington was the first president of the society. Benjamin Franklin was a member—as were many more of the most powerful and influential Americans, including several other American presidents."

"But what's the connection to the XYZ Affair?" Natasha asked.

"I was just about to get to that," Grant answered. "Also among the members were all three diplomats who were the principals in the so-called XYZ Affair."

Grant squinted his eyes as he accessed old files of information in his mind.

"Charles Cotesworth Pinckney, John Marshall, and Elbridge Gerry—all three were members of the society."

~

The train began to slow and a whistle blew as it chugged into a simple station platform. Outside, Natasha could see there were a few people selling small things. One elderly lady sat at a vegetable stand. A man with a brown hat and a beard tended meat behind a small barbecue.

A few people unloaded and a few people climbed aboard. A plume of smoke puffed out of the train and it jerked forward as it started down the tracks.

Grant continued, "It seems like I remember reading a speech in which John Adams warned of how the society might be dangerous for the young Republic, as it could be too influential as to be able to sway presidential elections whichever way it seemed fit. The fear was that such an influential society could undermine the Republic."

"Do you know why it was named the Society of the Cincinnati?" Grant asked.

They didn't answer. As a former teacher of history, Grant was clearly in his realm of expertise and happy to show off his knowledge of such obscure trivia.

"During a time of great distress, the Roman senate sought to appoint a man who would lead Rome through the crisis, but relinquish power afterward. They found such a man—Lucius Quinctius Cincinnatus. He was appointed Magister Populi by the Roman senate and assumed lawful dictatorial control of Rome.

"Cincinnatus took power, led Rome through the crisis, and then relinquished his power to return to his farm and family. His willingness to relinquish power was thought to be ideal and the sentiment was echoed in the presidency of George Washington."

"The reluctant ruler—so to speak," Alexei added.

"Yes," Grant continued. "The society named itself after this noble idea of willingness to relinquish power for the good of the people. However, when you think about it, there is actually another side to the story. There is the man who relinquished power, Cincinnatus, but there is also the elite group who bestowed the power upon him in the first place.

"A society of kingmakers. They can bring a man to power—and they can take him out of power," Alexie interjected.

Grant nodded his head.

"Kingmakers—the puppet masters. Revelation speaks of the rise to power of a one-world dictator, so the idea does not seem to be unrelated.

And if the Society of the Cincinnati had some connection with the overthrow of the Vatican in 1798, that also would not surprise me.

~

At Rome's Central Station, Alexei hung up the telephone. He stood inside a small red telephone booth and looked out the door to Natasha and Grant.

"The commander of the Swiss Guard is a man named Karl Wiley. I am going to call him right now."

"Alexei, be very careful what you say," Grant warned. "Don't let them know where we are until you're certain he'll be on our side."

Alexei nodded his agreement.

"Yes, if Francis learns of it, he is powerful enough to do whatever it takes to eliminate a threat against him. For his own good—and ours—he mustn't know who we are quite yet."

"Grant is right, Alexei," Natasha added. "I have an idea. Alexei, you make the call. Tell the switchboard operator that you have an emergency message for Commander Wiley. When he connects you, ask him if he would like to know the meaning of the pigeon mail. That should get his attention."

While they planned the call, Alexei took a series of deep breaths.

"No! Wait!" Natasha exclaimed.

Alexei was startled and put down the receiver. Natasha always trusted her instincts.

"We lose too much control over the telephone. It's better for us to make this an e-mail conversation."

"You are right," Alexei agreed. "We will be able to craft our words more carefully, react better to his responses, and be more in control."

"But how can we make sure to e-mail him without one of his underlings screening it first?"

"Yes. We need a way to get in front of his eyes only," Grant agreed.

"That gives me an idea," Natasha said as she remembered what a friend in the State Department had taught her. "We need a safe place to connect to the Internet."

"No, we don't. We can just use your phone," Grant suggested.

"Right, but we need to go someplace where we can be comfortable— and possibly wait a number of hours to make this work. After all, there's no guarantee of when he will be in front of his computer."

Natasha looked down at her phone and her face lit up. She had an idea that enhanced their plan.

"Let's just get somewhere safe and comfortable."

Natasha looked at Grant and Alexei to see if they had any suggestions.

"I think we need to stay off the grid for now," Natasha said.

"I have an old girlfriend here in Rome," Alexei answered. "I will tell her we need a place off the grid. She can rent it for us."

"No," Grant said. "I think it's dangerous to contact anyone we know in Rome."

"He's right," Natasha chimed in. "Francis is powerful enough to get Tom framed, send helicopters after us, and have a mercenary army to attack your monastery. Plus, he's got this remote viewing power. Staying off the grid means staying away from anyone else we know."

"Wait here."

Alexei left them and walked up to the ticket counter. He had a conversation with the lady behind the counter and then returned.

"The train to Rimini has excellent cell phone coverage. It leaves in thirty minutes. We can get a cabin."

Natasha remembered her journey from Rome to Rimini, but was able to shake off the memory.

"That's a good idea," Natasha agreed.

Once aboard the new train, Natasha sat down and went to work on her computer phone right away. Grant and Alexei peered over her shoulders. She explained what she was doing.

"I'm setting the advance search filter in the search engine to allow e-mails."

She clicked the drop down menu, and then typed "Karl Wiley" in the search box. Thousands of possibilities showed up. She went back to the advance search criteria and added the words "Vatican" and "Swiss Guard."

The narrowing of the search worked. She began to open the e-mails, right clicking on them, scrolling to the properties, and scanning for the IP address.

"This is his home computer, this is his office computer. And *this* one is the IP address for his Eurofone account. We can interface directly with his cell phone."

"Fantastic!" Grant praised her.

"Impressive," Alexei agreed.

"We are now looking at the screen of his cell phone," Natasha announced.

She double-clicked on the instant messaging software. She typed: *Pigeon mail messages are work of powerful Vatican imposter. Assassination attempt imminent. Tell no one. Have you broken the code? Please respond.*

Natasha sent the message.

"That is good," Alexei said, looking over her shoulder.

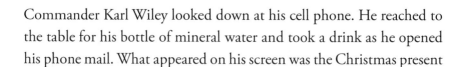

Commander Karl Wiley looked down at his cell phone. He reached to the table for his bottle of mineral water and took a drink as he opened his phone mail. What appeared on his screen was the Christmas present that he had hoped for. Finally a clue to the cryptic note that had been found on stray Vatican pigeons.

He reached back toward the table to put his water back, but he was so distracted by the message that he missed the table and dropped the bottle on his lap. With a startled jerk, he caught the bottle and put it back firmly on the table. He looked down at his cell phone again and began to type.

Natasha waited and stared at the screen as if she were willing her message to get to the commander. Her phone made an electronic boink sound.

The commander's response came back. *Who is this?*

Natasha responded: "*I only want to help and to also stay safe. You can call me Bird Dog for now.*"

"*Bird Dog: Can you decode the messages?*"

"*Affirmative. I have broken the code.*"

A minute later, a new e-mail appeared. It was a string of digits ranging from zero to six.

532410 3042334 2035046 12444.

Natasha smiled as she began to decode. First she created the magic square for each set of numbers.

A B C D	E F G H	I J K L	M N O P	Q R S T	U V W	X Y Z &
0 0 0 0	1 1 1 1	2 2 2 2	3 3 3 3	4 4 4 4	5 5 5 5	6 6 6 6

5 3 2 4 1 0	3 0 4 2 3 3 4	2 0 3 5 0 4 6	1 2 4 4 4
U M I Q E A	M A Q I M M Q	I A M U A Q X	E I Q Q Q
V N J R F B	N B R J N N R	J B N V B R Y	F J R R R
W O K S G C	O C S K O O S	K C O W C S Z	G K S S S
P L T H D	P D T L P P T	L D P D T &	H L T T T

Natasha looked down at the boxes. She gained speed as she went. She read her conclusion aloud to Grant and Alexei. UNITED NATIONS JANUARY FIRST. They looked at the decoded sentence very seriously and the knowledge sunk in just a bit deeper that this situation was more real than it had ever been.

Natasha started to type her response in, but Alexei put his hand on her shoulder.

"No," he whispered. "If you tell him the exact translation, they will crack the code without our help. We need to give him as little information as possible."

Natasha looked back at Grant and Alexei.

She typed, "This message details a *where* and a *when*."

Wiley answered, "How do you wish to proceed?"

"He's playing it safe," Alexei remarked. "He knows he needs us and wants to make sure we come along nicely."

"So how would you like to proceed?"

Alexei sighed and scratched his chin.

"This is as far as I can go with you here in Rome, Natasha. I cannot enter Vatican City. You two must to be my eyes and ears."

Natasha typed, "At 2100 hours, send a driver to Central Station, he can hold a sign for "Bird Dog." The vehicle needs to be tinted so no one will be able to see us. There are two of us. A diplomat and a counselor. The driver should take us directly to your office, but we need to avoid all other people. Just you and your office for now."

"Agreed," Wiley replied.

~

When they arrived at Wiley's office, he motioned them to sit down in front of his desk. Wiley appeared as she imagined. He was a tall, blond Swiss with a hooked nose and a direct stare. Wiley sat behind his desk and took a long, hard look at them. Finally he spoke.

"So who is this imposter?"

"Before we tell you, you must promise not to immediately say or do anything about it. Surveillance of this man will be the only way to catch his co-conspirators and to get the proof you will need."

"All right then. Who is it?"

"The individual is a man I have known for many years. It is Francis Charles."

Commander Wiley's reaction seemed odd to Natasha. He didn't seem very surprised.

"That seems rather impossible. What evidence do you have of such an allegation?"

"You are the one who has the evidence actually. Let me see the message," Natasha demanded.

Wiley pulled an enlarged photocopy out of the file and handed it to Natasha. She studied it for a moment before pronouncing.

"Commander Wiley, as a professional handwriting expert and as someone who is familiar with the hand of Francis Charles, I can tell you for certain that this is his handwriting."

"Unless I know exactly what this message states, who cares if he wrote it?" Wiley answered. "You said it details where and when. Now it is your turn to trust me. Give me the cipher so that I may verify the details."

Natasha wrote it out for him and then showed him how she decoded the numbers.

Wiley snatched the paper and held it up in the light as if he were a cashier checking for a watermark. He was thinking it over.

"This is quite serious. Very few people on the planet have any idea that he had planned an appearance at the United Nations this week. Francis Charles would be one of them."

Wiley put his hands together under his chin with the tips of his fingers tapping underneath his jawbone.

"Just the leaking of this information is a most serious crime."

Wiley picked up the phone.

"Your analysis had better be correct. Send Brandioni to my office right away."

Wiley looked at them again.

"Mr. Brandioni is our handwriting expert."

"Can he be trusted?" Natasha asked.

"Most definitely."

"No. Wait!" Grant urged. "We can't take that chance. It must be an independent analysis."

Wiley picked up the phone again.

"Cancel Brandioni."

He looked at Natasha and Grant somewhat impatiently.

"What do you suggest?"

"In order for an independent handwriting expert to match the handwriting on this message to the handwriting of Francis Charles, they will need an extensive handwriting sample," Natasha advised.

Wiley rubbed his eyes.

"But *you* did not need an extensive sample," Wiley challenged.

"I have an extensive handwriting sample. I've received handwritten cards and letters from this man for two decades. His handwriting is very distinctive. It's what inspired me to study handwriting in the first place."

"This is a problem," Wiley responded. "All of his work for the Vatican is of course in print."

"Yes. The most likely place to find an adequate sample would be his personal home office," Natasha added.

Wiley bowed his head again and then looked back up at Natasha.

"The problem is twofold. If we detain him and search his home and we don't find incriminating evidence, there will be nothing more I will be able to do except for perhaps tender my resignation. Francis would be able to simply call off his plans and cover up his trail. Of course, we would miss out on the opportunity to find his co-conspirators. Hmm."

There was silence for a moment.

"On the other hand, if we could get firm confirmation that the evidence we will need is in fact within his home, we could proceed more confidently."

Wiley looked down at his desk and placed his hands together in front of his face. He shook his head as if acknowledging that he could not readily identify a solution.

"What if I could get you the evidence?" Natasha suggested. "If I were able to find it, I could photograph it, and that would be proof enough at least to proceed more seriously."

Wiley picked up the phone.

"Have Mr. Andreason call me on line one immediately."

"Who's Andreason?" Natasha asked.

"Mr. Andreason is in charge of security for Francis."

"But wait. What if your question tips him off and he warns Francis?"

"Don't worry. Mr. Andreason is trustworthy."

The phone rang and Wiley answered.

"Commander. It is Andreason, sir."

"Andreason, I need you to answer a question for me."

"Yes, sir. Please."

"Mr. Andreason. The subject of my question is of the utmost importance. You must not speak to anyone of it. Do you understand?"

"Yes, sir."

"Good, Mr. Andreason. Please tell me. Does the Cardinal Secretary of State keep any pets?"

"No sir. No pets."

"Are you certain? No cats or hamsters or birds or fish?"

"Well... now ...."

"Mr. Andreason!" Wiley urged.

"Yes, sir. Sorry, sir. Yes. His personal assistant Nicholas keeps pet doves. We have seen him perform illusions with them from time to time. He is an amateur magician of sorts."

"I see. But no other pets then?"

"No, sir."

"Thank you, Mr. Andreason. That is all. Speak to no one of this question."

"Yes, sir."

"That is all, Mr. Andreason."

Wiley hung up the phone and looked at Natasha.

"How did you take over my cell phone?"

Natasha didn't answer. She simply smiled.

Wiley continued, "According to Mr. Andreason, Nicholas keeps pet doves in the flat."

Wiley looked down at his desk again and shook his head with disapproval.

"Miss Azshatan, there is no evidence here. Certainly not enough to obtain a search warrant. Without a legal search of his home for evidence, anything we would find would be useless. I'm afraid all we can do is to cancel the Holy Father's visit and restrict the cardinal's access to the itinerary. Of course, we can also watch him closely."

Natasha shook her head.

"No," she said. "He'll know we're onto him."

"Perhaps you underestimate us?" Wiley responded.

"Perhaps you underestimate Francis Charles?"

Natasha had an idea.

"You say that Nicholas is an amateur illusionist who performs with pet doves?"

"Yes," Wiley affirmed. "It is what Mr. Andreason says."

"Have his doves been tested for Asian bird flu? After all, bird flu could possibly not only endanger the secretary of state, but also the Holy Father, since they work so closely together."

"I like the way you think, Dr. Azshatan. Of course, we have a legitimate reason to inspect and test these birds. We would be derelict in our duties unless we ensure those birds do not carry disease."

Wiley picked up the phone again.

"Mr. Andreason, ask the young man to surrender his birds. You may tell him that we simply need to ensure that the birds are not carrying any diseases. That is all he needs to know. Bring the birds to my office as soon as you have them."

"Yes, sir," Andreason answered. "Do you suspect disease, sir?"

"Just a precaution, Mr. Andreason. Get this done quickly."

He hung up the phone. Wiley stood up and looked out his window toward the apartment of Francis Charles. He spoke with his back turned to Natasha.

"When the birds arrive at the office, we will tag them with RF transmitters. It will look as if we are injecting a vaccination into the birds. Then we will release them."

"But what about Nicholas? He'll be expecting his birds to be returned to him," Natasha said.

"We'll have to tell him that the birds are being observed for an undetermined period of time and that they will be returned to him at such a time as we feel they pose no health threat."

"All of which is technically true," Natasha affirmed with a wide smile. "I like the way you think too, Commander."

~

After the doves were injected with the RF transmitters, they were released from the commander's office window. Wiley sat down at his desk and navigated to a Web site. He looked up at Natasha and Grant and signaled them to come around to his side of the desk. He pointed to the screen.

"This site is how we can track the birds. Wherever they go, we will see it in real time."

Natasha looked at the map on the screen and saw the red dots slowly moving out of the city.

"Looks like they're headed west," she said. "What will you do when they are out of your jurisdiction?"

"The only thing we *can* do. We will track them and arrange cooperation with local authorities. Believe me. We can count on the utmost cooperation."

Natasha looked at the screen and then at her wrist, once again forgetting that she had no watch.

"New Years is just three days from now. What if the birds have to fly a far distance?" Natasha asked.

"Then we will have to wait for them, but we don't have to wait here any longer. We can track these birds from our cell phones."

Wiley rapidly typed on his keyboard.

"I'm sending your phone the link to this page."

"No, thanks," Natasha said. "We're perfectly happy waiting here in your office."

She gestured with her hands at the multiple pieces of furniture.

"If we get tired, we can take naps. You have coffee and we have kielbasa and bread. So, I'm quite ready for the long night of watching these birds."

"Let us just pray that they will lead us to the terrorist."

~

William Jaimeson picked up the phone to call Douglas Blair. His wife Jessica answered. They exchanged greetings.

"He said he was headed out to the island to meet with you. He's not there with you?" she asked.

"Perhaps I'm mistaken, but I don't recall any such plans. When did he say we were supposed to meet?"

"This morning he told me 2:00 p.m."

William shot a glance to the clock on his wall; it was 3:40.

"Well, I'm sure there's an explanation. Please have him give me a call when you have a chance."

"I'll do that."

"Thank you, Jessica. Good night."

He hung up the phone and dialed the Blair residence, just a few blocks away. No answer. He got up from his brown leather chair and walked to the living room where Meredith was curled up on the couch reading one of her favorite books. A fire was burning in the fireplace and holiday music played in the background. He approached her, bent down, and kissed her on her lips.

"Meredith, dear. I'm taking a walk over to Doug's place. I shouldn't be gone too long."

Meredith rolled her head forward to touch her forehead to his. They looked at each other's eyes up close; they were seemingly crossed and cockeyed. They both smiled at each other.

"You better not take too long, William. Or I'll be very disappointed," she said and smiled.

He kissed her again, and walked out of the room, He threw on his coat, laced up his boots, and walked out the front door on his way to Douglas Blair's home.

Doug's Cadillac was parked in the driveway and the neighbor's fluffy orange cat sat atop the hood. The cat jumped off the hood and walked with William up to the front steps of the home. William rang the bell.

He looked behind him; he was still getting used to his Secret Service detail that followed him everywhere he went. Agent Franks and Agent Mathews seemed like good men. They kept their proper distance, too. Almost distant enough to forget they were always around every corner.

William rang the doorbell again, but there was still no answer. The cat looked up at him and let out a meow. Will moved along the porch and looked into the window. A fire burned vigorously in Douglas' enormously oversized fireplace. It was a massive fireplace made of large stone blocks. To load it with logs, one would have to step down into it. The fireplace's opening was about five-feet wide, and four-feet high. It burned long logs that were split length-wise into pie-shaped four-foot wedges.

William spied to see anything else, but there was nothing. He turned around.

"Mr. Franks, let's just walk around the home and see what we can see, shall we? Douglas is supposed to be here, but he's not answering the doorbell or the telephone. His car is parked out front, and the engine is still warm."

"Sir, would you like us to place a man here at the Douglas residence?"

"Yes. That's a good idea," William answered.

Agent Franks spoke into the small microphone in his hand.

"All right, sir. Let's go ahead and see if he's around back."

The ground was still covered with snow, but William didn't see any tracks. In the back of the home, a set of tracks went from the back porch to the woodshed. There was no sign of Douglas. The holiday lights suddenly lit up all around the house, making them feel as though Douglas had turned them on from the inside, as a neighbor would turn on the front porch light to greet a visitor at the door. William looked at the darkening sky and then at his watch, which read 4:15 p.m. The timer had turned on the lights.

He turned to the secret service agent.

"One of you stays here. Let's the rest of us go back home for now. Let me know when you make contact with Mr. Blair."

William began the short walk back to his own home. He played with the large gold ring on his right ring finger. It had grown loose on him recently and he had gotten into the habit of sliding it back and forth between his knuckles. The ring had been passed down to him from his father. An American Bald Eagle was artfully embossed on it and around the eagle, the Latin phrase *Societus Cincinnatus*.

~

Commander Wiley's radio sounded an alert.

"CSOS1 is on the move. CSOS1 is en route to base camp. Over. CSOS1 in route to base camp. Over."

Wiley picked up his radio.

"10–4. Over."

He stood up and cleaned the clutter from his desk.

"What's going on?" Natasha asked. "What's going on?"

"The Cardinal S.O.S. is on his way," Wiley replied.

Natasha looked nervous and surprised.

"Do you think…?"

"Don't worry," Wiley answered. "If he was using these birds to send these treasonous messages, then he will be quite disturbed that we have taken them from his home."

Francis Charles reached the door to Wiley's office. The Swiss Guard stood at the entrance. He looked at the guard as if to dare him.

"Try to stop me from opening this door. Who do you think you are?"

The guard stepped back; Francis flung open the door and barged into Wiley's office. He immediately saw Natasha and sneered.

"You! I should have known, Commander Wiley."

He snapped his attention to Wiley.

"This woman is utterly insane."

He turned back to Natasha and pointed his finger in her face.

"I've had enough of your games. Karl, I demand to know what is going on right this instant. What are your men doing taking my doves and what is this spy doing in your office?"

"*Your* doves?"

Karl put his hand out sideways to shield Natasha. With his other hand, he reached under the edge of the corner of his desk and pressed the lockdown button.

"I understood the doves belong to Nicholas," Wiley challenged.

Francis stood silent and looked at Wiley with a piercing glare.

"It's convenient you have come here, Cardinal Charles. Please have a seat. There is a matter that we need to clear up. Cardinal Charles, two months ago, a dove—in fact very similar to the ones we took from your home this evening—flew into the Holy Father's window. It apparently made a very loud noise. Upon coming to investigate the noise, the Holy Father discovered the bird to be dead.

"The Holy Father cupped the delicate dove in his hands and bowed his head in prayer. The Holy Father's staff and guests circled around to watch. He lifted his head from prayer, slowly opened his hands, and the bird was revealed to be miraculously alive. Everyone was stunned. Witnesses reported they could feel the energy radiating. The guard who told me his account gets chill bumps every time he tells the story."

Francis interrupted, "Yes. The Holy Father told me the story himself."

"Not all of it, I'm sure," said Wiley.

Wiley opened his desk drawer.

"The observant guard noticed a pill-sized capsule attached to the leg of the dove and called attention to it. We removed the capsule, and inside we found a coded message."

Wiley looked around the room.

"We ran the message through cryptology, and we even asked the FBI for help with it. No one could break the code. But tonight, Natasha Azshatan caught my attention when she deciphered the encrypted message."

He pulled the sheet of paper out and slapped it on the desk forcefully.

"She unlocked the code. You see."

He pointed to the letterboxes Natasha had written out on another piece of paper.

"The decoded message reads: 'United Nations January First.' You see."

Wiley looked at Francis eyes to see his reaction. Francis squirmed in his chair.

"Commander, I've suddenly become very bored of your story. We'll talk more about this tomorrow."

Francis walked to the door, but Wiley signaled his guard to block the exit.

"I wasn't finished yet, Cardinal Charles. You haven't heard the best part of the story."

Francis Charles turned around. Natasha was staring at him with satisfaction as Wiley delivered his next line.

"We know that it was you who wrote the secret message."

"That's preposterous! I suppose that it escaped you that the birds belong to my manservant Nicholas, who also has access to my handwriting. He's obviously the one who you need to speak to regarding this issue.

"Very sloppy, Mr. Wiley. Let me guess. Natasha the psychic investigating paleographer is your handwriting expert. She won't testify in trials anymore because as soon as the jury finds out she thinks she can talk to dead people, she loses all of her creditability. She's famous—or *infamous*, I should say. Her irresponsible testimony led to the acquittal of one of America's worst serial killers, Gilbert Carver. You two are the ones who will need attorneys."

Francis turned around to go. He waved at the guard dismissively to move aside.

"Have Nicholas arrested immediately. If you had any brain at all, you would know this is his doing."

Once again, Wiley shook his head at the guard.

"Don't open that door," he commanded.

Francis turned around again, but Wiley stood confidently.

"We obviously knew the dove had been trained as a mail pigeon—and we were interested to see where it would lead us if we let it free. So we injected it with an RF ID and tracked its flight. Do you know where it ended up?"

No answer from Francis.

Wiley continued, "This dove ended up in London and stayed put on the most interesting street. Do you know what street the dove lives at even to this day? No? The dove lives on the London Street of Paternoster. One of the oldest streets in London. Isn't that interesting?

"We released the other four doves that were taken from your home and guess what? They're headed on a course to England. The English authorities will raid whatever apartment the birds land at. Of course, when all four end up at the same location, it will eliminate coincidence. And what will they find in this Paternoster apartment? We believe it will be your coconspirator. We'll probably find pigeons there, too, that will probably, when released, fly to your apartment. And we'll probably find evidence of a terrorist plot to strike the United Nations building on January 1."

Wiley continued, "Until the birds arrive to Paternoster, I feel very comfortable placing you under arrest on charges of conspiracy to terrorism and conspiracy to murder. And I feel very confident in Dr. Azshatan's abilities. I feel very confident letting her into your apartment with my men and a search warrant. She will be able to find a handwriting sample that will do the job."

Natasha stepped forward and looked into his eyes.

"Checkmate!"

The Swiss Guard chained the hands of Francis Charles.

Wiley shouted, "Take him to prison!"

The Swiss Guard led Francis Charles out in handcuffs.

"You're making a mistake. It's Nicholas. Not me. I'm the secretary of state of Vatican City. Of course your accusations are misplaced—"

Wiley turned to Natasha.

"We better get you over to his apartment right away."

He picked up his radio.

"Bring Nicholas to my office right away. We must investigate if he has any role in this."

~

Captain Andreason escorted Natasha back to the palace apartment of Francis Charles. As they walked down the hall to his private library and study, Andreason waved the search warrant up near Natasha.

"We have a search warrant," he reminded. "So take all the time you need to find what you're looking for. My men, of course, will also be looking."

"Thank you, Captain. It may not be easy to find an adequate writing sample. I guess I'm hoping to find a handwritten journal or perhaps speeches he may have handwritten before typing. Or perhaps articles or essays he may have handwritten."

A large painting depicted a gentleman writing at a desk hung on the wall near his library entrance. The man held a feather pen in his left hand and looked about to dip it into its ink jar. The parchment was nearly filled with unreadable script. The man's face seemed familiar to Natasha. His cheeks were full and his forehead was prominent. He wore small round spectacles and was dressed in the fashion of late eighteenth century France. Suddenly, Natasha realized that the man in the painting reminded her of Francis Charles himself.

"Captain Andreason, who is the man in the painting?" she asked as they entered the library.

"I believe that is a painting of Giovanni Angelo Braschi," he answered thoughtfully.

"That name sounds familiar."

"He's better known as Pope Pius the VI. The painting depicts him practicing law before his ascendance to papal power."

"You mean he didn't make his way up through the priesthood?"

"No. He practiced law up until just three years before he was elected pope."

Natasha registered the information, noting to herself that it was Pius VI who had been dethroned by Napoleon's army in 1798.

"All right."

She opened the drawers in his desk and ruffled through his papers.

"Keep your eyes out for anything that looks like it might be his handwriting —and of course anything that looks like those pigeon messages."

Captain Andreason looked at Natasha from around a bookcase corner.

"Perhaps we will find what you are looking for where this stairway leads."

Natasha walked over to Andreason. It was a secret staircase hidden behind a false wall panel. It was steep and narrow and there was no light. Andreason pulled out a Zippo lighter and lit the staircase with the lighter's single flame.

"There's a combo lock on the door."

"Let me see," Natasha said.

She maneuvered past Andreason and looked at the lock. It was similar to a briefcase lock. It had four wheels that each rotated to display numbers zero through nine. Natasha looked at it for a minute. *He thought no one else would ever figure out the key to his code. Wasn't he just wrong?*

She pictured the cipher she had figured. Underneath the UVW were the four fives. Natasha rolled each wheel to display a number five and pushed the door lever. She felt the spring action of the mechanism opening. The door swung open. Inside was the secret lair of one of the world's wealthiest and most powerful immortals. The man currently known as Cardinal Secretary Of State, Francis Charles.

The circular room displayed treasured rare artifacts. Natasha noticed an ancient papal tiara among them.

In the center of the room, Natasha noticed the island, which showcased the special playing board with hand-carved pieces. None of the pieces were carved precisely enough for Natasha to recognize any one person. She did not even recognize herself as the empress, but that didn't matter to Francis—he knew who the pieces represented.

"Take a look at this game board," she said.

She caressed her fingers across the longitudinal lines and handled one of the wooden pieces that was definitely a Swiss Guard.

"It's not quite chess, but it looks similar."

Andreason walked over and picked up one of the pieces. It was a modern man in a suit and long dress coat. The man had his right hand raised in the position of taking an oath.

"I think he carves these pieces himself," Andreason stated.

Natasha walked along the display shelf that ringed the room. It was also a display countertop. She came across a leather document case.

"This is interesting," she said.

She unwrapped the leather strap and opened the leather cover to reveal a stack of extremely antique papers. The collection of writings was in Italian, French, and English, but all by the same hand. She scanned through. *These are the personal correspondence of Giovanni Angelo Braschi.* She continued to flip carefully through the pages.

"Miss Natasha, come look at this," Andreason called.

Natasha suspended her study of the ancient letters and joined Andreason.

"See how's he's got this magnifying glass mounted to this hobby desk. It would be just right for writing those small little messages."

Natasha agreed, but she was more interested in the antique papers. Natasha went back to the writings of Braschi. His writing style seemed related to Francis. Certain letters matched almost perfectly. For example, the way Francis' crossed his F. There was a unique squiggle. In addition, they both used the same squiggle to cross their lowercase T.

Andreason walked up behind Natasha and looked over her arm at the papers.

"Angelo Braschi again. Interesting. You know he kept doves too?"

"What?" Natasha asked.

"Pius the VI kept doves too," Andreason answered. "He is said to have tenderly released one just before Berthier's soldiers broke into his apartment and placed him under arrest."

"What happened to him after he was arrested?"

"That's an interesting question, Miss Natasha. He was said to have died in prison after only eighteen months. But the French somehow misplaced his body and his funereal was postponed for three years."

"How could they have misplaced the pope?"

Natasha sensed something significant surrounding the circumstances of Pius VI's death and subsequent misplacement of his corpse. Her mind raced. She pictured the painting of Braschi and the similarities to Francis Charles. The prominent forehead and the intelligent, dark eyes. She looked at the Braschi letters.

"Look at this," she said. "Braschi was writing to Benjamin Franklin regarding alphabet reform."

She flipped through more papers and found a letter with a broken wax seal. It had an eagle embossed on it.

Natasha's mind was racing, trying to make connections.

The aftermath of the so-called XYZ Affair lasted about three to four years. Braschi's body was missing about three years. Natasha's mind made the connection. Just as she had found the PATERNOSTER pattern on the wall art in Francis' office. Just as she had figured out the significance of the palindromes. And just as she had made the connection regarding the interchangeability of U and V being the key to a special apocalyptic cipher. Her synapses fired and her eyes grew wide. *Eureka!*

She went into vision—just as she had when she had seen the acts of Lucas Phillip Reynard. In her mind's eye, she saw Braschi releasing his doves. The dove carrying secret instructions for his escape from the

French prisons and a promise of an amazing treasure for men whom would secure his release.

Of course, Braschi's body went missing. Because there was no body. He had faked his own death, relocated to America, and assumed a new life in the new world.

Braschi and the XYZ affair are the missing link to how the immortal King David eventually became the American Francis Charles. Natasha snapped out of her vision. She turned to Andreason.

"He's got an escape plan. He's already ahead of us."

She stopped. Andreason was holding his pistol aimed straight at her at point blank range. Natasha shot a glance back at the game board, confirming that in fact one of the pieces was a Swiss Guard. *That would be Andreason.* She knew why he was pointing the pistol at her. It wasn't because she was under arrest for a crime that she did not commit. No. His intention was to make her an illegal prisoner. Natasha quickly surveyed the room.

"Mr. Andreason? What's the gun for?"

She held the leather document case in her hand. A leather strap and buckle were attached to secure it. Natasha grasped the end of the strap and swung the document case instantly so that it wrapped around the wrist of Andreason as if she was an expert with a bullwhip. The documents of Giovanni Angelo Braschi flew out in every direction and swirled around the room like flakes in a snow globe. Natasha yanked hard as soon as the strap had spiraled around his wrist and stripped the gun from his hand. With the strap wrapped tightly around his wrist, she pulled down on the leather and cinched it tighter, simultaneously using her right hand to bend his wrist backward. She forced Andreason to his knees, twisted his arm behind his back, pulled back his other arm, and tied his two wrists behind him.

Natasha retrieved Andreason's pistol and came back. Slowly, while aiming the gun at him, she reached out and caught hold of the top of his radio antenna. She pulled it off from its belt clip and repositioned it in her hand so she could depress the talk button.

She composed herself and spoke into the radio.

"Bird Dog to Base Camp. Over."

She waited for a response.

"This is Base Camp. Go ahead, Bird Dog."

Wiley's voice sounded a bit surprised to hear from Natasha from over the radio.

"Red alert. Red alert. CSOS1 to attempt escape imminently. Reinforce security around him immediately."

Natasha ran down the stairs as fast as she could. On the last stair she tripped and fell through the secret panel door in Francis' library. The library was dark; no one was there. She picked herself up and ran out of the apartment. Once on the street, she ran as fast as she could to Wiley's office. As she ran, she attempted to continue her contact with Wiley to confirm that he was acting swiftly in regards to her alert. After his first response, he did not answer any more of her radio calls.

"Bird Dog to Base Camp. Bird Dog to Base Camp. Over," she panted.

Natasha began to panic. *Grant Nuby was with Wiley. What if Francis broke through and took him over? What if he killed Wiley? Why isn't he answering!* Natasha's mind raced. *Wiley was her ally, the only one she could trust after the incident with Andreason. What if he were dead now and Francis Charles back in power—ready to squash his adversaries like insects?*

Get out of here. Just get the heck out of here. Turn around and go back out of these city walls. But she couldn't stop.

She yelled into the radio again. "Bird Dog to Base Camp! Over!"

Forget him! Get out of here while you still can. In her mind's eye, she imagined Grant Nuby turning into a werewolf and chasing her down through Saint Peter's Square.

The alarms in her mind were relentless. She found herself acknowledging how powerful the thought was, but her reasoning overpowered her fear. If she ran now, when would she ever stop running? Somehow, she pulled strength from somewhere deep inside. She was already running fast, but she broke free to a whole new level of speed—an Olympic sprinter summoning her last power to shoot ahead and cross the line first.

~

Grant Nuby sat in the background and listened as Wiley interviewed Nicholas. Wiley was pushing him hard to reveal what he knew. Nicholas insisted that he knew nothing of any of this. He acknowledged that the birds were his, but he didn't know anything about their capabilities to deliver mail. Wiley called for Nicholas to be taken to a holding facility to be further debriefed.

"I sense he is telling the truth, Commander Wiley," Grant said.

"I agree. He seems innocent for now, but he may have important details."

Just then, Natasha's voice came over the radio, alerting them to Francis' likely escape attempt.

~

The Swiss Guards escorted Francis Charles straight from Wiley's office. Instead of marching him to Vatican City's criminal holding facility, they marched him to the Vatican helipad where a large transport helicopter awaited them. Its rotors were already spinning as Francis and his loyal guards climbed aboard.

Wiley looked at the video monitor and saw the guards were off route and headed toward the helipad. He raised the alarm and ran toward the helipad as fast as he could, drawing out his pistol as he ran. He stopped suddenly. Natasha caught up to him as he stood there.

Wheezing and out of breath, she yelled in exasperation, "What are you waiting for? You're just going to stand there and let him escape?"

"The helicopter is armed with missiles. If Francis still wants to assassinate the Holy Father, he certainly has the means to do so."

He called into his radio to abort the pursuit, but the radios were jammed. The helicopter lifted off and immediately flew out of Vatican airspace to an unknown destination. It was a perfect and simple escape for Francis Charles.

Wiley and Natasha ran back to his office. He immediately dialed his liaison to Scotland Yard, urging him to raid the flat on Paternoster Street before Francis could tip them off.

Wiley hung up the phone and turned to Natasha and Grant.

"We are in your debt already. You have undoubtedly helped us thwart Charles' plan against the Holy Father. And I can promise you this. I believe your husband is innocent and you have my word that I will do everything possible to affect his release. Even if it takes a phone call from the Holy Father himself. There's just one more thing I have to ask of you?"

"What?" Natasha asked.

"I need you to be my eyes and ears in England and to make yourself available to Scotland Yard if they need you. They've agreed to your presence at the Paternoster site. The jet is waiting for you. Miss Natasha, Mr. Nuby, will you go?"

"We're on our way!" Natasha said solemnly.

She took a rubber band off of Wiley's desk, gathered her hair, and snapped it on to the back of her head. She pulled her bag off the floor and hung it off of her shoulder.

"Absolutely!" Grant agreed.

He extended his hand to Wiley in a firm handshake. Wiley nodded at them.

"Then go. And Godspeed!"

Natasha and Grant ran out of Wiley's office and down to the waiting jet. As Natasha boarded and seated, it occurred to her that she hadn't slept since those few short hours in the balloon. Once again, her only chance to sleep would be high up in the clouds. Just before she passed out, she thought, *This is definitely a red eye.*

~

In London, Inspector Ivor Patterson met Natasha and Grant at the Paternoster apartment. He was a pudgy freckled man, dressed in a crisply ironed Scotland Yard uniform.

"We missed him. I'm sorry to say," he told them as he introduced himself and shook their hands. "But we found loads of those coded messages—and the birds, too. The birds have been RF tagged and released. We're monitoring closely, but unfortunately the messages have been shredded. We're scanning the shreddings right now, but our program is designed to find English word combinations, and use algorithms as well as microanalysis to assemble the pieces of the puzzle. The problem is that not only are the messages shredded, but they are also undecipherable strings of numbers. We will need every tool in our toolbox—and I'm not shy to reach out for help. Commander Wiley told me that you can read the code quite fast. So if you're ready to go to work, I have a table set up for you."

"Microanalysis?" Grant asked.

"Yes. It's rather like ballistics—only on paper shredding. Each blade in the shredder is unique at the microlevel."

Natasha understood immediately. It would be like matching two pieces of paper that had been cut in half with a pair of wavy-bladed scrapbooking scissors. Some scissors have sharp, angled waves and others have round, lazy waves.

"I get it—so I'm the shortcut at the end."

"At least until we can write a program to read the cipher. But I don't even know if that's possible—with the unique aspects of this particular code. Wiley said you're a genius. So yes. You are the short cut."

Natasha sat down at the desk.

"Grant, you can help with this, too."

"No. I already know where this is taking us—and I think you do, too. Good-bye, Natasha," he said softly and hugged her.

He exited the apartment, went out onto the street, and left in a taxi to go back to the airport. Natasha looked back down at her work. The computer had reassembled three of the messages so far; Natasha began decoding them right away.

The first message was "I would love a dove. Send twenty to Rome's farmer's market."

The second message was "Pocket change."

The third one was "What else do you need?"

Ivor walked over and looked over Natasha's shoulder.

"That was fast, Natasha. Looks like you decode them faster than we can get them to you."

He handed her four more pages. Natasha looked up at him.

"How many of the messages do you have?"

"We estimate we may be able to restore as many as forty," Ivor answered.

Natasha picked up the one she was working on and waved it.

"I can tell you right now that Francis Charles didn't write this one. Let me show you something."

She showed him the second message.

~

Four more hours passed at the home of Douglas Blair. The neighbor's orange cat had long since abandoned the warmth of Cadillac's engine— and the fire that warmed the Blair home had long since burned out.

~

Brian Jones walked into Heathrow International and checked his luggage. As the American prepared to walk through the metal detectors, he emptied his loose change, keys, and cell phone into a tray. On the other side of the detector, he retrieved his items from the tray.

Five other American businessmen checked luggage and passed through the security screening on their way to board the same flight as Brian Jones. AeroEuro Flight 900 to Rome. None of the security screeners noticed that the six businessmen were wearing professional makeup and wigs. None of the security screeners noticed that the loose change these men emptied from their pockets as they passed through metal detectors didn't quite chime a normal tone.

Brian Jones, Keith Thompson, John Sanders, John Colgate, Jackson Hobbs, and Randal Fauntleroy. The six men boarded without the slightest hint of a suspicious eye. Except for one man—one man felt something was wrong. His logic told him he was crazy, but his intuition told him otherwise. Flight 900 departed Heathrow on time.

∾

Natasha looked up at Inspector Patterson.

"Do you see how he writes his numbers so precisely? Just like a professional font. See. Now look at this one."

Natasha showed him the "pocket change" message.

"This handwriting is messy in comparison. Tell whoever is sorting to prioritize shreds with perfect penmanship."

"Excellent, Natasha."

Natasha continued to decode. She found an important one. *If notified, target Vatican instead.*

She shouted, "Inspector, we're looking for an international flight from either London or Paris to Rome. Cross-reference with the name Ahmad Ahmid. The target has been changed. Their Plan B is to strike the Vatican."

"Exceptional, Miss Azshatan."

The inspector immediately flipped his phone open and called Wiley.

"One other thing, Inspector. Use dogs at the gates to detect plastic explosive—which I believe will be hidden in false coins."

"Exceptional, Miss Azshatan. Right away!"

Ivor dialed again and gave full instructions to his team.

"Please, Miss Azshatan, continue. We need to know what is written on every scrap of paper."

Another inspector walked up to Ivor and whispered in his ear. Natasha went back to work.

∾

Grant Nuby stood up after takeoff and walked to the lavatory. As he did so, he looked for the others that he knew must certainly be on the plane.

Over the years, he had experimented with his condition. Even though he lost control while he was possessed, he found that if he focused on certain tasks just before his mind was taken over, the demon somehow had to perform the list before it could go on to its own agenda.

The way Grant understood it was that, at first, the demon is still trying to fit into its new brain and until the takeover is complete, the brain more or less goes on autopilot. Many times, Grant had awoken from an episode of his demonic possession only to find that he had accomplished impossible tasks that he could not remember.

But that's a last resort.

He made his way to the cockpit and approached the stewardess. He was sure that if he notified the captain, they would take measures to land the plane immediately.

It was too late. Amid Ahmad, a.k.a. Brian Jones, exited from the lavatory and began taking over the airplane.

Grant was frail and no match for these trained warriors, but he knew the fate of this plane if he did nothing.

He tuned out the words of Amid Ahmad and focused on the other members of his team. He visualized what he would do to each of the terrorists if there were no limits and let the demon take over.

With the speed of a Tasmanian devil, Grant lunged across the plane to where Amid Ahmad had just stuck the plastic explosive to the window.

A booming voice reverberated out of the demon-possessed Nuby, shouting, "Go to hell!"

Grant snatched the explosive from the window and embraced the astonished Ahmid. He embraced Ahmad with a bear hug as tight as a boa constrictor and pressed the detonation button.

It was a small, muffled explosion. A fine mist of red blood sprayed in all directions. Ahmid Ahmad's head rolled down the aisle, his eyes still wide open in shocked horror. Grant fell to the floor. He looked up at the faces of some of the people whom he had saved and uttered a single word: *Atonement.*

He closed his eyes and peacefully released his spirit. Flight 900's passengers rose up against the remaining five terrorists.

~

One of the younger investigators ran into the room and interrupted Patterson and the other inspectors.

"Turn on the news," he yelled.

He ran over to the television and turned it on. Natasha stopped decoding and watched the television news coverage. The headline banner at the bottom of the screen read: *The renowned psychic medium Grant Nuby sacrifices his own life to thwart terror attack.*

At first, Natasha was stunned. The room roared with a victorious cheer. She smiled and, overwhelmed, burst into tears. Ivor Patterson offered his hand to pull her from her chair and gave her a hug.

Natasha's cell phone rang. It was Wiley.

"I'm sorry for your loss, Natasha. I know he was your friend."

She tried to smile, but burst into tears again.

"He was. He was. But I know that, more than anything, he would have wanted to go out like that. I think he found peace."

"Natasha, something else has happened and I need you back here right away."

Natasha could tell from his tone that the matter was serious and urgent.

"What is it?"

"I'll tell you when you arrive here in Vatican City. Please hurry to the jet—time is critical."

"All right. The Vatican requires my assistance on another matter."

~

The Swiss Guardsman escorted Natasha to where Karl Wiley stood working in the middle of Francis Charles' home office. The apartment was full of guards poring through papers and examining every small detail.

Wiley looked up from the document that he and a guardsman were reading.

"Natasha! There's no time to waste. The Holy Father was abducted and his life is in danger."

Natasha was totally shocked. She had expected that the urgent matter had something to do with Francis Charles, but she hadn't expected this.

"I know you have a gift, Natasha. Please, now more than ever, we need it."

Natasha put her hands over her face and stretched them back across her temples. She looked around the office and combed her fingers through her hair. Her eyes came back to Wiley.

"Grant, Alexei, and I theorized that Father Elijah had discovered powerful secrets within the pages of the Bible, which if revealed, would interfere with Francis' scheme to achieve his aspirations of global dictatorship."

Natasha breathed deeply and continued to look around the room. She bit the tip of her finger.

"But now with his plans completely blown and his true identity known, what motive would he have to abduct the Holy Father?"

"He is a very logical sort," Wiley said. "We also asked the same question. He must have a reason."

Natasha nodded.

"Why else would he make himself the target of such an intense manhunt?"

She turned to the direction of the narrow staircase.

"I need to look around his secret room."

She climbed up the narrow dark staircase and Wiley followed her.

"That was impressive work you did on Mr. Andreason," Wiley remarked as they entered the circular room. "We found him tied up and comatose on the floor."

Wiley smiled and looked at her. Natasha stepped across the room to the display shelf and picked up the papal tiara.

If Elijah was endeavoring to authenticate the Vicarious Filii Dei theory, the holy grail of that quest would be to find a tiara with that title inscribed onto it.

She said, "I researched the subject a little. A quest to find such a tiara would be fruitless, since the whereabouts of only a few of the tiaras are known. Only five have survived and none of them bear an inscription. One of the tiaras that survived is the one that Napoleon endowed to the successor of Pius VI. Napoleon supposedly had an inscription engraved onto that tiara, but whatever it said, it was considered offensive and was removed. But I was thinking …"

Natasha turned to Wiley. "It turns out that from the middle of the Dark Ages, every pope in history possessed many tiaras. They were a traditional gift from royalty—so there should actually be *hundreds* of these tiaras. None of the tiaras survived the fall of the Vatican in 1798."

"Where did they all go?" Wiley asked.

"That's one of the greatest unasked questions in all of history. Where is the missing Vatican treasure of 1798? Hundreds of priceless jewel-encrusted triple crowns, all manner of gold and silver and treasures and relics and secrets.

Elijah was not killed because he was about to reveal his Antichrist theories, he was killed because he stumbled across a path leading to the greatest missing treasure of all time. A path which would also intersect with the ambitions of a powerful immortal, hell-bent on world domination."

She walked along the circular edge of the room and looked at the paintings, artifacts, and books. She noticed a photo of the Holy Father taken at a time before he was elected.

"Wiley, before Andre Saracini became pope, he was perhaps one of the world's foremost paleographers."

Natasha bit her lip and stared out in thought. Her eyes brightened and she turned back to Wiley.

"That's why Francis abducted him. That's why Francis is obsessed with these Latin and Greek palindromes. They contain clues to the whereabouts of another treasure room. A treasure vault that stores not only the lost Vatican treasure of 1798, but also the missing treasures from the temple in Jerusalem.

"Think about it. In 1797, Pius VI sued France for peace—*months* before the invasion. Plenty of time to have the treasure moved. Moved and consolidated."

"Dear God!" Wiley exclaimed in a low whisper.

He stared at a painting leaned up against the wall, which depicted the Ark of the Covenant.

"Natasha, you're talking about the Ark of the Covenant!"

"The Ark of the Covenant *and* something much more dangerous—The Rod of Aaron."

Natasha pointed to another painting. It depicted Moses with his outstretched arms waving a stick as he commanded the sea to divide. She pointed to the stick.

"It's the original magic wand, splintered from Eden's tree of life and, according to sacred writings, more powerful than you can imagine."

"How do you mean?" Wiley asked.

"Moses waved it into the air to execute just about every miracle that he performed—from turning Egypt's water into blood to the parting of the Red Sea."

Wiley took his eyes off of the painting and looked back at Natasha.

"Why would Francis be obsessed with the palindromes?"

"Wiley, suppose you compose a clever proverb and wordsmith it in such a way that it is also one of the world's most sophisticated palindromes—it would pretty much guarantee the preservation of that proverb. Now, if you hide secret clues within the wording of that palindrome, then those secret clues will also survive all down through the ages."

"So—within the palindrome, a proverb; within the proverb, a clue."

"Eureka!"

Natasha's eyes widened in epiphany and she ran down the narrow stairs to the study; Wiley followed behind her.

She breathed deeply and exhaled. She pointed to the large work of art across from the office desk.

"Look! The Five Wounds of Christ."

SATOR
AREPO
TENET
OPERA
ROTAS

Natasha hurriedly snatched a writing pad and a pen from the desk.

"The letters in this palindrome are hiding another meaning!" Natasha shouted, her voice quivering.

She wrote out each letter: "*Satan, ter oro te reparato opes.* Satan, I bid you thrice: Return my treasure back to me!"

Wiley turned white.

"Unbelievable. This man really is the Antichrist."

"Grant told me that he told you everything and, even though

outwardly you seemed skeptical, he sensed that you believed. Now, I'm sensing that you believe. We need to start calling this man by his name. His name isn't Francis. It's Davad, Hebrew for David and, coincidentally, also a palindrome. He is the man known to the world as King David."

Wiley put his hands on his hips and stared at the magic square. Natasha cracked her knuckles and stared at the paintings. There was something else nagging at her. The magic square seemed so full of surprises. First, the double paternoster cross, then this satanic anagram. She shook her head. As hard as it was to believe, she felt as though she was being guided to believe that it would bear out one final clue. To think so wasn't logical, but the influence upon her mind was pervasive and she recognized that she was being influenced.

The Four Horseman of the Apocalypse. White horses and black horses. Of course. The thought seemed from nowhere, and unrelated, but the Apocalypse is what we're dealing with.

She ran across the room and took a knight from a chessboard and held it up to the magic square. Starting at the letter O, she moved the knight over the letters as if in a game of chess. She read the letters out loud as she went. Wiley wrote them down, as she called them out. O R O T E P A T E R O R O T E P A T E R.

Natasha turned to Wiley, took the writing pad from him, and translated it out loud. "*Oro te Pater, oro te Pater.* I beg you, Father. I beg you, Father."

She circled the unused letters and showed Wiley. The leftover letters spell the Latin word *sanas*, which means, "You heal."

Father we beg you. You heal. Of course it was clumsy, but what did it mean as far as being a clue for where to start looking for Davad's lost treasure room? What did this phrase have to do with anything? Did it play off of any of the other palindromes?

Natasha remembered the Fountain of Aya Sophia. A sophisticated Greek palindrome was inscribed over the fountain. She pulled out her phone and accessed the memo in which she had copied it. *The palindrome translated "wash your lawlessness, not only your face." But it was inscribed over a fountain wasn't it? Yes! Of course, in Biblical times the sick would go to the fountains and beg to be healed. What else?*

Natasha hurried to the bookshelf, pulled out an atlas, and opened it to Turkey. She pointed down at the map of Istanbul.

"Since the beginning, I've felt that Istanbul has some significance to this whole mystery. Here we have an ancient fountain with a sophisticated palindrome and a fountain where the sick would go in order for God to heal them. I also had a dream that I was scuba diving with father Elijah—he had an artifact and a treasure map. I remember seeing an underwater cityscape with vast domed structures and medieval towers. In the dream, I thought it was Atlantis, but now I know it was Istanbul."

Natasha's eyes widened. She hurried back to the wall of books and her eyes rapidly scanned it. She pulled out a huge art book and rapidly flipped pages until she came to the painting she was thinking of—another painting of the Ark of the Covenant. It depicted the Ark on a giant flat rock in the middle of a wheat field. At the base of the Ark were six golden rats.

"Look! When the Philistines took possession of the Ark from the Israelites, they were cursed with a plague of rats and disease. The Philistine priests believed the source of the plague was the Ark. Hoping to stop the curse, they returned the Ark to the Israelites, leaving it to them in a field with six golden rats as an offering to the God of the Israelites."

"Now clear your mind, Wiley."

"All clear."

"What do you think of when I say the phrase 'Plague of rats'?"

"The bubonic plague."

Natasha nodded her head.

"The bubonic plague started at the docks of Constantinople right around AD 538."

Natasha took another volume from the shelf and opened it on the desk. She flipped through the book, found the passage, and read it out loud.

"In the first Holy Crusade in AD 533, the Byzantine Belisarius seized the treasure from a royal ship fleeing the Algerian harbor of Hippo Regius. It was then shipped to Constantinople, the capital of Byzantium. In AD 534, Emperor Justinian brought the Vandal king into Constantinople. The historian Procopius of Caesarea clearly describes the treasures of Jerusalem being paraded at head of this triumph."

Natasha looked up at Wiley.

"Everyone in Constantinople who knew about the secret location of the Jerusalem treasures died from the plague. Even Emperor Justinian was not immune. The only clues to the treasure's location are these Greek palindromes.

Wiley was bent over, looking at the book. He straightened out and stretched his back.

"This all leads you to believe that the lost Jerusalem treasures are hidden somewhere in modern Istanbul?"

"Yes," Natasha answered. "And Istanbul is where Davad has taken the Holy Father. They are there. I know it!"

Wiley put his hands together and rested his chin on his fingertips. He shook his head negatively.

"This is an impossible situation, Natasha. Our diplomatic ties with Turkey are strained at best. Shall I call their ambassador and tell him the Holy Father was kidnapped by King David in order to help him on his quest for a magic wand so he can become the Antichrist? It sounds crazy."

Natasha looked down at the floor. *It did sound crazy. And what would even sound crazier would be this business about the Ark of the Covenant.*

"Natasha, we can't send our army in there either. It would violate international law."

Wiley pulled an asthma inhaler from his pocket and held it up for Natasha to see.

"The Holy Father is far from immortal. He could die without his medicine. A dusty city like Istanbul, I don't even want to think—"

"If the Holy Father has been kidnapped and taken to Istanbul, you will have to save him. I will support you from here in any way possible."

Natasha took the medicine and tucked it into her pocket.

"Please book me a commercial flight right away. The Vatican's jet is too high profile. It would make the news in Istanbul and take away my only advantage—the element of surprise."

"Absolutely, Natasha! If anyone can do this, it is you. May heaven help you. Go and Godspeed!"

~

Alexei met Natasha at Istanbul International. Natasha explained her theory to him as his driver shuttled them through the city's nightscape on the way to Aya Sophia. Natasha looked ahead through the windshield. The temple glowed; its mega-domed structures and tall narrow towers seemed almost extraterrestrial. She wondered if Emperor Justinian could have ever imagined the temple lit up at night.

"Those hooligans!" Alexei whispered hoarsely. "Wiley sends you here all by yourself."

"Not exactly," Natasha explained. "He gave us an unlimited budget—and if we confirm the exact location of the Holy Father, he will send an incursion of Swiss Guard."

"He should have sent some with you right now."

Natasha looked out the window. The neon streets signs glowed on her face blue then green then red. Alexei tapped her on the knee to get her attention.

"Natasha, I found something very disturbing in my Bible. It's about the palindrome 'wander in darkness, consumed by flame.'"

Natasha looked down and saw the one page Book of Jude. The page in front of Revelation. She took the Bible from Alexei and read the passage.

> Beloved, I found it necessary to write to you exhorting you to contend earnestly for the faith which was once for all delivered to the saints.
>
> For certain men have crept in unnoticed, who long ago were marked out for this condemnation, ungodly men, who turn the grace of our God into lewdness and deny the only Lord God and our Lord Jesus Christ.
>
> And the angels who did not keep their proper domain, but left their own abode, He has reserved in everlasting chains under darkness for the judgment of the great day;
>
> Woe to them! For they have gone in the way of Cain, have run greedily in the error of Balaam for profit, and perished in the rebellion of Korah. These are wandering stars for whom is reserved the blackness of darkness forever.

Natasha looked up to Alexei.

"I see the connection. It's another example of how the apostles feared of the hijacking of their faith."

"It is more," Alexei continued. "Do you see the second-to-the-last sentence? 'Perished in the rebellion of Korah'? The rebellion of Korah was a rebellion of 250 leading Israelites against Moses and Aaron. Moses used the Rod of Aaron to call down fire from heaven to destroy those that were against him. Then God told Moses to put the Rod of Aaron inside the Ark of the Covenant, next to the Ten Commandments, in order that those who perished in the fire 'may not die!'"

Alexei took the Bible from Natasha and quickly turned the pages. The Bible's pages flickered and glowed with each passing neon light.

The Lord said to Moses, "Put back Aaron's staff in front of the Testimony, to be kept as a sign to the rebellious. This will put an end to their grumbling against me, so that they will not die."

Natasha grabbed the Bible back from Alexei and read the last sentence again.

Alexei continued, "According to Jude, it is these, the ones who perished in the rebellion of Korah, that are destined to infiltrate the Church. It is these rebels that even though once killed by the wrath of God by fire, who were also cursed by the same God that they would also not die. It is these souls, which wander in the night, consumed by fire."

Natasha's face froze in horror.

"Davad, the immortals from the rebellion of Korah, and the fallen angels are all after the same thing. They've joined forces to take possession of the Rod of Aaron. If they succeed, they will be an unstoppable army of the damned."

The van stopped at an intersection. The glowing light from the street lamp cast crimson across the faces of Natasha and Alexei and illuminated the pages of the Bible in red. Natasha flipped the Bible to the book of Revelation and read it aloud.

> "And they gathered them together to the place called in Hebrew Armageddon."

～

The van stopped in front of Aya Sophia and Natasha and Alexei climbed out. Natasha pulled on her backpack and gazed at the moonlit wonder. The windows that ringed its dome cast out dim light and its enormity eclipsed the starry night sky.

Natasha ran to the fountain and Alexei followed. It was a short run through the gardens to the fountain. Natasha stopped in front of it. The garden and the fountain were slightly illuminated with landscape lighting, but the atmosphere was filled with shadows. She slung off her backpack and pulled out one of four emergency flares taken from the van's roadside emergency kit. She struck the flare alight and handed it to Alexei who then aimed its light at the amazing palindrome inscribed across the fountain.

Natasha gazed, waiting for inspiration. She flipped opened her phone and wrote down the proverb with the English translation underneath of it.

νιψον ανομη ματα μη μοναν οψιν—Wash your sins, not only your face.

She stared at it. She felt helpless, but hopeful. *What is it? What am I missing?*

"Alexei, what if instead of one reading it from left to right, one started reading it in the center, and then out in both directions? In this case only the second half of the proverb would be read, but it would be read twice."

She took the flare from Alexei and used its burning red tip as a pointer.

"Begin reading at the T in the center."

νιψο νανομ ημ α τ α μη μοναν οψιν
ecaf ruoy ylno ton   < >   not only your face

Alexei translated, "Not only your face, not only your face."

"If this is the right way to read the clue, then it's being repeated twice for emphasis."

Alexei took back the flare and shined it up on the inscription.

"Maybe you are correct, Natasha. Just like you said earlier. The proverb is preserved within the palindrome, but a secret clue within the proverb."

Natasha stared at the fountain. *So why is it telling me this at the fountain? Because at the fountain, one would normally wash one's face. But the "Not only your face, not only your face" is directing me to fully immerse myself. Not only my face, but my whole body.*

"We're at the fountain. The 'not only your face, not only your face,' is a command for full immersion. It's directing us to the larger body of water."

Natasha pointed to the Basilica Cistern. She flung her backpack around her shoulders and ran toward its entrance. Alexei ran beside her, the flare in his hand streaking a red glowing trail.

"Alexei, since the cistern is a hundred times larger, it's much more appropriate to be fully immersed in."

"Not only that," Alexei answered. "The Emperor Justinian baptized his army in the Cistern. Baptized by full emersion."

They reached the entrance and Alexei shined the flare to illuminate the inscription over the enormous doorway. Natasha thoughtfully pondered the words. It was also a palindrome. She wrote it out the same way as she had the other and showed it to Alexei.

"It translates 'Whoever you are, let the law be your guide.' But, if we read the clue out of it like the last one, starting at the center, and reading out in both directions, then it repeats the phrase, 'The Law be your guide, the Law be your guide.'

σονιοκα τε χ ετ ακοινοσ
Ediug ruoy eb wal law be your guide

"What law?" Alexei asked.

Natasha smiled.

"The Law of Archimedes. That's what law?"

Alexei looked puzzled.

"The law of buoyancy?"

"It's the only law that I know of that has anything to do with a place like this. A place entirely dedicated to the collection, treatment, and distribution of water. What other law has anything to do with water?"

Alexei didn't have an answer and Natasha felt relieved. She smiled and took a deep breath. *This idea of a secret chamber feels right. But is it right? Or is this your overactive writer's imagination? There's only one way to find out.* She grasped the door handle and pushed her weight into opening it, but it didn't budge. The door was locked.

Alexei pulled out his army multi-tool knife and brandished it toward Natasha.

"Tough soldiers no having use for tweezers and toothpicks in their knives."

He pulled out the tweezers, bent back the thin metal, and slid the slender end into the lock. He applied clockwise torque, while simultaneously slipping in the hooked end of the toothpick. He pushed up the tumblers within the lock while maintaining clockwise pressure.

"These things from pocket knife are the soldier's lock-picking instruments."

He pushed up the final pin and the lock turned over. Alexei pushed the tweezers and toothpick back into their respective slots and kissed the knife.

"Big thanks to army knife," he said and swung open the door.

Natasha entered first, shining the flare ahead to the stone stairway that led down to the pool. The cool, humid air smelled musty. No theatrical lights, no eerie music as when she toured with Grant. No tour guide, no chattering of tourists, or shuffling steps. They stepped down the stairs in ghostly silence.

At the bottom of the stairs, they walked to a far corner near the edge of the cistern pool. Alexei held the flare up to light the area. Natasha crouched down.

"I need your knife," she told him.

"What are you thinking, Natasha?"

Alexei handed her the knife and Natasha opened up its scissors.

"I think the entrance to the secret chamber is hidden underwater here in the cistern somewhere."

She cut two 3 x 12 centimeter strips from a clear plastic freezer-bag. She pulled a roll of duct tape out of her backpack and attached a strip of the tape along each edge.

"What are you doing?" Alexei asked.

"Goggles," Natasha replied. She pulled her cell phone out and placed it in another plastic bag and tucked it into her hip purse along with her pistol and the asthma inhaler.

"Take whatever you can with you in your pockets. We'll definitely need your knife, the three flares, and the duct tape. Natasha handed Alexei the tape. He squished it flat and pocketed it.

The flare burned down to its end. Alexei placed it onto the stone floor before it burned his fingertips. He pulled out the second flare, struck a light, and stuffed the two remaining flares into his beltline.

Natasha took her clear plastic strip and taped it across Alexei's eyes. The tape made an airtight seal across his brow, along the bridge of his nose, and under his eyes. He looked like an old man in a homemade Zorro costume.

When she finished, she handed him her clear plastic strip with affixed duct tape. She held her hair back from her face as he secured the improvised goggles. Natasha looked at Alexei in his priest robe and improvised goggles. The flare cast a red flickering glow and Natasha almost laughed at the thought that he looked like some kind of absurd comic book hero. She realized that she also looked just as unusual, dressed in a black, skintight athletic shirt and black spandex pants.

"Are you ready?"

"*Da, pashlee!* Yes, let's go!"

"Follow me."

Natasha took the flare from him. She pivoted off the edge of the pool and submerged herself into the dark cistern waters. The maze of underwater marble columns was eerily illuminated by the flickering glow of the flare.

Natasha took a deep breath and swam underwater to the far eastern side, surfacing twice for air along the way. At the corner, she waited for Alexei and caught her breath by leaning back and floating.

Alexei surfaced and rested a few moments. Natasha took another deep breath and dived down. Along the bottom, the stones were enormous—

one meter high, one meter deep, and 1.5 meters long. She searched for a bottom stone that would have some natural feature to grip.

Natasha felt a rush of adrenaline as she noticed one with the features she expected. The second stone in from the corner had two graspable natural features that were spaced conveniently if their purpose was to act as handles for the stone.

With the flare still in her left hand, she pointed to her eyes and then to the stone. She handed the flare to Alexei and placed both hands on the stone. She pushed down and felt the stone give ever so slightly. *Eureka!* She felt her heart skip a beat. *This is really happening. This is crazy.* She pushed down again and dislodged the buoyant stone just as she had visualized. She swung it open and swam into the secret chamber. Alexei followed behind her.

When Alexei came through, the flare lit up the area around them. She swam over to where the small underwater cavern became shallow. Alexei appeared a moment later gasping large gulps of air. He held the flare up and illuminated the chamber.

They were in subterranean cave room. A terraced rock floor gradually stepped out of the water and then leveled out. Natasha looked up at a stalactite-covered ceiling. The light from the flare danced off of the moist rock walls. She stepped up the terrace and was amazed. The room was stacked with unimaginable treasure. Gold coins, jewels, and all kinds of priceless artifacts, including hundreds of jewel-encrusted papal tiaras. She marveled as she panned around the room.

"*Bolshna Moy.* My God!"

Alexei crossed himself. In the center of the room, an empty pedestal demanded Natasha's attention—at its base were six golden rats.

"The Ark was here!" she declared. "They've taken it."

Alexei was mesmerized by the immense treasure. Natasha noticed a dark hole where the light did not reflect off of the walls. It was clearly the primary entrance and exit.

"Come on! We don't have any time!"

"He already has the Rod of Aaron and the Ark! What can we possibly do?" Alexie asked despondently.

Suddenly, red sores appeared across Alexei's hands and face. He looked at the disease on his hands.

"*Bolshna Moy*! Davad has initiated the plague of sores—a third of mankind will die!"

Natasha looked at him and a tear leapt from the corner of her right eye. She gulped and swallowed her own fear. She laid calm hands on him and cradled his head in her palms.

"The question is not 'What *can* we do?'—it is 'What *must* we do?' All of heaven is on our side. We must have faith."

Alexei visibly summoned his courage and nodded affirmatively. He threw the remnant of the flare into the water, ignited the third flare, and handed it to Natasha.

"You lead a way, my dear. I am to be right behind you."

"All right then! We must hurry!"

~

Natasha ran down the stone corridor. She heard the voice of Davad—at first just barely, then louder and louder. There was the sound of cheering and applause and then the voice of Davad again.

"We will do what God either will not do or cannot do! We will save the earth from mankind and mankind from himself!"

A thunder of applause echoed down the corridor. Natasha reached the end and looked forward to empty space that was lit with the flicker of torchlight. She extinguished the flare. The voice of Davad and the sounds of a cheering crowd emanated from below. She was at the top of an ancient auditorium. She snuck into a balcony-like area and looked down.

The audience circled around in balconies 360 degrees, each level higher, and each level farther out from the center. The audience looked like it was made up of four hundred cardinals in crimson capes. The costumes were not modern, but rather styled after some earlier versions that Natasha did not recognize.

Davad stood at the center stage at the lowest point, draped from head to foot in pearl white pope's attire; on his head, he wore a magnificent triple crown. In his right hand, he waved the sapphire Rod of Aaron.

In the center, the Ark of the Covenant lay showcased and, off to its right side, Pope Andre Saracini was laid out on an altar as a spectacle—powerless and fighting for his life with every asthmatic wheeze.

Alexei caught up to Natasha and looked down.

"The rebels of Korah!" he mouthed silently. "The Rod of Aaron must stay in close proximity to the Ark or they will perish."

Davad continued his speech. His voice boomed powerfully with the tone and tenor of a motivational speaker.

"The plague will destroy a third of mankind, but two-thirds will live. The human race is ready for our leadership. They will see clearly that only a world united in common cause can reverse catastrophic global climate change."

Another round of cheers and applause thundered.

Alexei looked up at Natasha and quietly quoted, "Exodus 4:17. Take this Rod in your hand so you can perform miraculous signs with it. God told it to Moses. We must take this stick from him somehow."

Natasha knew he was right. *The Rod was a relic from the original tree of life. It had power all on its own. This was demonstrated when Moses threw down the Rod in front of Pharaoh and it became a serpent. Pharaoh matched the miracle when his own priests threw down their rods, which also became serpents. But the serpent that was the Rod of Aaron, acted on its own will to eat the others.*

Natasha crouched down low to where Alexei sat leaned up against the wall. His face was covered in sores and his sweat-drenched neck reflected the torchlight. He breathed in raspy, phlegm-tattered breaths.

Alexei struggled to speak.

"Where two or more are gathered, there I will be," he quoted the words of Jesus Christ and performed the sign of the cross.

Natasha repeated Grant's words, "That's the power of intercessory prayer; pray unceasingly."

Natasha held Alexei to her bosom and looked upward, tears streaming down her face.

She cried out in a hoarse whisper, "Jesus! All my life I have pushed you away as only myth and an academic curiosity. But I have now seen your power as well as the power of evil. I believe in you! In the name of the Father and of the Son and of the Holy Spirit, save us!" Natasha whispered into Alexei's ear, "Don't you die on me. Don't you dare!"

She placed him carefully on the ground and looked down to the altar. Barring a miracle, the Holy Father would die without his medicine. Curled in a fetal position, he was unable to utter a prayer to save even his own life.

If I throw the inhaler, it would take a miracle for him to catch it. He's an old man in a weakened state—about to pass out from lack of oxygen.

In her mind's eye, she envisioned the inhaler hitting his fingertips and cruely bouncing out of his grasp and onto the floor.

Natasha thought of another idea, reached into Alexei's robe and pulled out the last flare, the roll of duct tape, and the knife.

She wrapped the end of the duct tape roll around the pocketknife and pulled out a sufficient length of it so that she could lasso it to the chandelier of torches. She pushed the flare stick through the center of the tape spool so that it was like a tire with an axle sticking out on each side. She held it in her left hand and she swung the length of the duct tape rope in circles with her right hand.

"God help me!" she breathed as she lassoed the chandelier.

Natasha placed a hand around the flare stick on each side of the tape roll and, an instant later, she jumped off of the balcony and rode the unrolling spool of tape all the way down. She landed safely next to Pope Andre and administered his life-saving dose of medicine.

An uproar sounded immediately. Natasha struck the flare alight and waved it in her left hand. She pulled the pistol out of her hip bag and aimed at the encircling immortals in an effort to guard Pope Andre.

Andre breathed another life-giving breath and stood on top of the altar, his long silver hair windswept and his deep blue eyes burning with the power of the Holy Ghost. The hum of angelic voices flooded the room and filled the atmosphere.

Andre summoned all of his vitality and boldly commanded, "In the name of the God of Israel and of Isaac and Jacob, and in the name of Jesus Christ and of the Holy Ghost and in the name of the God of the souls of all mankind and as the representative of Christ on earth, I rebuke Satan and his angels and cast them down into the bottomless pit. And I command that the spell of immortality be broken upon the rebels of Korah and upon the fallen Davad. By the power of God you are cast into eternal darkness."

Natasha looked at the beings that filled the cardinal costumes and watched as they burst into piles of dust.

Davad waved the Rod of Aaron and shot a blue, laser-like force field that protected him and the remaining fallen beings. From where the Holy Father stood to where the blue field divided the room, the unholy beings continued to burst into dust plumes like a falling chain of dominos.

Davad pushed his open palm outward and moved the protective field farther out. It covered some of the already perished rebels and revived their piles of dust into living beings once again.

Pope Andre pushed his right hand out to push back the blue barrier.

"For God so loved the world that he gave his only begotten son, that whosoever believes in Him should not perish, but have everlasting life!"

The hum of angelic voices elevated to a higher pitch. Natasha looked around and saw beautiful and ghostly glimpses of angels shimmering like holograms of rainbow light.

She looked beyond the blue light barrier that shot out from the Rod of Aaron and saw as it changed into a monstrous, vicious serpent.

The serpent opened its mouth wide, exposing two huge fangs and a split tongue that shot out of its mouth like a blue arc of electricity. In an instant, the serpent plunged its fangs into Davad's hand and shot him full of the poisonous venom of damnation and electrified his body. Blue fire shot out of his eye sockets and his flesh evaporated under his skin. The rippling skin sucked in against his smoldering skeleton and, a moment later, he burst into dust. The serpent in his hand dropped to the ground and slithered to where Pope Andre bent down and picked it up by its tail and it once again became the Rod of Aaron.

The remaining rebels of Korah and other followers of Davad burst into piles of dust like exploding kernels of popcorn.

Natasha turned her attention to Pope Andre. He looked at her with a warm smile and grateful eyes.

"Thank you Dr. Azshatan!"

He opened his arms and embraced her and she embraced him in a gentle, reverent hug. "Please, Holy Father, hurry."

Natasha led him up to where Alexei lay on the cold stone floor, his lifeless body covered in bloody sores. Natasha fell to her knees, held Alexei, and sobbed. It felt like she was holding her own father.

"Pope Andre, is there anything you can do?"

He reached down and caressed the top of her head. He held the Rod of Aaron out and knelt down next to Alexei. The Holy Father performed the sign of the cross and then slowly lowered the Rod to rest across Alexei's forehead between his eyes and down the bridge of his nose. The Rod glowed blue and the hum of angelic voices again filled the air. A blue aura enveloped Alexei as the sores on his skin vanished. His chest hitched as he suddenly breathed in and his eyes opened in wide surprise.

Natasha smiled down at Alexei and petted his head. She looked up to Pope Andre.

"Thank you, Holy Father!"

The Holy Father put his hands on the sides of her face and temples.

She felt a radiant warmth flow from his hands into her body. He smiled down at her with loving eyes.

"Thank you, my angel. Power-hungry tyrants—and even immortals disguised as mortals—have always aspired to conquer the Church from within. The Apostles Paul and John warned us of it as you know. But the forces of good, holy, and pure have almost always prevailed. Most people don't understand that the Church's darkest times are the result of such attacks."

Natasha smiled and he looked into her eyes.

"Don't worry about anything, my child. As the Lord Jesus once said, 'The flowers don't think about how to clothe themselves, but yet they are clothed so beautifully. And the birds worry not about the next day's food.'"

"Thank you, Holy Father."

"Will you pray with me, Dr. Azshatan?"

He reached his arm sideways and embraced her as he prayed.

"Dear Lord Jesus. Thank you for your child, Natasha Azshatan. Thank you for her genius and abilities, and for her loving heart. I pray for her well-being both now and for the future. Let your spirit always guide her and teach her the things that she should know. And give her peace and answers to her questions. In the name of the Father and of the Son and of the Holy Spirit. Amen."

As they stood up, the Holy Father kissed her on the forehead.

"Your husband is a most excellent man. The Lord has already answered your prayers for him. He'll be home as soon as they can process the paperwork, my dear."

An incursion of Swiss Guard rushed in and surrounded them.

Pope Andre addressed them, "This woman and this man saved my life. Please attend to them."

He looked deep into her eyes.

"Good-bye for now, my dear. You are in my prayers, and I am in your debt."

He was rushed out by his entourage of Swiss Guards. He stopped momentarily, turned around, and waved good-bye, before disappearing as his wall of guards closed ranks behind him and ushered him out of the stone chamber.

~

It was a crisp, sunshiny, winter's day in Seattle. Natasha marveled at the beauty and majesty of Mount Rainier. A fresh layer of snow blanketed the countryside, but the roads were clear and safe. Natasha had arranged the Hummer option with the limousine company. She felt safe and protected and enjoyed the ride back to Jerrell's Cove. She couldn't wait to get back home to reunite with Tom.

When Natasha entered her home, she was disappointed. The house was cold and empty. No Tom to greet her and hold her. Just then, her cell phone rang.

"Natasha? Jeremy Benton. Happy New Year!"

"To you, too. So, what's going on?"

"I'm at the Federal building right now. Tom's free. They're processing him right now. I'll have him home to you in a couple of hours."

"Oh, thank God."

She smiled and looked upward to heaven.

"He'll call you as soon as he gets a chance."

"Great! Good job, Jeremy!"

"I don't think it was me, Natasha. Chalk it up to a miracle."

"Well. Thanks again anyway, Jeremy. You were really here for us when we needed you."

"See you soon."

"All right. Bye-bye."

Natasha turned the heat up in the house and drove to the store. As she was shopping for groceries, Natasha sensed a familiar spirit. It was a happy spirit—the spirit of Elijah. She sensed him smiling at her and embracing her. She could picture his blue eyes. Natasha stood in the bread aisle and enjoyed the moment. She consciously thought that she wanted to visit and leave wreaths at the gravesites of Father Elijah, Jim Worley, and Sheriff Darwood.

However, there was something else she felt like Elijah was trying to show her. He was trying to influence her to buy something else. It was something that had to do with the sign of the cross.

The sign of the cross, sign of the cross. To protect me from the evil spirits? No. For something else. I think I know what he's trying to get me to buy.

On the way home, Natasha stopped at the graveyard and laid the three wreaths.

"Thank you, Elijah. Thank you for inspiring a deeper spiritual curiosity. I believe in miracles. I believe in people and the spirits of people. And I believe in the Christianity that Paul and John fought to preserve."

"I'll keep an eye out for you," she said as she walked back to her Subaru.

At home, Natasha switched on the oven, turned on the radio, and began baking fresh cookies. The phone rang.

"Babe! It's me!" Tom announced. "I love you!"

Natasha burst into tears. Her voice momentarily locked.

"I love you too, honey! So much!"

"I'll be home in less than an hour."

There was silence for a moment. Natasha was so overcome with emotion that she couldn't speak. She gulped and took a deep breath.

"Can't wait, love. See you here."

"Okay. I love you, honey!"

"I love you, too."

The line went dead.

~

Natasha happened to be watching out her living room window when Sheriff Green drove past on his way to meet with William Jaimeson at the Blair residence. She wondered what he was up to this late on New Year's Eve.

William Jaimeson waited for Green on the front porch of Doug's house. He rocked back and forth in a wicker rocking chair. He was eager to resolve this matter with Douglas one way or the other. A Secret Service agent stood guard two meters to William's left, diligently scanning the night air for anything that could be a threat.

Green pulled up into the driveway and approached the front porch. The Secret Service intercepted him, but William called out to them to let Green alone.

"Congratulations, Mr. President. We're all so proud of you."

"Thank you, son. I am proud of you, too. Thank you for the fine work you are doing here at Jerrell's Cove and for your assistance this evening. As you can see, my chief of staff is nowhere to be found. His car's engine was warm four hours ago, but still no sign of him."

Green dangled the house keys.

"Barbara O'Brian cares for Mr. Blair's home when they're out of town. I stopped by her place on the way here to pick up her set of keys."

Green said nothing more. He just opened the door and walked into the house.

Inside the house, the air was warm. "Mozart's Requiem" floated down the stairs and softly filled the atmosphere.

"The fireplace was burning four hours ago, too," William commented. "It was like Douglas was just here."

Green walked over to the fireplace to get an idea for himself how old the fire was. He noticed a blemish on the fireplace mantel, and scratched it with his thumbnail to see what it was. Suddenly it was apparent to him.

"*In girum imus nocte et consumimur igni*," had been written in blood on the fireplace stone. The blood was difficult to notice because it had been baked onto the stones by the heat.

Green looked down into the smoldering ashes in the fireplace and saw a charred and melted syringe. The cremated remains of a human body smoldered.

Will had not yet approached the fireplace. He was standing back and observing the room as a whole.

Sheriff Green turned around.

"Sir, I think I found Mr. Blair."

The answering machine blinked with one unheard message. She pushed the play button.

"Natasha, it's Grant. I don't have very much time. I'm about to board this plane and I don't think this will turn out well for me, but I had to call you to say good-bye. You have been a true friend. Please remember me well—that I was a good man. And there is something I must tell you about regarding the killings at Jerrell's Cove. Isn't it suspicious how the murders seemed to be customized so conveniently to attract your attention? How many murderers leave bloody handwritten Latin Palindromes as clues to taunt investigators? Natasha, I know that I did not kill those men. The killer is someone whom you already know. Remember my advice. Stay positive and pay attention to your dreams. Good-bye."

Natasha looked around. The house seemed so empty and Grant's message creeped her out. She couldn't wait for Tom to get home. She walked to the kitchen and put some water on to boil for hot chocolate.

She turned around to go back to her bedroom and what she saw petrified her. Once again, she felt the most horrible sense of evil.

Bright red, bloody letters spelled out one more palindrome for her.

AH, SATAN SEES NATASHA.

Natasha froze in pure terror, knowing that Satan was indeed watching her. She heard the bloodcurdling high-pitched voice of Gilbert Carver as he appeared from behind the corner.

"Ah, Satan sees Natasha!"

He smiled slyly. He was hiding something behind his back. Natasha tried to think rationally. She knew a little about this man—actually too much. If she showed she was afraid of him, she would be like all the other woman who had feared his grotesque appearance. Since childhood, he had suffered from the unstoppable progression of Elephant Man's Disease. His head was a misshapen wad of dough; he was lumpy from multiple tumors growing all over his body.

Gilbert suffered even more severely from ridicule as his parents forced him to attend public school despite his horrific deformity. At the age of thirteen, his deformity hit its peak. Natasha remembered him recount in court how he was traumatized by the sight of his own mother vomiting from his appearance. She left him and his father the day after his thirteenth birthday.

"I did it for you," he said in his high-pitched voice.

He swayed like the demon she had battled in the library. He was obviously influenced by a similar evil spirit.

"Gilbert?"

She tried to smile.

"I did my research, Natasha. I made a mystery just for you—with special handwriting clues for you to solve. But you didn't guess it was me, did you?"

Natasha stared at him.

"Gilbert, what are you holding behind your back?"

Gilbert's face contorted and, with an evil smile, he brought forth from behind his back the severed head of Douglas Blair. His hand was buried deep up the remains of the neck and into the skull. A butcher knife protruded from the temple of the head. He grabbed the hair with his left hand and pulled the skull off of his right hand with a sickening sucking noise.

"I needed to dip the pen into the ink jar."

He held out his finger.

"You want to play a game? I can chase you around the house with my bloody hand."

He lurched toward her, sticking out his bloody finger.

"No, Gilbert!"

Gilbert pulled the knife out.

"Too bad. We're going to play anyway."

He cackled and started walking toward her. One of the tumors on his head was bulging larger and it seemed as though it was about to burst through his skin.

"Satan will give me a new life if I kill you! It's the final task!"

"No, Gilbert. No. Please stop."

Natasha backed toward the kitchen counter, hoping to grasp a knife or some other weapon. She didn't want to underestimate his power—as she knew he was under demonic control.

She couldn't find anything and ran out of the kitchen. She threw the Christmas tree down as she passed down the hallway.

"Ahhhh. Satan sees Natasha!" he chanted repeatedly. "Ah, Satan sees Natasha. Ah, Satan sees Natasha. Ah, Satan sees Natasha. Natasha ran to the master bedroom and tried to lock the door, but the lock was glued shut.

"I hope it's okay! I've made myself at home here the whole time you were gone."

Natasha looked at her bed—it was messed up and feces smears spattered the middle.

Like he craps in his sleep.

Gilbert kept coming closer. He fought his way through the bedroom door.

"You deserve to die, Natasha!" he hissed and swung the knife at her. "Don't make it harder. Just kneel down on the floor and I can make it painless."

"No, Gilbert! No!"

He lunged at her. Smiling and chanting, he lunged at her again. Natasha stepped back on one of her high-heeled shoes and tripped backward. Gilbert jumped on top of her and put the knife at her throat.

"Okay, Gilbert. Okay. I will give my life for you," Natasha said as sweetly as she could. "You have had a difficult life and I would like for you to have the chance for something better. Thank you for the opportunity to do such a good deed."

Gilbert pulled the blade from her neck and sat up across her pelvis. The tumor over his left eyebrow was pulsating like a sack of about-to-hatch spider larvae.

"Just please. Make it fast and painless like you promised."

Drool dribbled involuntarily out of his mouth and spilled off his chin.

"Stab me in the heart as hard as you can!" she cried.

Gilbert smiled.

"Thank you, Natasha."

He raised the knife like an ax man about to split wood, holding the knife with both hands. He raised it over his head for maximum strength and velocity. A blue vein that went across his brow and into his tumor pulsed in sync with the tumor. As he raised the knife, the tumor erupted into a spitting volcano of puss, splattering Natasha's face. She contorted in revulsion.

He swung the knife down at her chest. Natasha had no intention of letting him plant the knife into her heart and squirmed sideways. The knife buried into her right collarbone and stuck. Natasha vomited violently into Gilbert's face—a huge stream of forceful vomit. Gilbert recoiled and Natasha pulled the blade from her clavicle and swiped across Gilbert's exposed throat like a tennis backswing. His head dropped down, blood bubbled down his neck, and he fell over sideways, dead.

Natasha screamed in horror, frustration, exhaustion, and victory. She screamed out and cried in spasms. When she was finished, she crawled to the nightstand phone and dialed 911.

~

Tom arrived home to the scene of ambulances, sheriff's cars, and Secret Service standing on the front porch.

When he walked in, the EMT was finishing the stitches. The wound had been extremely minor. Since the tip of the blade hit the clavicle, nothing more than the very smallest portion of the tip of the blade had actually punctured her skin. It was a miracle.

Natasha got up and ran to Tom and bunny-hopped into his arms, covering him with kisses.

Tom lifted her onto his hips and spun Natasha in circles.

In that moment, Natasha didn't want to tell Tom about what had happened at the Vatican, or about her meeting with Kirov, or her fight with the demons, or how she figured out the PATERNOSTER encryption. She just wanted to hold him tightly and tell him one thing. She wanted to tell him what Elijah had revealed to her while she was in the grocery store; the thing about the sign of the cross.

The sign of the cross had been the results of her pregnancy test.

Tears burst from her eyes and she smiled widely as she whispered in his ear.

"We're going to have a baby!"

Tears leaked from the corners of Tom's eyes as he held Natasha tightly. He smiled widely and kissed her on the lips.

"Now, that's what I call a New Year's miracle!"

Natasha buried her face in his neck, kissed it, and shed more tears of joy.

~

William Jaimeson arrived a short time later and asked her about Francis Charles. Natasha left out the parts about Francis being immortal and a possible fulfillment of Antichrist prophecies. Although she feared the dark potential of Jaimeson, she sensed that he was unaware of such potential. For the present, he was a charismatic leader focused on his well-intentioned agenda. Jaimeson seemed genuinely disappointed and astonished at the news. He gave his condolences and, before he left, invited Natasha and Tom to his inauguration ceremony. Natasha and Tom agreed, and made reservations at the Four Seasons for January 24.

During the inauguration ceremony, a dove landed on Natasha's lap, startling both her and Tom. Natasha looked at its leg and saw what she expected—a message capsule. She opened the capsule and unrolled a short handwritten note.

The audience was cheering. William Jaimeson was on his way up to the podium. Natasha pushed her glasses up the bridge of her nose and read the letter.

My Dearest Natasha,

I shall remember you forever. Please look in on Nicholas from time to time in my absence. I rescued him from an Orphanage in Rimini and he has always been the son I never had.

As for me, I'll be fine. As you can imagine, I have powers and wealth beyond comprehension.

You may call me "ΔΑVΑΔ" (DAVAD) henceforth. As you may have figured, a palindrome in the Hebrew tongue.

Go in peace.

ΔΑVΑΔ

Natasha's heart raced and her mind swirled. She looked up again. William Jaimeson was swearing to protect and defend. Cameras were flashing in all directions.

Many people who attended the inauguration ceremony of William Jaimeson would later agree with Natasha's account; that his eyes glowed red in the moment he took his oath of office.